SHOOTING the SPHINX

SHOOTING the SPHINX

AVRAM NOBLE LUDWIG

A TOM DOHERTY ASSOCIATES BOOK · New York

FORGE®

SHOOTING THE SPHINX

Copyright © 2016 by Avram Noble Ludwig

A Forge Book
Published by Tom Doherty Associates, LLC
175 Fifth Avenue
New York, NY 10010

www.tor-forge.com

Forge® is a registered trademark of Tom Doherty Associates, LLC.

The Library of Congress Cataloging-in-Publication Data is available upon request.

ISBN 978-0-7653-8113-2 (hardcover)
ISBN 978-1-4668-7798-6 (e-book)

Our books may be purchased in bulk for promotional, educational, or business use. Please contact your local bookseller or the Macmillan Corporate and Premium Sales Department at 1-800-221-7945, extension 5442, or by e-mail at MacmillanSpecialMarkets@macmillan.com.

First Edition: June 2016

Printed in the United States of America

0 9 8 7 6 5 4 3 2 1

This book is dedicated to those courageous people in Egypt who faced down tyrants twice, then were so cleverly tricked out of democracy. May they find it again some day.

ACKNOWLEDGMENTS

For a debut novelist, the excitement that comes with seeing your first advance check, your first uncorrected proof, your first blurb, your first book cover, and your first encounter with a pleased reader fills you with a childlike glee and a deep sense of gratitude to everyone who believed in your book.

First and foremost, I have to thank Bob Gleason, my editor, who agreed to read this manuscript unsolicited over a glass of wine at a book signing and ten days later told me he wanted to buy it. I have to thank Margaret Mclean, one of Bob's authors, who introduced me to him, and Megan Carroll, who introduced me to her. Bob's capable editorial assistants, Elayne Becker, Kelly Quinn, and Paul Stevens, at Tor/Forge shepherded me through the process of publication. Elisa Pugliese helped me with an initial cover design, and Dan Cullen designed the final cover. Ed Chapman and Meryl Gross copyedited the book. Eftihia Stephanidi took my author photo. My agent, Richard Abate at 3 Arts, handled the negotiation. And finally I have to thank the founder of Tor/Forge, Tom Doherty, an old-school publisher who decided to take a chance on an unknown author.

The idea for this story was born at the Sundance Film Festival, where I saw the Oscar-nominated documentary *The Square,* about the Egyptian Revolution, by my friends Jehanne Noujaim, Karim, and Dina Amer. That film took me back to Cairo and started my mind churning over old memories of making movies there. My old friend and partner in crime, director Doug Liman, first sent me to Cairo to shoot a helicopter shot of the Sphinx for his movie *Jumper* and again to do more filming for the political thriller *Fair Game.* My gratitude also goes out to William Martin, Ambassador Joe Wilson, Whitley Strieber, Geraldine Brooks, and John Gill for their words of encouragement. And I must credit Fred Gilbert for a stanza of his old British music hall song "I'm the Man Who Broke the Bank at Monte Carlo," which some may remember from *Lawrence of Arabia.*

My life has had various other directions than novel writing, yet I've always craved to write and be read. It's taken thirty years to get to this point. Many people have aided me in that quest and helped me to get ready to write this work.

Naomi Wolf edited my writing before this. Her rigorous notes made me a novelist. Malaga Baldi was my first agent and believed in me professionally before anyone else. Patricia Marx, Adam Langer, and Jane Rosenman taught writing classes that I took at the 92nd Street Y, as well as all my classmates there who edited my earlier work.

Thanks to my friend Mary Frances Young, who was the first

person to read *Shooting the Sphinx* and encouraged me by asking again and again for more chapters, spurring me on to completion even as the end of the book was being written. She told me that the ending was not right and had to be redone. Finally, this story started out as a play and might have stayed that way but for film director Oday Rasheed, who read it and told me he wanted to make a movie out of it. He worked with me as I wrote a film script, but there was just more to this story than a movie could hold.

DRAMATIS PERSONAE

Ari Basher, a film producer
Charley Foster, an aerial camera technician
Sal Montevale, a helicopter pilot
Don, an aerial cameraman
Frank Solomon, a top Hollywood director
Elizabeth Vronsky, an executive producer
Tom Cucinelli, a movie teamster
Hamed, Ari's driver in Cairo
Farah Aziz, a graduate student and revolutionary
Samir Aziz, Ari's fixer
Rami, a popular singer and revolutionary
Walid, a fixer at Cairo International Airport
Mohamed, a street urchin at the pyramids
Glenn, Elizabeth Vronsky's husband
General Hanawy, president of Petroleum Air Charters
Mustapha Shawky, his number two
Farouk, an archaeology student and guide

Dr. Hamoud Nesem, minister of archaeology

General Moussa, chief of customs at Cairo International
  Airport

Omar el Mansoor, the head of Studio Giza

Ali, ticket taker of the Sphinx light show

Major Horus, a helicopter squadron commander

Khaled Nahkti, the biggest movie star in Egypt

Leela, Samir's wife

Yasmine, Samir's daughter

Mahmoud Abbas, president of the Palestinian Authority

Sharif, ex-minister of tourism in Jordan

Prince Amir, brother of the King of Jordan

Princess Jala, his wife, an ex-journalist

Wael, a driver

Detective Kek, of the Cairo police

PART ONE

Allah has not promised us tomorrow.

—Old Arabic proverb

Chapter 1

Ari Basher hopped out of a van into a blast of rotor wash at the Thirtieth Street Heliport. He hiked up his jeans and tried to keep the grin from devouring his face as he let himself into the gate through a tall chain-link fence. He loved to fly.

A sleek white corporate Sikorsky S-76 had just touched down, the rotors still spinning overhead. A bored CEO in a business suit stepped out of the aircraft. He cast a grim dry glance right through Ari, who politely held the gate open for him. Ari wanted to ask, "Dude, why so serious? You get to soar over all the bus riders on your daily commute."

Instead Ari called out, "You're welcome!" The businessman faltered, dazed by the radiance of Ari's confident exuberance.

"Thank you." He cracked back a wan creaky smile of his own, rusty from disuse. Ari knew that he'd won the CEO over as he disappeared into his typical black SUV.

On the other side of the large corporate Sikorsky, Ari found his ride, a smaller Eurocopter, and his team: Don, Charley, and Sal, the pilot.

Charley Foster, a gruff, elfin ex-Navy F-16 mechanic, who had worked on aircraft carriers for years, was threading film into a special aerial camera inside a gray three-foot ball mounted on the nose of the chopper.

Sal Montevale, a compact, bushy-white-haired Vietnam vet, who had been an air cavalry pilot and was now the dean of New York aerial photography, sat in his cockpit waiting. Ari waved. Sal had flown on Ari's first job in the film business, twenty years prior, in the Hamptons. The star of the picture was supposed to steal a helicopter and buzz a crowd of extras at a lawn party. When the star stepped into the chopper, they had called "Cut" and slapped a curly blond wig on Sal's head; Sal was the one who'd taken off, buzzing the crowd with low, shaky moves as if he didn't know how to fly. The result was some great acting as the extras had run for their lives like Viet Cong in a village about to get hit.

Don, the cameraman, sat in the backseat, a monitor and camera control console in his lap. Mellow and unflappable, Don was an Australian surfer who had somehow risen to become the top aerial cameraman in the world. They would all be spending a lot of time together in the coming weeks, so Ari expected that life story to come his way over a beer—or ten—in the hotel bar.

"How we doing, Charley?" Excited to get in the air, Ari walked around to the front of the chopper and peeked over Charley's shoulder at the camera.

"I said we'd be ready by the time you got here, and we're ready, so back off."

"I love you, too, Charley."

Charley shut the round three-foot SpaceCam housing, then grabbed his fist with his hand, a signal to Don that the camera was ready to fly. Don moved his controls up, down, left, and right. So did the ball on the nose of the chopper—like a giant eye with a tiny pupil. Ari spun his finger in the air as a signal to start the engine, but Sal was already flipping switches and easing the throttle in. The whine of the turbines spooling up and the smell of jet exhaust put the grin back on Ari's face. He opened the door and stepped up into the right-hand seat beside Don so they both could see the monitor.

"Can you believe they pay us for this?" Ari winked at Don.

"Don't tell the studios how much we dig it." Don put his finger to his lips. "Or those greedy buggers might just start charging us to come to work."

Sal pulled on the collective and the rotors bit into the air, lifting the chopper off the ground. Ari hadn't been in a chopper in a while, and the first sensation of helicopter flight always startled him a little. As a private pilot, he was used to flying a plane and feeling like he was sitting on top of something. A helicopter always made him feel a different center of gravity, a different weight, like he was hanging from a coat hanger stuck in the back of his jacket. Ari pulled a rough sketch of their flight path out of his pocket.

"Sal, the director wants us to try this. To loop around over the middle of the George Washington Bridge."

"Sure." Sal studied the drawing for a second. "Got it."

Don, too, memorized the pattern and nodded. Then he focused the camera downward, practicing moves: zooming in and out on moving cars below on the West Side Highway.

They flew over tiny little people jogging in the park, biking on the streets, coming and going. Not one of them having as much fun as I am right now, thought Ari. Ain't my life cool?

"Here's your bridge," said Sal. The GWB loomed up in the windshield, an elegant massive structure, its two giant cables strung over pylons rising out of the Hudson River between the Palisades of New Jersey and Washington Heights on the New York side.

"Ready, Don?" asked Ari.

"Set."

"Roll it."

Like a dragonfly in slow motion, the little helicopter flew right over the middle of the bridge, its lowest point, then banked around and came back.

"You get it?" asked Ari.

"I can do better," said Don. "The shot takes a long time to develop."

"Can you fly it faster, Sal?"

"How much?"

"As fast as you can. We're going again."

Sal repositioned the chopper in the sky. He pushed on the stick and the craft surged forward, nose down. Again they crossed over the dip in the suspension bridge and banked hard left. Ari felt two Gs on his ass, then three as the weight of his body literally tripled in the tight turn. He watched the screen, figuring that he had about six takes in him before he lost his lunch. The chopper leveled out of the turn and crossed back over the bridge, returning to its starting point.

"How was that?" asked Sal over his headset.

"Eh," said Ari. He wasn't thrilled. "Let's try it again."

The three men did the shot a few more times, but they knew collectively that it wasn't special, just adequate. They shared one of those rare moments in movie-making when the best plans, the best people, the best equipment just don't add up. The editor will end up hacking off the front and back of the shot and pick a fairly boring piece of footage, where the audience can see the whole bridge and know what it is. All this for nothing—movie-making was just like that, hours and days of work for seconds in the finished film.

On take six, Ari looked out of the window to fight his nausea. He could taste a little bile on the back of his tongue. Sal and Don seemed fine and ready to go again. Ari looked down at the Palisades: sheer granite cliffs that dropped three or four hundred feet into the Hudson.

"We've got to tell a story in every shot," he said, almost to himself. "Sal, Don, cut. Forget this. We've got it as good as it's going to get, and it's going to wind up on the cutting room floor anyway."

Sal and Don looked at Ari like scolded children. The best of the best always internalize failure. Ari pointed down at the Palisades.

"What if we start along the edge of those cliffs, really tight, and we don't know where the hell we are. We could be in the middle of the Rockies for all the audience knows, then we bank, we find a piece of the bridge, see the river, follow the traffic really close, then descend down underneath the roadway; and, *voilà!* New York City is revealed as we drop beneath the bridge!"

"Could work," said Don, starting to visualize the shot in his mind. Sal grunted in agreement. He eased off the stick, banking wide over the river to come right to the edge of the cliff.

They skimmed over the tops of barren winter trees sticking up from the craggy rock ledges, then banked out over the Hudson alongside a massive suspension cable dipping down below the roadways and their flow of traffic, to finally drop and find the distant Empire State Building dead on in the middle of the shot. The entire bridge looked as if it were balancing like a teeter-totter right on the very tip-top of the art deco building's giant antenna, an optical illusion.

"Yeah!" cried Ari. The three men grinned at each other like demons. They had bagged the big one, caught movie magic in the camera. "We got it!" Ari reached out and slapped his pilot and his cameraman on the shoulder. "We got the shot!"

Chapter 2

Ari sat in the darkened screening room watching his aerial footage with the other producers, the key crew on the film, and the director, Frank Solomon. There had been a lot of "oohing" and "ahhing" at the George Washington Bridge shots, but only one opinion in the room mattered: Frank's.

The film business was the last true feudal society, replete with droit du seigneur, courtiers—even court jesters. All things and all people revolved around the director in this aristocracy of creative commerce.

Up on the screen, the next shot started at the top of an art deco radio mast, which, of course, turned out to be the needle of the Empire State Building. The camera passed right over the antenna's tip and then tilted down a thousand feet to reveal tiny cars and buses on Fifth Avenue below. The effect stole your breath.

Frank gasped in the front row. Elated, Ari knew the shot would make it into the movie.

"Is that all?" asked Frank.

"One more," said Ari, holding up his finger. Empty sky popped on screen. A green spike came up from the bottom of the frame, then several other spikes appeared. They grew until everyone realized that what they were seeing was the crown of the Statue of Liberty. Her face rose slowly up, filling the screen. Her blind eyes were almost grotesque, even horrifying.

"That close-up's a little too close." Frank stood, signaling the end. The lights came on. The projector stopped rolling.

Ari looked around the small screening room. About a dozen producers and studio execs, the editor, the cameraman, the production designer, wardrobe, hair and makeup: every department that had something to do with the look of the film was present and waiting for a chance to ask endless questions of the director.

Ari knew that he would only have a minute or two at most before the others jumped in, distracting Frank with tomorrow's shoot questions, all more immediate than his own. In order to steal the director's attention, Ari had come equipped with props: six plastic pyramids, a toy helicopter, and a kitschy little golden plaster statue of the Sphinx.

"How'd you like the bridge shot?" Ari walked up to Frank.

Frank didn't nod, or even smile. He rarely paid anyone a compliment, but something on his face, some tacit shift in his expression betrayed that he did like Ari's shots—very much.

"Good," was all Frank said. Yet Ari knew that one quiet "good" from Frank was worth a hundred superlatives from everyone else in the room. The producers started to crowd around.

"Great stuff."

"Terrific!"

"So much to choose from," they said on the coattails of Frank's approval.

"When do you leave for Cairo?" asked Frank, shutting off the compliments.

"Now," answered Ari.

"So soon?"

Elizabeth Vronsky, the executive producer responsible for the business side of the film and its budget, stood up. She was taller than most of the men in the room and had a cool confidence in her ability to shoot down any risky idea. This ability always put everyone in that room, including Frank, on the defensive. She spoke for the studio in Hollywood. If Frank was the king of this film, Elizabeth was the queen.

"The problem is . . ." began Beth. Ari dreaded his precious minute getting sucked up by what might go wrong with his work, instead of what had to be done. ". . . that we might miss our date at the Sphinx. We just got permission for only one day next week. We don't know if we can get it again or how long that might take—"

"Frank." Ari cut her off by walking past her to the control console at the front of the screening room. "How do you want me to do the shot?" He quickly set up the little statue of the Sphinx and the plastic pyramids on the console, then held up the toy helicopter.

Frank drifted over, drawn to the statue of the Sphinx.

"One possibility," continued Ari, "is that we start tight on the head of the Sphinx," Ari held his toy helicopter up to the little gold statue mimicking a possible flight path, "so tight we don't know where we are. . . ."

Frank reached down and picked up the tourist trinket

Sphinx. He brought it up to his weary eyes to study closely for a moment, his large impassive face dwarfing the little hand-painted golden lion like a witch doctor with a voodoo doll.

"Where did they pick this up?" asked Frank.

"In Cairo," said Ari.

Frank's cell buzzed. He didn't even have to look at it. "That's our leading lady. I made a promise to come over to her hotel to discuss her lines for tomorrow, and we have a four thirty A.M. shooting call." Frank stifled a yawn, girding himself to that thought, then tossed the Sphinx to Ari. "Astonish me. You always do." Then Frank walked out of the room.

"No pressure," said Beth.

"Oh, man." Ari picked up his model pyramids. The other producers descended on him.

They all chimed in at once. "What day is your permit for?" "Do you have enough time to pull this together?" "What's your backup plan?"

"I get the shot," insisted Ari. "That's my backup plan."

"And I've got something for you." Beth started for the door. "Come to my office." She didn't wait to see if Ari would follow. He just did.

Chapter 3

Beth's assistant was waiting outside the screening room door. She held up a folded check request form between her hands almost as if in prayer.

"What's this check for?" asked Beth as she started walking down the hall to her office. Ari and the earnest young novice fell in beside her.

"They want to rent a camera crane for Monday," said Beth's assistant.

"No," said Beth.

"But if we don't get it picked up tomorrow, it won't get on the truck for Monday morning—"

"Tell them to call me."

"But . . . it's Friday night," stammered the assistant.

"So what?" Beth turned on the fresh young thing. "I'm still here. You're still here." Beth pointed at Ari. "He's still here."

"Beth," Ari wanted to calm her down. "It *is* Friday night."

Beth turned her glare on Ari, then tore the check request in half and gave it back to her girl Friday.

"I said no." With that, she disappeared into her office.

Ari gave it a second, then patted the quivering assistant on the shoulder.

"Don't worry, kid, Beth's not angry with you. She's not even angry at these clowns for asking for a crane at the last possible second in the work week. She's angry at . . . someone else." Ari winked at the assistant. "We're all under a lot of pressure. Go fill out another check request. In half an hour she'll get around to signing it."

Ari took a deep breath, as if jumping into an icy pool, and then slipped into Beth's office, shutting the door and locking it behind him.

Beth was already dialing the combination of her big safe, which was about the size of a wardrobe. She always wore new high-tech running shoes, crisp jeans, and a tight Lycra jacket, the zipper slightly open to accentuate her long neck. Her erect posture made her seem even taller. She wore no makeup, yet had a perfect white complexion, which was prone to red blotches just before she got angry. Ari had seen big macho union grips, electricians, and teamsters reduced to fidgety little boys under the gaze of her piercing gray eyes. Her straight red hair was always twisted into a bun with a pen stuck through it. She was a study in casual precision.

With a clank, she pulled the handle and yanked open the heavy gray doors of the tall safe. Inside were stacks of hard drives, hundreds of them, containing in digital form all of the

footage of the movie. On a small part of one shelf sat bundles
of cash. She picked up some packets of hundreds and turned
back to Ari, who reached out for the money.

"Such a pleasure doing pleasure with you," he joked, hoping she had calmed down a little.

"Don't you ever contradict me in front of my staff again."

"Beth, lighten up. Why tear up the kid's forms? She's just
going to have to fill 'em out again when the key grip calls you
in fifteen minutes to kiss your ass."

"And you cut me off while I was talking to Frank." Her ice-
gray eyes went wide.

"So that's what we're really mad about here?" Ari tried not to
betray his own nerves. "I only had twenty seconds of his attention."

"Just because you're the director's pet doesn't mean you can
cut me—"

"Hey," he interrupted, "I thought I was *your* pet?"

"Don't you pull that charm stuff on me." She gazed at him,
her anger wavering.

He thought, she's either going to slap me or . . . He moved
in toward her slowly, almost imperceptibly. Whenever Beth got
mad, Ari fell into a hypersexualized state. He could usually
stop himself from acting on it, but sometimes he was overwhelmed with a sensation of falling or spinning and felt a
strong urge to reach out and hold on. He kissed her suddenly,
backing her up between the doors of the safe, biting any other
words of anger out of her mouth.

They kissed roughly, like vipers, for a few seconds, then, her
anger spent, she caught her breath and held out a packet of

hundred-dollar bills, swaying, a little woozy in his arms. Pink blotches blushed onto her cheeks and earlobes.

"Only ten thousand?" asked Ari.

"That's the most you can bring, by law." She composed herself, tore a petty cash chit off of a pad and pulled the pen out of her red hair, which spilled down around her shoulders. "Sign for it." He let go of her. "Ari, we've got to stop doing this."

"I agree." He didn't mean it.

"I'm a married woman."

"Right."

Beth collapsed into her chair. The months of high stress were wearing on her. Ari suspected that under normal conditions, she might not have noticed him, but in crisis, in emergency, he seemed to thrive, to enjoy himself. He had a perfect calm. Beth and others often drew relaxation from his presence like a drug. "Are we making the right move in Cairo?"

"Of course." He leaned over her desk, close enough to kiss her, and signed the piece of paper.

Quivering with tension, she breathed in the charged air between them. He could taste her fear. "You will pull this off?" She looked into his blue eyes, searching for an answer. Her tough tomboy exterior was paralyzed.

"When have I ever failed you?" He smiled his most radiant smile, trying to make all her worries seem trivial.

"Are we thinking with our brains and not our . . ."

"Balls?" He prompted her with a most immature possibility.

She rolled her eyes, her anxiety falling away. "Not exactly the word I was looking for." Beth slapped him gently on the face a few times, a love tap. "Just promise me."

"Anything."

"Don't make me look bad with the studio."

"Baby"—Ari slid his fingers around her cheek, over her pink ear tip, and into her red hair—"no one could ever make you look bad."

"Oh god," she groaned, "who writes your lines?"

He answered her with another kiss while he checked his watch out of the corner of his eye.

"What the . . . ?" She caught him. "Were you just looking at your . . . ? What time is your flight?" Worry suddenly creased her brow.

"We still have a few minutes." He grinned, then swiftly unzipped her jacket and pawed voraciously at the buttons on her white blouse.

"Are you crazy?" She slapped his hands away. "People know we're in here."

"We'll just have to be quiet then." He popped open the last button and reached behind for her bra.

"Stop that!" she whispered. "Is your car here?"

"What car?"

"To the airport? Oh my god, we didn't call you a car?" She reached for the telephone and started dialing.

"I don't need no stinkin' car." He took the phone out of her hand and hung it up. "Saving you money, babe. Always thinking of you." He pushed her down on top of her desk and she surrendered to the calm caress of his roving hands.

"But . . ." She stopped him. "How are you getting to the airport?" He simply answered her with a kiss as he pulled down his pants. He had no more time for talk.

Chapter 4

A rental truck pulled up in the dark outside the glaring light of the International Terminal at JFK. Ari hopped out of the cab. A couple of big teamsters climbed down after him.

"Hey, Cooch," Ari called to the driver, Tom Cucinelli, "you and Vinny meet me at the Lufthansa counter with all the camera cases, will ya?"

"But the cops?" said Cooch.

"They can't tow you. It's a five-ton truck."

"But Beth doesn't like us getting tickets."

"Blame it on me. Tell her I told you to because I was running late. Tell her exactly like that and she won't say a thing," Ari called over his shoulder as he walked in.

At the Lufthansa desk, Ari presented the ticket agent with a list: seventeen camera cases and their weights. Three of the cases weighed over one hundred and fifty pounds, and the heaviest weighed over two hundred.

"That will be fourteen thousand six hundred and ninety-one dollars in excess baggage fees," said the tall blond ticket agent, in a slight German accent. A fine-looking fräulein in her sharp Lufthansa navy blues, thought Ari as he produced his Amex card and held it out to her. The agent tried to take the credit card, but Ari didn't let go.

"And all this gear will be put on my flight?" asked Ari.

"We cannot guarantee that all will be transferred through Frankfurt on to Cairo." She seemed to have a certain frosty satisfaction in saying that. "The Cairo leg is almost full, and checked baggage is the priority."

"I am checking it." She's a passive-aggressive masterpiece, thought Ari. "I'm paying fourteen thousand dollars to check it."

"Any object over eighty-five pounds, we consider not checked baggage, but air freight. We cannot guarantee arrival at the destination for at least seven business days."

"A week?" He knew that that would screw things up in Cairo big time.

"Maybe longer," she said with a dry hint of sadism.

Ari started to experience his vertigo sensation. A flirtatious smile took possession of his face. "I need this stuff in Cairo on Monday, all of it, together. It's for a helicopter shot of the Sphinx."

Whenever things started to go wrong, Ari's charisma instinctively buoyed him. His smile had become so hardwired into his personality that he couldn't control it anymore. He couldn't turn his charm off. He imagined leaning forward and kissing her right at the counter. Somehow she read his thoughts and she blushed.

"Checked luggage must be our priority," she replied, flustered but unmoved from a Teutonic adherence to the rules.

He wanted to reach out and pull the hairpins out of the curled braids of gold hair that crowned her head. He had to consciously quash the impulse. Stop it, he told himself.

"Does any airline treat two hundred pounds as checked baggage?" asked Ari, wishing he were on Air France.

"Well . . ." She melted a little and glanced over suggestively at the EgyptAir counter.

A few minutes later, Ari, his two teamsters, and two skycaps were standing next to two luggage carts piled impossibly high with black cases before a dark-haired, green-eyed EgyptAir ticket clerk with the bangs of a Cleopatra haircut.

"Not a problem, sir," said the Egyptian clerk.

"But the heaviest is over two hundred pounds and takes four men to lift." Ari smiled his smile.

"Not a problem." The clerk smiled back bigger, broader—a love fest.

Most of the cases were too large to fit through the scanner, so all seventeen had to be wheeled straight past the TSA scanning area, lined up against a far wall, and opened in order to be hand searched. A male TSA agent with a hangdog face walked with Ari down the line of cases, about sixty feet long.

"It's a SpaceCam," explained Ari, "a gyrostabilized camera that mounts on a helicopter."

The TSA agent stopped. "And what's that?" He pointed down at one case, containing a lawn mower engine mounted inside a metal frame.

"That's nothing. Just a portable generator."

The TSA agent shook his head. "You can't fly with it."

"Why not?" asked Ari. "It's been completely drained of gasoline."

"Against the rules."

"Do I look like a terrorist?" Ari turned on the charm again.

"And what does a terrorist look like?" asked the TSA agent.

Ari frowned. "Cooch?"

"Yeah, boss?" said the teamster.

"Send this back where it came from." Ari closed up the case and dragged it off the wall.

Luckily for Ari, the EgyptAir flight was almost empty. He found a whole row of seats in coach on which he could stretch out. He took a pill, put in earplugs, and slipped a blindfold over his eyes. Getting away from the daily grind of months of sixteen-hour workdays on the main unit of the film did have its advantages, he thought as he sank into a deep exhausted sleep.

Hours later he roused from a dream. The plane was flying through flames. Flames licked at the windows. The plane banked and weaved to avoid giant clouds of fire in the night sky. The pyramids lit up. The Sphinx came to life and leapt from the top of one pyramid to the next to escape the mounting conflagration erupting from burning, shifting desert sand-storms of fire rising up into the blackness like orange tornados.

In a sweat, Ari opened his eyes. His ribs ached from the rise between the seats he lay across. He tugged at the flash of a turquoise skirt on a passing flight attendant. Stunned, the Egyptian stewardess spun around.

"Sorry, sorry." Ari pushed himself up, a little panicked. "I smell smoke. I think the plane might be on . . ."

"No, no," the flight attendant reassured him. "Look out the window."

Ari peered out into the blackness. Dozens of small fires dotted the night below. The plane was descending.

"What are all those bonfires?" asked Ari.

"Just another Egyptian celebration," she explained as she turned away. Her crazy 1970's turquoise stewardess skirt disappeared down the darkened aisle.

Chapter 5

Ari shivered in the cool night desert air as he stepped out of the plane onto the rolling jet stairway. The night sky was pitch black, starless and moonless. He scanned the runways, the tarmac, even the terminals, all very dark for a large international airport. Ari stepped aside letting the Egyptian passengers file by out of the glowing hatchway behind him. He turned back and looked along the underbelly of the plane. The baggage handlers opened up the cargo bay doors and started pulling out luggage. Lingering until he was the last of the slow groggy line, he followed the others down the steps glancing over his shoulder at the baggage piling up on the carts. Where are my cases? He thought. Where the hell are they? They're so big wouldn't they be the last things to load and the first to pull off?

At the bottom of the jetway stairs, Ari squeezed into the only available spot on the crowded people mover as the glass folding doors closed behind him.

"I can't believe I'm in Egypt. I can't believe I'm in Egypt!" said a teenage girl with a Long Island accent as Jewish as any in the Five Towns. Ari turned looking for a Jewish girl, but saw instead a petite dark-skinned Egyptian-American on tip-toes, craning her neck to see out the window, holding on to her parents. Her father, a short stocky balding man with a black goatee, held her arm to keep her from falling.

"Wait 'till you take a drink of water from the Nile, darling," said her mother with her own thick Long Island accent. "Then you'll know you're in Egypt."

At passport control, Ari put down fifteen dollars for his Egyptian tourist entry visa, a large stamp that covered half a page in his well-thumbed passport. They do things big in Egypt, he thought, as he went to find baggage claim.

The terminal had a 1970's architectural vibe. Scattered around were gangs of porters loitering, sitting on large wooden wagons that looked like they must have been in use since the 1930s. The nearest gang of porters noticed Ari. Without a word exchanged, they gravitated toward him when the big black cases started to arrive, slid through a portal in the wall by baggage handlers. The porters stacked all sixteen precariously high on their cart.

"Mr. Basher?"

Ari turned around. He saw his name on a piece of paper held up by a smartly dressed young woman with chic cat's-eye glasses. She was evidently his contact.

"Please call me Ari." He flashed his smile. "Are you from the Press Ministry?"

"Yes, oh my . . . ," she said. Ari followed her gaze up at the towering wall of stacked cases. "That is a lot of equipment."

"Too much?" asked Ari as the porters pushed the squeaky, groaning cart under the omnipotent smile of President Hosni Mubarak. His framed portrait hung on the wall above.

"This letter"—she held up a paper written in both Arabic and English—"says that you are making a documentary. I don't know if the customs man will believe it."

As they walked in front of the sixteen cases to the customs desk, Ari saw Western tourists wheel their suitcases straight through, but the wealthy Egyptians pulled out of line. Customs officials directed them to lift their expensive luggage onto a table to search for dutiable items. What's wrong with this picture? thought Ari. The rich are actually getting soaked.

The towering wagonload of equipment cast a psychic shadow over the entire customs section. All the customs agents seemed to lean in and cast furtive glances toward Ari and his mountain of gear. A ferret-faced agent working the line, selecting who would get searched and who would walk through, took the Press Ministry letter and slowly read it. He looked up at the tower of cases, did some sort of abstract mental calculation, and said, "Tomorrow."

The Press Ministry woman started arguing with him. But Ari could see that the man was afraid of her letter, afraid of the pile of equipment, and afraid of making a decision.

"What's the problem?" asked Ari.

"He says you must come back tomorrow," translated the Press Ministry woman, "when his supervisor is here."

"Why?"

"To get your camera."

"Oh-oh." Ari began a fervent protest in English. "But . . .

but . . . I've got to use this equipment tomorrow!" His contact from the Press Ministry joined in in Arabic, to no avail.

Unmoved, the customs agents directed the porters to wheel the half ton of camera gear over to the wall where it would spend the night under the watchful eye of Mubarak.

Chapter 6

Ari had to brace himself into the corner of his car's backseat to keep from flying over to the other side. Ari's driver, Hamed, started a light rhythmic tooting on the horn as they flew around a traffic circle in downtown Cairo at breakneck speed. A cacophony of horns rose up, all playing a discordant tune in the night.

"Everyone's honking," observed Ari. "Why?"

"Yes." Hamed had a bright effervescent enthusiasm and curly hair that bounced up at every bump in the road. "The horn is necessary."

"But no one is in the way."

"In Cairo," explained Hamed, looking back over his shoulder at Ari, "the horn does not mean 'Get out from my way.' It means, 'I'm here beside you. Don't forget about me.'"

"Ah. Look out!" Ari pointed. An old flatbed truck, belching black diesel exhaust, cut them off. Hamed hit the brakes. Ari caught the back of the front seat as he flew forward, his cheek mashing up against the headrest. On the back of the moving truck, which was now in front of them, twenty young men stood on the flat open bed as if on a giant surfboard; a few, bolstered from falling off by their comrades, were waving a large Egyptian flag and looking like the famous marines on Mount Suribachi. The truck horn belted out its one-note tune, "I'm here, don't forget about me."

Hamed veered off down a side street, as the truck, sporting its jubilant flag wavers, did another lap around the traffic circle. Ari watched them wistfully out of the back window until they disappeared. He wanted to tell Hamed to follow them, but Hamed turned down another dark street, which ended in a cul-de-sac.

Ari stepped out of the car and looked up at the architecture around him. But for the pervasive darkness, he could be standing in Paris. The antique, ornate detail of the Belle Epoche was everywhere; balconies with wrought-iron railings; apartments with French windows and high ceilings. From atop the building in front of him, his destination, Ari could hear voices, a man and a woman yelling at each other. He walked inside.

The lobby had a faded glory about it. An ornate elevator shaft rose up through the center of the building like a hundred-foot-tall birdcage wrapped in a square staircase. Ari pushed the button, but heard no whirr of machinery. Evidently the elevator was stuck on a high floor. Resigning himself to the long climb, he started up the worn white marble stairs.

The staircase was clean but dingy. The trace dust of fine desert sand had infiltrated the city in its every crack and nook. About halfway up the stairs, Ari heard a door bang open. The yelling resumed, the man's Arabic distinct and audible this time. Then Ari realized that the woman was responding in English.

"So let them fire me! Let them dare." A bold young voice echoed down from the hallway above. "If it's only money I want, I can go to Dubai tomorrow and make three times as much. What I don't want is to work for a company that would threaten to fire me for blogging on my own time!"

"Blogging what?" The man's voice had switched over from Arabic to English. "What are you blogging?"

"When will you stop yelling at me, Samir? When?"

"When you are married and living in your husband's home, then I stop yelling! Until then, you are my responsibility. When someone thinks of firing you, they won't warn you again. What are you blogging?"

She didn't answer, but Ari heard the slap of angry footsteps come out onto the landing. He heard the sliding gate of the old-fashioned elevator open and close. The elevator started to descend. The violence of the words, the sexist prerogative, and the challenge to it left Ari a little spellbound. He felt like he had eavesdropped on something unthinkable in his own Western mind, the voice of Arab machismo that entitled a brother to dictate to a sister well into adulthood. Who was this woman who wasn't having any of it? Who was this sister in open rebellion?

Ari watched the elevator loom over him as he climbed up onto the next landing. He could see her legs, and he halted in front of the elevator gate to watch. Dressed like a student, she wore tight jeans and a purple blouse open over a tight T-shirt. She was tall. As tall as me, he thought. No head scarf over her long, almost black hair, which had a slight tinge of red, a henna sheen. She locked eyes with him through the cagelike diamond pattern of the sliding brass gate. Her brown piercing eyes held a smoldering rage that quickened his pulse.

"Hi there." Ari flashed his brilliant smile.

She blinked several times, surprised. He had confused her rage. She didn't seem to know what to do with anything other than anger at that moment. "Uh . . . hello," she said awkwardly as she dropped in the descending elevator beneath him. He watched shamelessly, waiting for her to glance back up at him, which she did. They locked eyes for a second. He winked. Then he continued climbing the stairs to the top, enjoying the little charm bomb that he'd tossed inside the elevator.

On the landing, he looked up and down the hall at signs on doors. Each was in Arabic except for one, PAN EGYPT FILMS. As Ari tried the doorknob, he heard the sound of the call to prayer on a loudspeaker from a nearby mosque. The door swung open. Ari stepped inside.

The walls were bright white and freshly painted. Ari wandered through an anteroom toward an open door and into a main office. The wooden furniture was new, and in the Arabic style. Through the door, Ari could see a big wooden desk covered with a sheet of glass, a MacBook, an ashtray, a burning cigarette, and a neat pile of papers with red ink corrections on them. When he reached the open office door, Ari lifted his fist to knock, but Samir Aziz was unrolling a small red prayer rug on the white tile floor.

Ari froze. He had never, in person, seen a Muslim pray. Samir was in his early thirties, clean-shaven, with his hair cropped short and a gray spot about an inch round on his forehead from kneeling five times a day with his head to the floor. Samir was fit, wore a maroon shirt, tan slacks, and brown loafers that he had already kicked off beside the rug. He stepped to one end, stood up straight when he noticed Ari in the doorway, and said, "Welcome."

"Oh, excuse me," said Ari. "Don't stop."

"Once you start, you cannot stop." Samir slipped on his shoes, walked over to Ari, and held out his hand. "Have you had anything to eat?"

Ari shook his head. "Oh no, I ate on the plane. Besides, my stomach's asleep."

Samir looked at him skeptically. "We will get you some real Egyptian food."

Samir had the same smoldering brown eyes as his sister. Ari wanted to ask about her as they walked out, something indirect that might open a window of insight into this furious Arab machismo, but Samir turned out the light. The moment had passed.

Chapter 7

"So they took everything?" Samir pressed the old elevator button. The elevator didn't move.

Ari nodded. "All sixteen cases."

"Not seventeen?" Samir was alarmed. "One is missing?"

"No, no." Ari reassured him that nothing had been stolen. "When I was checking in in New York, the TSA agents took the generator."

"Why?"

"They were dicks." Ari started to explain the American slang. "That means—"

"I know what is dicks." Samir cut him off.

"Assholes."

"Yes, in Arabic we have a whole dictionary for that word." They chuckled. Samir pressed the button again, harder this time, poking it. The elevator still did not move.

"Someone forgot to shut the gate properly," Samir said with

a tinge of resentment. Ari assumed that in Samir's mind he blamed his sister. "That person's carelessness means that we must walk down the stairs." He ushered Ari to the staircase. "Anyway, a generator is the least of our problems. We can easily rent another. Your SpaceCam, on the other hand . . ."

The unfinished sentence hung in the sober air between them all the way down the stairs and out into the street.

"So when the woman from the Press Ministry found you . . ." Samir broke the silence.

"Yes?"

"Was she wearing the hijab?"

"The what?"

Samir made a circle with his hand around his face. "The scarf over her head."

"No, no scarf." Ari shook his head.

Samir winced, then slapped the wall of the building beside them with his palm, hard.

Ari was again startled by this macho overreaction. "What's the problem?"

"I told her to wear it to create respect," said Samir.

"Respect for . . . ?"

They turned the corner and found themselves amid round café tables on the sidewalk. Each tabletop had a tile mosaic of a swirling Arabic design. Four men smoking an enormous hookah passed the pipe between them. The sweet apple scent of their tobacco wafted through the night air. The men turned and looked at him. Ari was the only Westerner. He could feel all eyes checking him out.

"Respect for what?" asked Ari again. Samir heard the

question, but he didn't answer. He walked inside the café. Ari followed him past beaded curtains to a quiet section in the back. They took the very last table.

"Tell me everything that happened once you stepped off the plane," demanded Samir.

Ari recounted the whole trip as they ate. When he finished the story, he wiped up some scattered bits of rice with a final morsel of lamb. Samir took out a cigarette and flipped it around several times in his fingers.

"Why didn't you take Lufthansa? They land at Terminal Two. I have a man at Terminal Two."

"I had no choice," said Ari, remembering the cool blond ticket agent. "We might not have seen those cases for a week."

"At Terminal One, I have no control. Cigarette?" Samir offered one to Ari, who shook his head.

"No thank you. I don't smoke. Look, Samir, film is an existential universe. We can't look back. The only question is, will we be able to get our camera out in time to shoot?"

"I don't know."

"You don't know?" Ari wasn't used to hearing those words in the movie business.

Samir started tapping the unlit cigarette on the table. "That is right."

"But you're my fixer. Can't you fix it? A good fixer can fix anything."

Samir took out a tarnished old brass Zippo lighter and lit his cigarette. "You don't know what it's like to live in a military country. Our permission has to be signed by Tantawi himself."

"Who is Tantawi?"

"The defense minister." Samir took a deep nervous drag, blowing the ember bright orange in the night. "When you first called me, two months ago, I applied the very next day, even before you gave me the job."

"Really?" Somewhat surprised that Samir would do so much work on spec, Ari locked eyes with Samir. "And what if we hadn't hired you?"

"'Go to work and the job will come.'"

Ari was impressed with Samir's drive. This was Ari's own attitude to work. "If we miss our date on Monday, can we just get another date a few days later, or do we need to apply all over again?"

"I do not know."

There was that phrase again. "You don't know much." The recrimination had just slipped out. Samir flinched. Ari wished he hadn't said it.

"Do you accuse me of doing my job incorrectly?" Rising up an inch or two in his chair, Samir's spine was up.

"No one said anything about—" Ari backpedaled.

"You just did." Samir stamped out his barely smoked cigarette. "I told you I did not know the answer to that question on the phone before you boarded your plane in New York. Have you forgotten?"

Ari was shaken by Samir's vehemence. "Relax. I've done this kind of thing all over the world. It always works out."

"But this is Egypt." That smoldering rage came into Samir's eyes again, and Ari felt weak. He needed to assert control. He stood up and looked down at Samir.

"One way or another, we will get that shot." Ari flashed a quick burst of his own well-hidden aggression, then he changed the subject. "How are we doing on the university?"

"We can shoot there any day but that Thursday." Samir seemed relieved by the change. Good, thought Ari, he knows he's a hothead. "But there might be an issue with noise. . . ."

"What kind of issue?" demanded Ari.

"The students have been very active lately." Samir stood up and reached into his pocket for some money.

"Well . . ." Ari remembered his own college days, and flashed his smile, dropping the tension between the two men. "Students will be students. And the museum?"

"We can't shoot there on Wednesdays."

"So we'll do the airport scenes on that Wednesday." Ari glanced at the door. Hamed leaned against his car out in the street. "I'd better go check in with the studio now that LA's waking up."

Samir threw some Egyptian pounds on the table, and the two men walked outside. Hamed was leaning against Ari's car, also smoking.

"Hamed will drive you to your hotel." Samir spoke to both Ari and Hamed, instructing them. "He will pick you up at six thirty in the morning. He will tell you what to do."

"Where will you be?" asked Ari.

"Asking for another date at the Ministry of Defense, *inshallah*."

"And where is Shah Allah?" asked Ari.

"Excuse me." Samir stared back blankly.

"Where is . . . Shala?" Ari tried again with a different accentuation.

A smile broke open Samir's serious face, growing and growing until he burst into laughter so uncontrollable, so almost hysterical, that he doubled over from lack of air in his lungs. It was the first time Ari had seen Samir smile.

"What's so funny?" Ari asked, mystified.

"You will soon . . . ha, ha, hee, hee, find out." Samir put a hand on the car to steady himself, but he was racked again with a fresh wave of manic laughter. The few remaining café patrons drinking their coffee looked on in bemused curiosity until two policemen hurried by. Everyone gradually went back to their own business, amused. However, at the sight of the policemen, Samir sobered up immediately.

Chapter 8

Ari gazed out the window of Hamed's car at the multitude of Egyptians thronging the streets at night. Mostly men, but more than a few women, some with children in tow, bustling in and out of butchers, bakeries, laundries, restaurants, electronics stores as if it were the middle of the day.

"Hamed, the streets are full of people and it's one in the morning?" asked Ari.

"Yes, Mr. Ari. *Um al-Dunia*," Hamed replied over his shoulder.

"Excuse me?"

"You don't know what is *Um al-Dunia*? Cairo is 'Mother of the World.' Peoples in the street all night long."

Ari spotted a vegetable stand on the corner ahead. The owner seemed to be everywhere at once, stuffing an armful of cucumbers into the string bag of a woman wearing a black abaya, tossing a melon to a boy who threw back a coin; then, like a magician, seemingly out of thin air, he produced a glass of pulpy yellow juice for an old man with a long white beard.

"Hamed, pull over there. That fruit seller."

"But, Mr. Ari, you will have anything you want in your hotel."

"I want the real thing. Pull over."

Hamed did so, and Ari jumped out, surprising the fruit seller. Ari pointed at the half-empty glass of pulpy yellow liquid at the mouth of the white bearded man.

"What kind of juice is that?" asked Ari. He could already smell the sweet perfume of it.

The fruit seller held up a soft orange and yellow mango with little black spots on the skin, so ripe it was almost rotten. *"Mangojus?"*

"Yes, mango juice. One." Ari pointed at himself.

"Mr. Ari, the glass is not clean." Hamed had appeared right beside him, full of worry. "Rinsed only."

Ari pointed at the cheerful old man's white beard, which had a circle of yellow in the middle. "Ah," gasped the old man, refreshed.

"If he can do it," replied Ari, "so can I."

"This man drinks from the Nile," countered Hamed. "That you cannot do."

"I've shot in India, Haiti, Vietnam. I can take it."

But the fruit seller had already snatched up a knife, slit the bottom of the mango, and tossed the fruit into an ancient rubber press. He simultaneously pulled a lever and reached for a glass sitting upside down on an ornate copper drying rack holding six other glasses. As the first drop of mango juice fell, he caught it; then the deluge of fruit and pulp dropped in, filling the glass to the brim. In seconds the fruit had been crushed and was under Ari's nose. The seller proudly smiled at his own sleight of hand. He knew he was as much a showman as a fruit man.

Ari drank an explosion of taste just shy of the fine line between ripe and rotten, something the homogenized, pasteurized world of aluminum cans and plastic bottles could never deliver. Ari gulped down the whole glass.

"One more." Before he could see how, his glass was full again. The white-bearded man was grinning at him with mango-yellowy teeth. Ari thought, I'm finally here, and the Egyptians love me. Everything's going to work out. The camera will get out of customs, the Ministry of Defense will give me a new date, and whatever else they throw at me, I'll deal. Cairo is sweet, just like this glass of *mangojus*!

Then, to his delight, Ari heard music and singing. He couldn't help but sway slightly. He wanted to sing along, but didn't know the Arabic words. A gaggle of about twenty young people came around the corner, a handsome guitar player in their midst. They were cool. They were students. They sailed along on a deep certainty that they were right and you would naturally agree with them if they could just get you to join in.

The fruit seller tossed pieces of fruit to several protesters as they marched by. Strumming and singing in Arabic, the guitar player walked straight toward Ari. The song was a call and response. Ari couldn't understand the call, but the response was simply, "Ha, ha, ha." Ari found himself chanting that word with everyone else, as did the fruit seller and the man with yellow mango circle in his white beard. The guitar player was wearing a golden T-shirt that had a cartoon of the Sphinx with the singer's own head on it and the name RAMI in English letters above.

Rami stopped in front of Ari and strummed a final chord, ending the song. "Hey, man, are you a journalist?" he asked in English.

"No." Ari shook his head. "I'm a filmmaker."

"Are you here to film the revolution?" asked Rami, with a lick on his guitar.

"What revolution?" asked Ari bewildered. The gang of singing Egyptians clustered around him.

"You don't know about the revolution, man?" asked one of them.

"Come with us. We'll show you," said a tall one with a harmonica.

Who were these crazy kids on a street corner in Cairo, with long hair, speaking English, wearing funny T-shirts, and singing along with a guitar? "I can't," said Ari, though he felt the tug of temptation. "I've got to get to bed."

"The revolution comes while America sleeps." Half of the kids laughed, and then translated for the other half, who also laughed. Rami clucked his tongue with a shake of his head. He strummed his guitar and moved on. The pack of hip would-be revolutionaries followed him off down the street. A guy with a Red Sox baseball cap brought up the rear.

"Hope and change?" asked the Egyptian Red Sox fan.

"Hope and change," agreed Ari.

"Go Red Sox! *Inshallah!*" added the Boston fan.

It didn't seem like the right moment for Ari to mention he was from New York.

A phalanx of thirty tough-looking men in leather jackets, along with a couple of police in uniform holding walkie-talkies, came around the corner slowly shuffling along after the kids. The police looked sullen and self-conscious, a marked contrast to the joy of the moments before.

"There are more police than protesters," noticed Ari uneasily.

"Let them come." The Red Sox fan turned to go. "We laugh at them." The fan caught up with the rest of his merry comrades down the street, who were already chanting out their fearless refrain:

"Ha, ha, ha!"

PART TWO

It makes the heart to tremble when you open an undiscovered tomb.

—**Dr. Zahi Hawass, leader of the Supreme Council of Antiquities**

Chapter 9

As the concierge is very proud to tell you, the Mena House Hotel, built in 1869 next to the pyramids, was first a hunting lodge for the Egyptian King Ismai'l Pasha. The chandelier in the old lodge is so tall that it rises up through the second floor, through a gallery of balconies especially designed for beholding it. Ari couldn't help but gaze upward as he passed beneath the unique lamp, staring up at a white glass globe with an Arabic pattern etched in gold overlay. His eyes were so tired from his twenty-hour journey that he could hardly focus them. The chandelier seemed to spin over Ari, although it could not move.

"This way Mr. Basher."

The porter took Ari up one flight by elevator, then out onto the balcony around the chandelier. Its forty columns of suspended turquoise stones and glass refracted the white globe light at their center. His eyes saw with the hazy glare of sheer exhaustion. He felt as though he had stepped inside a kaleidoscope, all the glass bits of color suspended in midair. His voyage had finally become a hallucination. He staggered toward the pillow that he knew awaited him down the corridor.

Once inside his suite, Ari was about to tip the porter, but he noticed a pyramid that somehow seemed to be sitting on the balcony outside the room. He knew this was some sort of optical illusion. He had seen the massive pyramids from Hamed's car, and his conscious mind understood that the closest pyramid was at least half a mile away from the hotel. This one seemed close enough for him to touch.

"It is the pyramid of Khufu," said the porter with a proud little bow.

"Yes." Ari tipped him. "I must get some sleep."

Alone, Ari kicked off his white tennis shoes and began to peel off the rank clothes he'd worn for the past thirty-six hours.

"Laptop," he reminded himself. He slid it out of his backpack and set it to recharge on an old Moorish carved wooden desk. An Ethernet cable sat at the ready like a coiled snake that could lunge out and strike him in the night. He plugged the cable in and turned on the machine.

He craved a shower, but the bed loomed before him, immense, larger than king size, he thought. A giant bronze headboard shaped like a scallop shell etched with finely detailed filigree patterns, eight feet in diameter, hung on the wall. Ari could see his golden face reflected, and like Narcissus, he fell toward himself, with a bounce onto the bed. As his head settled deep into a crisp white pillow, his computer rang.

"Uuggghhhh." Ari arose, imitating a mummy in a monster movie, and staggered toward the ringing knowing that Beth was the only person it could be.

Ari pasted on a smile and hit accept. "Hey, babe!"

Beth's face popped up on his screen. "Darling!" She sat at her desk, holding a cup of coffee, daylight streaming across her face. "How was your flight?"

"Eleven hours in coach," he mumbled, wondering how he should tell her about the SpaceCam.

"Coach?" she asked with a slight hint of suspicion.

"I had to switch flights."

"Why? Did we make a mistake with your booking?"

"No mistake. But I got a whole row, four seats. I could stretch out."

"Wow, lucky you."

"I wouldn't go that far." Ari decided that now was the moment. "They took the camera in customs," he confessed.

"What?" The warm glow dropped off of Beth's face. A poised catlike energy took its place. "The whole SpaceCam?"

"Everything." Ari waited for her reaction.

"Oh my god! You're supposed to fly on Monday. What are we going to do?" He could see her mind whirr into action.

"You know me. I'll put on my smile, go back down to the airport, and charm their pants off." Ari tried to seem relaxed about all of it. "Like I did to you."

Beth's nostrils flared. She was both angered and grudgingly amused at what she knew was more than a joke. "Are they women?"

"Uh, no."

"Did you tell anyone at the studio?"

"No, Beth." Ari had to quash this idea fast. "Let's not freak anybody out. Let's tell them all on Monday morning when they've got other things to think about."

Beth shook her head. "I don't work that way."

"Look, if I send an e-mail now, the damned SpaceCam'll be all they'll think about all weekend long. I'll get a million calls. There will be stress. And stress where it can't do me, or you, any good. Wait till I get back to the airport tomorrow and figure out what's really going on. Look here, girlfriend." Ari picked up the computer and carried it to the balcony. "What do you see?"

"I'm not keeping secrets, Ari." He aimed the computer outside. "Surprises give you cancer . . . Oh my god, oh my god, oh my god! Is that a pyramid outside?"

"Yes, the great pyramid of Khufu!" He had successfully diverted her, for the moment.

"You lucky bum! You have pyramids in your backyard." Then her producer face came back on. "How much is that hotel room costing?"

"You approved it."

"I did?" She was dumbfounded.

"Yes. Back when you thought you might come along. I noticed you didn't mark up that line item. Look at the bed: Pharaoh size. The sheets are like . . . to die for. If you roll over here, you can even see the Sphinx from in bed."

"Don't torture me."

"Why don't you jump on a plane and come over and join me?" he teased.

"Very funny." She made a face. "You're not the center of the universe. One of us has to finish this film. I still have movie stars to babysit on the set in New York."

"Look, Beth." Ari grew serious. "How much cash do you have on hand in the safe right now?"

"Why?"

"Do you have twenty thousand?"

"I might." She became still, poker-faced. "What happened to the ten grand I gave you?"

"I still have it. See?" Ari reached into the waistband of his pants and unzipped a hidden pocket. He pulled out the bundle of one-hundred-dollar bills she had given him. He rifled the money like a deck of cards before the camera on the laptop. "Can you get another twenty grand to the SpaceCam guys to give to me?"

"Ugh. On a Saturday morning?" She groaned. "Everything's always last minute with you. It's illegal to carry more than ten thousand, cash, on your person out of the country."

"Oy vey. So split it in half. Give ten to Don and ten to Charley Foster. They'll give it to me when they see me."

"Why don't you get it from your fixer?"

"Things happen fast in the field. Look, I probably won't need it, but I'd rather have it and not need it than need it and not—"

"Don't bribe anybody, Ari."

"C'mon, Beth."

"It's against the law. The Foreign Corrupt Practices Act. The Feds're cracking down on all the studios now."

"I'm a big boy. You don't have to tell me how the game is played."

"I didn't hear that." Beth put her hands over her ears as her cell phone buzzed. "Shit." She moved her coffee mug and looked at the phone incredulously.

"Who?" asked Ari.

"Brad Pitt's manager is calling me."

"On Saturday morning at . . . what the hell time is it over there?"

Beth didn't even notice Ari's question. She was completely focused on the phone.

"Darling?" asked Ari, trying to woo her attention back.

"What?" Beth was annoyed by the distraction.

"I love you." Ari felt a pain deep in his gut and a powerful contraction in his stomach.

Beth looked back into the camera in disbelief. "What did you just say?"

"That wasn't the first time."

"Almost."

He breathed through his teeth to relax his insides. "Don't forget the money."

"Don't play with me, Ari." She shook her head, fondly disappointed. " 'Bye, you bum." She had reached over to shut off the conversation, but stopped when Ari doubled over in pain. "What is it? What's wrong?"

"Ugh!" Ari jumped up, unbuckled his pants, and ran for the bathroom.

"Ari? Are you okay?"

Ari yelled from the bathroom. "I had some bad mango juice!"

"La, la, la! Too much information!" Beth yelled to him in a sort of singsong way as she reached for her computer keyboard and the screen went blank.

Chapter 10

Holding an empty plate, Ari moved through the sumptuous breakfast buffet at his hotel. Except for the absence of bacon, Ari could have been in any five-star hotel in the world. He passed a sous chef cooking omelets, another making crepes and waffles and pancakes. Ari hovered near a row of chafing dishes holding Middle-Eastern food.

"Would you like some eggplant?" asked a server.

"No thank you." Ari shook his head at a steaming ragout.

"Some beans?"

"Oh no." Ari shook his head again. "I'll just take some of that plain white rice there. No, no, just a spoonful. Less than that." The mystified server doled out a small pile of rice. The two of them stepped over to a station of fruit juices. Ari spotted his nemesis.

"Some mango juice, sir?" asked the server.

"I shouldn't really." Ari lingered longingly. "Maybe just half a glass."

Ari ate looking out at a green manicured lawn and palm trees. He could have been in LA, but for the pyramids and the faint acrid smell of some distant fire that one often smells in the third world, the burning of garbage. After a few half-hearted bites, Ari went to find his ride.

In the driveway a security guard with a mirror on a stick and a bomb-sniffing German shepherd were making a cursory check of Hamed's car. Ari got right in and the dog and man abandoned their task.

Hamed drove to the airport through heavy but fast-moving ever-honking pre-rush-hour traffic. They parked in the lot and walked up to the modern glass-and-steel terminal. Inside, Hamed and Ari passed by a huge palm tree growing up to the ceiling. They threaded their way through the bustle of white robed Arabs from the Gulf and colorfully dressed Africans, until they reached the farthest corner of the modern terminal. There in the wall was a panel—not really a door, but a door-sized rectangular cut in the wall. Hamed pulled out his cell and dialed. The wall opened.

A short, wizened Egyptian stood on the other side expecting them. Behind him, a steady stream of grayish drone people scurried up and down the corridor holding forms or chits out in front of them with singular purpose. In a hushed urgent tone, Hamed spoke to the man in Arabic. Ari figured out his name was Walid. Walid beckoned, but Ari hesitated.

"Mr. Ari, you go in. Walid will stay with you. I wait here," said Hamed.

"Okay . . ." With trepidation, Ari left the comfort of his driver/translator and stepped through the portal. Walid, who seemed to speak no English at all, swept Ari into the tide of

bureaucrats. They were off into a netherworld part Soviet so-
cialism, part British colonialism run amok, as if those two
forces had mated and produced some metastasized progeny
alive well beyond its historical moment, like that old Japanese
soldier who never surrendered still in his cave forever on some
South Pacific isle.

Ari's eyes had to adjust to the dark corridor. Bare lightbulbs
hung from old wires out of light fixtures long ago broken.
He found himself on line with the drone people shuffling
between walls gray from decades of dust. The architectural
detail had a 1930's feel. There were windows into darkness
and doors leading nowhere. Ari figured that he must be in part
of an old terminal that had not been torn down but engulfed
by the modern buildings around it. The Egyptians, the original
builders of history, must never demolish anything, he thought.

Walid led Ari down a busy well-worn flight of stairs to a
small dark office with windows that opened out into a narrow blackness.

"Oh, good morning, Mr. Basher," said the young woman
from the Press Ministry with the cat's-eye glasses. "Please sit
down. Would you like some tea?"

"Tea?" asked Ari.

"Mint tea?"

"Thank you, that's very kind of you."

She seated Ari in a chair next to her desk, which was covered in neatly organized piles of paper. She disappeared for a
moment, then returned with a tea in the Arabic style: fresh
mint tea in a small glass mug on a glass saucer, a sugar cube
on the side.

"Thank you." Ari looked at her without blinking, never

taking his eyes from her face. He adopted a slight smile, which he increased with an ambiguous hint of flirtation whenever she glanced at him. This made her anxious to turn her attention to her desk, the result Ari was hoping to create.

"You do remember," said Ari, "that my permit to fly around the Sphinx from the Ministry of Defense is for tomorrow only?" Get on with it, he thought, and get me out of here.

"Yes, yes, of course, Mr. Basher." She nervously ran through the papers on her desk. He noticed that today she was wearing the hijab over her chic haircut, but her cute cat's-eye glasses poked out with a hint of stylish defiance. She selected a paper and excused herself.

Ari looked down at his tea in the small clear glass. He picked up the sugar cube. As he had no teaspoon, he dropped the cube into the tea and tried to stir it with his pinky, but the greenish liquid was too hot. Ari just watched the sugar dissolve.

After a while, he drank his tea. He looked around the dimly lit room and decided that this part of the building must have been built during the 1950s because one wall was entirely of aluminum-framed windows that swung open into the black void. When Ari lost any expectation that the young woman would return, she did so. Ari set his teacup down and stood up.

"Mr. Basher, please come with me."

She took him out into the hallway, up several flights on the busy staircase, then to a corner office also looking into that same black void. An older middle-aged woman sitting at the desk was surprised when Ari walked in wearing his disarming smile. The young woman approached the older one and leaned

forward, whispering in her ear. Ari guessed from slight ges-
ticulations that she was telling how the SpaceCam had been
taken in customs the day before.

Ari got the distinct impression that the two women didn't
know what to do with him and were arguing over some
course of action that frightened them. Glancing every so often in his direction, he would smile and they would force
polite smiles back. Their whispers reached a soft crescendo.
The middle-aged woman picked up the phone and made a
phone call. Some minutes later the fax machine rang and a
fax came in.

"Very well," said the middle-aged woman. "I will take this
to the head of customs, General Moussa." She started for the
door, then she stopped, remembering something important.
"Would you like some tea?"

"Tea?" Another cup of tea, thought Ari. That's the last thing
I want right now. "Thank you. That would be so very . . . kind."
And he flashed his million-dollar smile.

Chapter 11

Ari looked at the tea leaves in the dregs of his cup. He slowly swirled around the viscous sugary syrup, studying the sweet muck, as he had nothing better to do. He stood. He walked to the windows and looked out at what once must have been an exterior view of the runway or the desert, but now was a black wall of shadows. What if I don't get the SpaceCam today? What will Frank think . . . ? Stop it, he commanded his brain. What if we miss our date with the military? Stop it, or you'll lose your cool, and you need to be cool.

His thoughts grew hazy, unfocused, liquid; indeed, he tried not to think. That would only make him nervous and look at his watch; better to detach from time and park his brain for a while until the middle-aged Press Ministry woman in the hijab returned. She finally did so, holding up the fax.

"I'm so sorry, Mr. Basher, but General Moussa needs to see the original letter, not a facsimile."

"The original letter?" Ari didn't understand. "The letter we already sent to you?"

"Yes. But it is not here at the airport."

"Where is it?" Ari wondered if that essential piece of paper had been lost.

"At the Press Ministry downtown."

Problem solved, he thought. "Can't you . . . request it?"

"Yes, Mr. Basher, this is the customary procedure."

"How long does that take?"

"Several days."

"Several? Several?" stammered Ari as he started to experience a new kind of vertigo, bureaucratic vertigo. "But we'll miss our date!"

"What date?" asked the Press Ministry woman.

Why doesn't she know about the date to fly over the Sphinx? wondered Ari. Should I tell her? If no one told her for a reason, you'd better not tell her now. "I will get the letter. I will get it from the Press Ministry and bring it here." Ari pointed at the fax. "Who has the original?"

She wrote the person's name on the fax. Ari dashed out the door, almost slamming into Walid, who was hovering in the corridor. They joined the teeming throng of chit holders. Ari, clutching the fax of his own letter, his own chit, tried to pass the shuffling crowd, but this was impossible as everyone else had the same intent, to get their little pieces of paper through this rat's maze and get on with their lives.

Finally, Walid opened the portal and let Ari emerge from that netherworld into the bright modern terminal. He explained everything to Hamed as they ran outside to the lot and jumped in the car.

The two men drove away from the airport. They raced alongside thirty-, even forty-year-old black Fiat taxis. They passed trucks piled high with bales of cotton, three-wheeled carts made out of motor scooters, and even horse-drawn wagons rolling along on automobile tires. Toward the city center the traffic slowed to a crawl. Ari thought of getting out and walking, but the pace would pick up for a few moments and fool Ari's hope.

He looked at his watch. Two o'clock. How was that possible? Had each cup of tea consumed an hour?

"This drive'll kill the whole day," Ari said to Hamed. "I have to hand-deliver them a letter that they have in their own headquarters. Insane."

They passed the minaret of an ancient mosque. The call to prayer sounded. Several taxis pulled over to the side of the road, some of their drivers dashing into the mosque, others unrolling mats on the ground, then facing toward Mecca and starting to pray.

Traffic stopped short. Hamed pounded the horn. A great cacophony of honking erupted. Hamed leapt out of the car and started yelling in Arabic.

"What is it?" Ari got out and stood up on the car to see what was blocking traffic. A quarter mile ahead was a bridge that spanned the Nile. A small blockade of protesters stood in the middle waving banners and Egyptian flags. The protesters must have timed it with the call to prayer as their signal.

Under his breath, Ari cursed them. He was relieved to see a few police running across the bridge from the other side. There was yelling and shoving, then more police and the blockade broke up. Traffic started crawling again.

They turned by the river and followed it for a few blocks, stopping outside a big modern building. Its many balconies rose up overlooking the Nile.

"We are here," said Hamed. "The Ministry of Information."

Hamed ushered Ari in through security, but couldn't leave the car alone on the busy street, so he left Ari to fend for himself. Ari showed his fax to anyone who would take a moment to speak with him. He found the office of an almost identically chic young woman also wearing glasses and a hijab. She, too, fed him tea, made him wait while she vanished with the fax and came back, then brought him upstairs to the office of yet another middle-aged woman also wearing a hijab and glasses. More tea. A furtive whispered conversation. A phone call. They went out and came back half an hour later bearing the original letter identical to the fax. Ari thanked them each profusely. He dashed downstairs, ran outside, and hopped back into Hamed's car.

They beat their way back through traffic. They were racing the clock. The business day soon would draw to a close. Somehow they made it out of downtown without obstruction, back to the airport. They ran through the terminal to the little door.

Ari stepped back through the portal into the bureaucratic netherworld, shuffled through the corridor, and ran up the stairs. He reached the office of the middle-aged Press Ministry woman, who took the letter, gave him tea, and again disappeared.

Had he made it in time? Ari wondered. Would he be able to claim his sixteen camera cases to shoot his helicopter shot tomorrow, the assigned date on his permit to fly around the Sphinx? He started biting his fingernails.

In a very short time, the head Press Ministry woman came back holding the letter as if it were somehow unclean. "There is a problem."

"That's not the right letter?" Ari reached out for it, smiling his biggest smile but feeling like hell.

"No, the letter is correct." She looked at him sternly as if he were a naughty child. "It gives you permission to bring your camera into Egypt to shoot a documentary. However, all this equipment is obviously for a Hollywood movie. The Press Ministry cannot help you."

"But, but . . ." The smile was frozen on Ari's face. He racked his brain for the best thing to say. "Uh, honestly . . . it really is uh . . . based on a true story."

A porter came in and cleared away Ari's tea.

Chapter 12

Dejected, Ari sat on a bench in Terminal One staring up at the arrivals sign. Samir walked up, nodded to Ari, and sat down next to him. Their mood was somber.

After a while, Samir spoke. "Have you read Kafka?"

"Read him? He wrote my day." Ari faced Samir, his fixer. "How did it go at the Ministry of Defense?"

"The same as you."

"So we're not going to make our date tomorrow." Ari inhaled deeply. "And the military won't give us a new one?"

"No . . ." said Samir in a clipped, defensive way, as if expecting an argument.

"So we have a problem."

The words on the arrivals board started to flip over. The latest flight from New York showed AT THE GATE status.

"Your men have arrived." Samir stood up, avoiding a response. "Don and Charles."

"It seems to me"—Ari stood as well—"that we are going to have to start doing something differently."

"Yes." Samir nodded. A suggestive silence hung between the two men.

Ari said nothing, but rubbed his fingers together in the universal sign of bribery.

Samir glanced around the terminal. "It's best not to speak of such things."

"I'll leave it to you then."

Samir peeled off and walked away toward the gates. Ari caught up to him.

"Speaking of money . . ." Samir veered abruptly into the mens' room.

"Yes?" Ari followed him into the empty bathroom. They were now alone.

"The money did not arrive in my account today." Samir pulled out a cigarette. He looked at Ari in the mirror.

"Ugh." A financial crisis of confidence is the last thing I need right now, thought Ari. "I'm sure it'll come tomorrow," he said in a soothing tone.

"Tell me, Ari," said Samir, flicking open his brass lighter and taking a furious drag. The tip of his cigarette burned red. "How did you pick me for this job? Did you first call Studio Giza?"

"Of course." Ari admitted to having called the biggest and oldest film studio in Egypt.

"So why didn't you pick them over me?" Samir studied Ari carefully. Samir's suspicion of not getting paid would increase or decrease in the next minute. He would certainly quit if Ari gave a wrong answer.

"Studio Giza didn't call me back for two weeks. You called back the next day. You were direct, no nonsense. You got your bid to me in a week. One hundred and twenty-five thousand. Our accountants looked it over. It made sense. And, most of all . . . I trusted my gut."

Samir took another drag. He tipped his ash into one of the sinks on the counter. "Your gut?"

"Right here." Ari slapped his stomach twice. "My insides, my instinct. Also, I like to work with a guy who is on his way up and works harder than somebody who's already on top." Ari stepped over to the counter close to Samir. Ari knew he had to crush any doubt that might have arisen in Samir's mind. "Are you worried about the money?"

"Yes," admitted Samir. "I'm not Studio Giza. I must pay people in advance."

"You think we're not going to pay you?" Ari unzipped the secret pocket in his pants and pulled out the packet of one-hundred-dollar bills Beth had given him. "Here's ten thousand dollars." He slapped the green bills down on the red Formica counter. "In a few minutes, I'll have twenty thousand more. Go on, take it."

Samir glanced at the door nervously. Anyone could walk in. Ari was playing a game of chicken: Here's my wad and I can throw it on a bathroom counter if I want. If I can throw it around like that, there must be more to come, was Ari's implication.

Samir didn't touch the money. He took another drag on his cigarette. "Ariel Basher. What kind of name is that?"

Ari smiled his big smile. He was glad Samir had moved onto the topic of Ari himself, where he could always play his

strongest card. "It was Beshert, which means 'Destiny' or 'Fate'
in Jewish. When my great-grandfather came to America, they
changed it."

"Why?"

"The officials wrote it down wrong, or they couldn't spell
it, or they wrote it the way it would sound in English—who
knows? I'm 'Fate.' Ariel Destiny."

"It suits you." Samir was amused for a moment, just for a
moment, then serious again. He gazed down at the money.
"And Ariel? That was the name of the president of Israel."

"It's an ancient name for Jerusalem," explained Ari.

"Have you been there?" Samir asked. Ari could feel the hidden weight of the question, Muslim to Jew.

"I shot two movies there. I even shot in the Arab quarter
before . . ." Ari wondered if he should have mentioned that.

"Before what?" Samir was probing, evidently testing Ari for
some sign of Israeli nationalism.

"Before suicide bombs, before 9/11, before everything went
crazy. You can't do that today," said Ari.

"Why not?" Samir studied him for any hidden racism.

"Just use an Arab crew, you mean?" asked Ari.

"Not Israeli," said Samir.

"Right." Better get off this subject, thought Ari. "Like we're
doing here on this film. This is the coolest job we can do.
Shooting the Sphinx from a chopper? The first to try. How
cool is that?"

"No one has ever done it." Samir was pensive, considering
Ari's words.

"It will make your reputation with foreigners, with the

studios." Sell him, seduce him, flatter him, thought Ari. "And you got that right away. You were quick."

"To do something that has never been done before . . ." Samir was speaking more to himself than to Ari. Ari saw his opening.

"The first time is always hard. For anything, it's hard. Samir the Hammer, I chose you because I knew you would never give up." Ari knew he had said the magic words. Like everyone else, Samir wanted to be wanted for himself, for his own eccentric skills, for his honor.

Samir ground out his cigarette on the floor, then he slid the bundle of money back along the countertop to Ari. "Keep this. If I need it later, I will ask you for it, but get me the wire transfer confirmation, please, so we do not lose time."

"How much is this payment supposed to be?" asked Ari, picking up the money and stashing it.

"Twenty-five thousand dollars," said Samir.

"It will come tomorrow," said Ari.

"*Inshallah*," they both said simultaneously.

Chapter 13

Ari spotted Don, the lanky Australian cameraman, and the squat technician, Charley Foster, as they walked toward the customs desk. They both recognized the stack of sixteen cases piled up against the wall outside the impound storage room, still guarded by President Mubarak's gigantic portrait. From the sour look on their faces, they both understood that something had gone wrong. The customs officials waved them through without a search. Ari and Samir stepped up to greet them.

"Don, Charley, this is Samir, our fixer."

Charley rudely ignored the introduction. "And is that our camera?"

"So we're not flying tomorrow?" asked Don in his Australian drawl.

"No," answered Samir.

The three Westerners moved away from Samir slightly. Ari, Don, and Charley were the most disparate of men: a New York

Jew, an Australian surfer, and a Texan Navy vet. Off the job, they probably would never see each other. They probably wouldn't even like each other, but one fundamental principle drew them together. They had come halfway around the globe to get something and bring it back with them. For centuries the mantra of Western man was not just "hunt and gather" but also "extract." This was the highest imperative, the very foundation of Western civilization. Whether they knew this consciously or not, every Egyptian was either a collaborator or an adversary, but never an equal partner, never one of them. Only they could return to the West bearing their prize.

There wasn't much else to say. Ari, Don, and Charley piled into Hamed's car and went back to Giza. The traffic had thinned for the night, so the trip to Mena House was quick. Ari gave them an hour to check in and clean up. Then he went to Don's room for a visit. Charley handed Ari a beer.

"I see you guys found the local bodega." They toasted, clinking their bottles together.

"How'd Frank like the New York footage?" asked Don.

"Loved it." Ari knew he had to lay it on thick, as he was about to hit them with a pay cut. What else could he do? Things had gone wrong. "The George Washington Bridge shot was fantastic."

"And the Empire State Building?" asked Don, beaming proudly.

"Spectacular."

"Statue of Liberty?" Don pressed.

"Eh, not so much. But two out of three. That's"—Ari raised his bottle and clinked Don's—"not bad. Listen, guys, Beth is going to want you to cut your rate."

"Okay." Don nodded easily. Ari wasn't worried about Don. He rode the wave, not the money.

"In half," added Ari.

"Come on man!" Charley, true to character, objected gruffly and raised his beer bottle as if to hurl it at the floor. He didn't. Charley was all bark, and Ari knew that, too.

"When's your next gig?" Ari distracted him.

"Not till the end of the month. In Malaysia, Kuala Lumpur."

"The Petronas Towers. A James Bond flick," added Don.

"Good," said Ari, "gives me a few weeks to maneuver."

"What's the plan?" asked Don. "How do you get our camera?"

Ari's answer was a question. "You guys got something for me?"

Don and Charley both reached into their pockets. Each man pulled out a ten-thousand-dollar bundle of hundred-dollar bills with the bank band still around them.

"We should keep this money and get on the next flight out of here," said Charley bitterly. But when Don handed over his bundle, Charley reluctantly followed suit. At the moment he laid the packet of bills on Ari's outstretched hand, a dramatic sting of music played outside through the open terrace door.

Charley jumped. "What the hell is that?"

"It's the light show." Ari laughed. "Come and get a load of this."

The three men stepped out into the twilight. The lights on the Sphinx changed from white to green. A booming voice with a posh English accent echoed from the Necropolis into the night.

"You have come tonight to the most fabulous and celebrated place in the world," the voice echoed off the pyramids. "Here on the plateau of Giza stands forever the mightiest of human achievements. No traveler, emperor, merchant, or poet has trod on these sands and not gasped in awe. For five thousand years I have seen all the suns men can remember come up in the sky. I saw the history of Egypt in its first glow, as tomorrow I shall see the East burning with a new day."

Charley and Don stared out at the Necropolis dumbfounded.

"I didn't know the Sphinx was a Brit," said Don.

"He also speaks French, Swedish, German, Italian. At nine o'clock tonight he's Japanese," added Ari. "He's an international lion of mystery."

Chapter **14**

Back in his room, Ari knew he would have to call Beth in a few hours and tell her that he had made no progress on the camera. With the time difference, he didn't want to wake her up at four in the morning and ruin her sleep. He tried to nap for a few hours, but the bed seemed too big, too empty. If only she were there, he could calm her down, but from a distance, he couldn't predict how she would react. She was fundamentally a "no" person. Her job was to say no to risk, say no to mistakes, and rein in crazy filmmakers from burning through millions of dollars without a plan. And he had none.

Ari flopped around on the bed for a while. Sleep was impossible. He put his clothes on and went out for a walk. He left the gates of the Mena House, turning down several offers of dilapidated taxis, and strolled out onto the ancient road down the side of the Necropolis. The vast expanse around the pyramids was closed for the night except for the light show. The Sphinx was speaking Japanese; Toshiro Mifune's voice boomed through the Valley of the Dead. Tourist police, some on foot, some on camels, patrolled the pyramids and the smaller tombs that were still under excavation to keep the grave robbers away.

Ari skirted the wall around the pink, then green, then purple Sphinx. The café was still open to serve the handful of Japanese tourists at the late show. Ari asked for a mango juice. His stomach had held so far today, but he had eaten mostly rice. He didn't want to sit in the empty café with the waiter staring at him expectantly. He didn't want to buy a ticket to the light show, so he walked out onto the sand and found a large fallen stone against an ancient wall. He nursed his glass of juice listening to the guttural samurai Japanese.

Ari didn't like to think about himself or his life. He wasn't introspective. He had stumbled into film as a career and loved it. He was bored easily and hated routine. Each film was a new set of people, a new family. Each day was a different location, a different scene. The relentless stream of novel and unique problems that everyone hated was exactly what Ari loved. He was a problem solver, and film was all logistical challenge. How do you get the shot?

This vagabond life of hotel rooms, campers, soundstages, airplanes, riding around in vans, to scout or to shoot—he didn't mind it. He was full of energy. People liked him. They wanted him around, especially women. He heard people talk about him sometimes. They called him adolescent, a big teenager. He didn't care. He did hate gossip. He had no memory for it. "What you think about me is none of my business," is what he used to shut people up when they were about to repeat something nasty about him to his face.

His last girlfriend, Molly, was a screenwriter on his previous film. He overheard her on the phone one day: "Ari's got a first-rate smile, but a second-rate brain." Yet, as a writer, she hadn't seen him doing the impossible, the cinematic equivalent of finding water in the desert. At least Beth understood him. All of his career, he had never had a failure, a real disaster happen to him. What would that be like if he couldn't get back the SpaceCam? He wondered what he was going to say to Beth.

Ari sighed and put his half-full glass down on the rock. He'd had enough mango. He heard a sound, a crunching of the dusty sand. Ari looked at the wall behind him. There, in a gap at the bottom, were two gleaming eyes—the face of a little boy. He peeked out of a black rectangle where a missing stone left a tomblike hole in the wall. Eyeing Ari's glass, the boy looked like a wild animal come upon suddenly.

"I'm hungry," said the boy in English.

Ari picked up the glass and handed it down to him. The child drank with a thirsty violence as if the liquid might escape. Ari took the empty glass back against some resistance. The kid seemed to want to keep it. Apparently feeling more at ease, the kid slithered out of the gap in the stone wall. He sat down next to Ari.

"I Mohamed," said the kid.

"I'm Ari."

Mohamed reached out his hand. "Shake?"

Ari shook his little hand.

"I like you," said Mohamed.

"I like you, too."

"Where are you from?"

"New York City."

Mohamed, still holding Ari's hand, leaned his little head against Ari's shoulder. "Take me with you."

"I can't do that." Ari looked around for some kind of an adult.

Sadly, Mohamed lay his head on Ari's lap. Somewhere on the other side of the wall, Ari heard the sound of a soft moan, then, in German, *"Ich liebe dich . . ."*

From the horror of recognition, Ari jumped almost involuntarily off the rock, sliding out from under the boy's head.

Mohamed clutched at his hand desperately, "Give me a dollar. I'm hungry."

Ari reached into his pocket and fumbled out his boarding pass and some receipts for airport food. He produced a dollar and, before he knew it, out of the night came a dozen boys about Mohamed's age. They surrounded Ari, leaping up trying to grab the dollar out of his hand. "I'm hungry! I'm hungry!" they all yelped plaintively. Ari had to hold the dollar bill straight over his head to keep it from being torn. He crumpled it into a little ball and stuffed it into Mohamed's fist.

Three tourist police charged out of the café in their white uniforms with oversized black berets. They raised long rubber truncheons over their heads and brought them down with a swift crack, bashing the legs of the little boys. In seconds, the boys had vanished, behind rocks, through gaps in the wall— gone so fast it was as if they were never there in the first place. But Mohamed, the police had caught by the shirt. They dragged him away on the sand toward the gate.

Mohamed was no match for them, but it took a surprising amount of effort for three grown men to pry the dollar from Mohamed's little fist.

"Noooo!" wailed Mohamed, bursting into tears. Ari cringed. Spellbound, he followed them to the street outside the café. A flatbed truck was parked there, a giant navy blue box on the back. One policeman opened the padlocked door. Maybe thirty boys lay on the floor, lifting their heads up groggily to watch another one tossed inside.

The door slammed on little Mohamed. Ari just stood there. He couldn't believe it. He refused to believe what he had just seen. He closed his eyes and opened them. The truck was still there. This was beyond his comprehension, beyond his limited ability to trust his own senses at that moment. But the box was still on the back of the truck. The police noticed Ari. He drifted toward them, some kind of objection stirring in his throat. They banged on the cab of the truck and hopped up onto the running boards. The driver started the engine and pulled away.

Ari stood and watched the blue box police truck as it drove its catch of the day all along the road around the Necropolis past the Mena House hotel.

Chapter 15

Back in his hotel room, Ari immediately Skyped Beth. Staring at his computer, he watched as it rang and rang. He knew he was waking her up. A dim image popped on the screen. Her hand, her face, her white breasts and tousled hair, and beyond, lying next to her, Ari could see the naked fat belly of Beth's husband, Glenn.

"Honey?" mumbled Glenn. "What the hell?"

"I've got a unit in Cairo," said Beth. She rubbed her eyes. "Must be something wrong. Go back to sleep, Glenn."

Then she noticed her husband's nakedness on the screen. Wincing, she hit a button. Her image and Glenn's disappeared. Ari could hear the thumping slap of her feet on the floor as she carried her computer through to some distant corner of her home. Oh my god, oh my god, oh my god, thought Ari. What a mistake. I should never have called her this early. You idiot! he berated himself.

"What is it, Ari? What's the matter?"

"Nothing." Ari couldn't even picture her face. He was stuck with the latent image of Glenn's fat white belly.

"Did you get the cash from Charley and Don?" Beth guessed at a potential problem.

"Yes, yes, thank you, I did."

"Did you get your SpaceCam?"

This was what Ari knew he had to tell her, but not yet. "Darling, please, could you turn on your camera?"

"Keep it professional, Ari." She was very tense. "This thing's on speaker. I'll take that as a no. No SpaceCam."

"Not yet."

"What's your plan B?"

Ari bristled. "I get the shot."

"But if you don't?"

"I get the shot." Ari repeated the words slower, forcefully, deliberately.

"I told the studio, Ari."

Now he was shaken. "When?"

"Yesterday, after we spoke."

"But why?"

"Ari."

"I thought we had agreed not to tell them until . . . this morning? Today, morning your time?"

"Bad news is radioactive. Best to get rid of it before it rubs off on you."

"On you, you mean." Ari's ire rose. "So I can't trust you? My own—"

"Ari, please!"

What was he going to say? Girlfriend, lover, boss? He didn't even know. She had been naked. Glenn had been naked. The thought revolted him. "Throwing me under the bus like that?"

Beth turned on her webcam. They could see each other again. She had tossed on a thin silk kimono that was not entirely closed. "They're not stupid, Ari. If you had waited until today, they would have figured out you were sitting on information. I did you a favor."

"Are they worried?" asked Ari.

"Not yet, but we're paying Charley and Don two grand a day to take a vacation?"

"I asked the guys to cut their rate when we don't fly."

"Thank you." She softened.

"In half."

"Very nice." She seemed pleased and leaned back; her kimono fell open. She didn't adjust it. "Did you really ride a camel?"

"Tomorrow. Open your e-mail. When would I have had time to do that?" He was hostile, offended. He never thought of Glenn, as if he didn't exist. On other nights Ari knew how to keep the boundaries that would never intersect with married life.

"How's the food over there?" she asked, another question to keep him talking, and Ari could see that she knew he was upset.

"Now I understand hummus." Ari opened up slowly, cagily. "I mean, I really finally get it for the first time. And the mango juice is so good. It costs about a dime. I gave a glass to a kid, big mistake."

"What's so bad about that?" She prompted him to talk, to keep him on the line.

"The tourist police beat him for . . . begging."

"Beat him?" The words hit her and she closed her kimono reflexively. "How old was he?"

"Ten, maybe eleven. They marched him out to the street where there's always a truck with a big blue box on the back—no windows, just a giant box. They opened the door. There are about thirty kids sleeping inside right now."

"Oh my god!"

"And they threw him inside the box and locked it."

"What did you do?"

"Me? I didn't know what to do. I was so stunned." Ari realized what was upsetting him more than anything else. "I just stood there and . . . I didn't do anything."

PART THREE

The genius of you Americans is that you never make clear-cut stupid moves, only complicated stupid moves which make the rest of us wonder at the possibility that we might be missing something.

—Gamal Abdel Nasser

Chapter 16

Hamed pulled up in front of a British colonial building that might easily have stood in Knightsbridge or Bayswater. Ari was not expecting anything so grand, yet the number of the address matched the one he was looking for. So did the name on the brass plaque: PETROLEUM AIR CHARTERS.

In the States, when Ari went to a helicopter charter company, it was always in some shack on the far side of an airstrip. This place was an imposing limestone building about the size of the White House, girded by a tall wrought iron fence twelve feet high with black spikes on top. Outside the gate, a Horse Guards–style booth housed a well-pressed policeman bearing a submachine gun.

Ari gathered his props—his little gold Sphinx, his plastic pyramids, and his toy helicopter—then walked up the steps into the echoing lobby.

What imperial purpose this building had served for the British he could only guess. He crossed a white polished marble floor and passed through black Georgian columns. A twin circular staircase with red Persian carpet runners led upward.

"May I help you?" asked the receptionist. She wore a navy blue Chanel suit and had her hair in a twist.

"I have an appointment with General Hanawy."

"Follow me, please."

The receptionist led Ari upstairs through a reception room. Green leather couches around a coffee table faced the secretary's desk. Ari assumed he would sit and wait but she kept leading him on toward a mahogany door. She knocked and pushed the heavy door open.

"Mr. Basher is here," she said.

"Send him in," said an imperious voice.

Startled by not having to wait, Ari was shown into the largest office for any one person that he had ever seen. On one side was a sitting room area with Edwardian furniture where one could have tea. Models and pictures of different aircraft all painted with the same red-on-white pattern adorned the room.

Ari walked past a conference table down toward the enormous desk at the far end, where two rows of leather-backed chairs faced inward in the Middle-Eastern martial style.

The general arose. He wore a dark Savile Row suit. Ari had to stifle an urge to burst out laughing. The resemblance that Ari saw was uniquely Egyptian.

General Hanawy was a taller, younger, more handsome, more statuesque version of President Hosni Mubarak, the movie star version. Ari found it quite surreal, but he had come to sell, so he forced his grin into a smile and kicked into action.

"Hello, sir, thank you so much for seeing me."

"It is nothing. Don't mention it," said General Hanawy with a regal gesture as if shooing away a bug. "Ahmed Maher was my teacher. He taught me to fly. He taught me the MiG-21 fighter jet. He taught me how to stay alive and how to kill the Israeli pilots. He put me in the squadron of Hosni Mubarak." The general pointed at a younger picture of himself in uniform with Mubarak as his squadron commander. "Without Ahmed Maher, I would have died in the skies over Sinai when I was twenty-two years old. And he has asked me to help you. What may I offer you? Whiskey? Wine?"

"Oh, no, thank you." Ari shook his head.

"It is not a problem. We keep those for our American friends. And there is always the proverbial mint tea," added the general, as a tea tray landed on his desk and the porter handed Ari his cup.

"So my teacher, Ahmed Maher, told me you are from Hollywood, California?"

"Oh, no, sir. I live in New York, but he is correct. I do work for the movies, and I'm a pilot. If you ever come to New York, I will take you flying," Ari continued. "I will fly you down the Hudson River, over Central Park, over the Brooklyn Bridge, next to the skyscrapers of Wall Street, out over New York Harbor, then we'll fly in a tight circle around the Statue of Liberty."

As different as these two men were, they were both pilots. They knew something about each other that regular people didn't. They shared the fellowship of addicts hooked on a drug they had to wait ever so carefully to use. The price of this drug was competence—and a thorough understanding of how not to use it. Within a minute's inattention, one could cause, then suffer, the most terrifying fate. Every time one stepped into the cockpit, then pulled up and off the runway, a specter of death hovered, always quickening the heart just a little bit—waiting for the slightest mistake or malfunction, and making one feel a little more alive.

"Ahmed Maher said you require some assistance with aerial photography?" asked the general.

"Yes, sir."

"And the Egyptian Air Force will not provide what you need?"

Sell him first, thought Ari, then tell him your troubles. "Oh it's complicated, but . . . If I may, sir?"

Ari leapt out of his chair and set up the pyramids and Sphinx on the general's desk. The general raised his hand.

"One moment." The general picked up his phone and barked an order in Arabic.

"Before you start, let me call in my number two." General Hanawy leaned in confidentially. "I am something of a figure-head here. He is really the one who runs this company, Mustapha Shawky. He is a good man. He was never in the Air Force, but all of his brothers were. His is a fine family."

A very short bald man with a moustache and a hand-tailored Egyptian suit walked in.

"Hello?" said the diminutive Shawky, looking at Ari and not knowing what to expect.

"Mustapha, this is Mr. Ariel Basher from New York and

Hollywood. Ahmed Maher Shehata, my flight instructor, sent him to us. He is about to make a presentation. Go ahead please."

Ari finished placing the pyramids and Sphinx on the desk.

"So, here's the Great Pyramid, and the others."

"As they would be situated," said the general.

"But the Sphinx would be below them," Shawky corrected him.

The general turned on Shawky annoyed. "Of course, that goes without saying."

Ari picked up the toy helicopter and mimed the action as he described it.

"So the shot would start very close, tight on the head of the Sphinx, so tight that we wouldn't know where we were. Then, as the helicopter orbits the Sphinx, we start to see the head and recognize it. As we pull back, we see the whole body. We come around back here and go right past the tip-top of the pyramid of Khafre and the pyramid of Khufu. Then we see the whole Necropolis—and the desert in the background."

"Impressive plan," said General Hanawy. "I can envision what you want to achieve. It will be very dramatic." General Hanawy turned to Shawky. "Can we do this?"

"We have the capability," said Shawky. "Our pilots are very good."

"The best," added the general.

"What kind of helicopter do you desire?" asked Shawky. "We have eight Eurocopters and seventeen Jet Rangers."

"Seventeen?" Ari had never heard of so many helicopters belonging to one company.

"We have a total of twenty-nine helicopters."

"Wow." This was practically an airline, thought Ari. "In the U.S., when you charter a chopper, you usually go to some shack by a hangar where they have one helicopter, maybe two. This is a very grand building. How can you afford to have so many aircraft?"

"We are owned by all the American oil companies," said General Hanawy.

"We can move men and equipment all over the Middle East and North Africa from Cairo International Airport," added Shawky.

"I see." Ari began to understand that this operation was a web, a nexus connecting giant oil companies to their wells. "What do you charge for a chopper?"

"Don't worry." General Hanawy raised his hand like shooing away a fly. "If we did this, we wouldn't be doing it for the money. We would do it for Ahmed Maher, my instructor."

Shawky stifled a pained expression at the general's largesse. "You have a gyrostabilized camera?"

Ari held up the model helicopter with the little camera ball mounted on it. "Yes, it's called the SpaceCam. In about three hours, our technician can mount it on the nose of a chopper."

"From a practical point of view, this is very possible," said Shawky.

"Oh, that's great." Ari knew he had them hooked.

"However, if Dr. Nejem called . . ." cautioned Shawky.

"Look, I could do this and I could probably get away with it," mused General Hanawy. "But people I know would be very angry with me."

"Dr. Nejem," repeated Shawky.

"If Dr. Nejem called, I would have to stop immediately. You can understand the importance of the minister of antiquities in Egypt. Why don't you go to the Air Force? They would have to approve it anyway."

"We've already got a chopper from the Air Force," said Ari.

"You have?" asked the general, taken aback. "Then what are you doing here?"

"The SpaceCam got stuck in customs," admitted Ari.

"Oh they are terrible." Shawky commiserated. "We have troubles with them all the time."

"And you have a permit to fly on a specific date?" guessed the general.

"Today."

"Typical," said Shawky.

"I'm wondering," began Ari, "if there's some way that we could hire you . . . or your company . . . as a consultant . . . to pull some strings . . . or consult on helping us get a new date from . . . the Air Force as soon as possible?"

"I suppose I could be of some service," said General Hanawy.

"They won't even rent us an American helicopter," complained Ari.

"What do they want to give you?" asked the general. "Not one of those old Soviet Mi-17s?"

"Exactly."

"Unbelievable." The general was disgusted. "That's not a helicopter. It's a bus with a rotor on the top. You can drive a jeep inside of it. You can put twenty-two men inside of it, with equipment. Have you flown in it?"

"No, sir."

"Very shaky, a lot of vibration. Not good for snipers. Photographers, like snipers, would like the helicopter steady, I would imagine. And you want to fly low?"

"As low as possible, about a hundred and fifty feet off the ground."

"If you fly that low in a ship that big, you will kick up so much dust it will be a cyclone around the Sphinx, like a sandstorm. The tourists will be running for their lives."

"And that would make Dr. Nejam scream like an eagle," added Shawky.

"The Defense Ministry can ignore him; when I was chief of staff of the Air Force, I could ignore him, but now, not so much."

"You were chief of staff?" Ari was about to hire a four-star general as a consultant. He couldn't believe his luck.

"I retired two years ago to take this job. Did Ahmed Maher not tell you?" General Hanawy looked perplexed. "How do you know Ahmed Maher?"

"General Sheh . . . ata?" Ari tried to remember his last name. "I went to the website of the Egyptian Pilot's Association," explained Ari, "and asked if anyone knew where to rent a helicopter. He e-mailed back and told me to call you."

"You never met him?"

"No, sir."

"Never spoke to him?"

"No, sir."

"You have no connection with any American oil companies?"

"Uh, no?"

"You are not a member of the CIA?"

"CIA? Me?" Do they think I'm some kind of a spy? wondered Ari. "I just, I just . . . met him on the Internet."

The two top executives of Petroleum Air Charters looked at each other bewildered. Ari got the distinct impression that his appointment had been given under the misapprehension that he was someone else.

"Thank you for coming to see us, Mr. Basher." The general stood up and held out his hand to shake. "We don't think there is anything further we can advise you with."

The meeting was over. Ari found himself back out on the street in about sixty seconds still juggling his gold sphinx, mini pyramids, and little toy helicopter.

Chapter 17

The team rode on camels up to the foot of the Great Pyramid, the Tomb of Cheops or Khufu as the Ancient Egyptians would have called it. Samir warned them, "When the camels kneel to let you down, hold on as tight as you can."

Ari, Don, and Charley didn't need the warning; they had seen some Russians dismounting, and one of them had been flipped over a camel's neck into the sand. Each camel made a plaintive groan as a herder tapped its belly with a stick to make it kneel. Ari was bucked forward in the saddle, then as the hind legs buckled, he was whiplashed backward. He slid down the side of the animal's hump and looked up at the immensity of the 2.3 million huge stone blocks above them.

They met their guide, Farouk, an Egyptian archaeology student with curly brown hair and long thin fingers that pointed precisely and lifted delicately. They were like punctuation as he spoke. He led the climb. Tiny ant people on a giant rock staircase, they dodged around, then scrambled on top of the massive blocks. "The largest of these stones weigh up to eighty tons, some quarried five hundred miles away in Aswan then transported by barge almost five thousand years ago," said Farouk.

Samir leaned into Ari's ear as they were climbing. "Do not speak about our movie," he whispered.

"But how are we going to discuss the shot?" Ari was annoyed. "That's our whole reason for climbing up here."

"Wait until we are alone. Farouk is a graduate student. We cannot trust him."

"Because he's a student?"

"No, because he is not the normal type of guide. He is upper class. He must have some family connections to get his job."

Ari was confused. Trying to read some basis for suspicion, Ari watched the elegant young Egyptian. "Trust him about what?"

"There are no secrets in Cairo," replied Samir cryptically.

As they climbed higher, Farouk continued speaking. "When completed around the year 2560 B.C., this pyramid stood 481 feet high and was the tallest man-made structure for the next 3,800 years."

"How'd'ya think they got all these blocks up here?" asked Don in his Australian drawl. "Not by helicopter."

"The ancient Greeks believed wooden levers were used to lift the blocks," explained Farouk. "We believe that up to one hundred thousand men divided into large work gangs pulling long ropes dragged each stone up ramps all day and all night over a period of twenty years."

About halfway up the side of the Great Pyramid, Farouk stopped. "We must not climb any higher," he announced.

"Why not?" asked Ari.

"It is forbidden."

They all looked up at the top of the pyramid, only another two hundred feet above them. The hunger to top it, a kind of summit fever, had seized them.

"Is it really forbidden?" Ari put on a sly look, probing the possibility of a bribe. "Or sort of forbidden?"

Samir winced and shook his head.

With stern disapproval, Farouk said, "Only Dr. Nejem can allow it."

"Dr. Nejem?" asked Ari. The name sounded familiar.

"The leader of the Supreme Council of Antiquities."

"Okay." Ari turned around to the view of Giza, and the city of Cairo beyond. It was surprising to see how very much a part of the city they were. "Is it permitted to walk around the pyramid on this level?"

"Certainly," said Farouk. He led the way. Ari hung back. Don brought up the rear.

"It's a funny sight, isn't it?" said Don to Ari. "We're right on the edge of the city. On one side, urban sprawl for miles as far as you can see. But behind us—"

"Desert." Ari finished the sentence as Farouk disappeared around the corner onto the other side of the pyramid. "So, Don, if we start the shot low and tight on the head of the Sphinx, so tight you don't even know what it is . . . Then we orbit around in front of it, pulling back to reveal the top of that pyramid." Ari pointed out the path in the sky that the helicopter would take. "Then we fly right past the top of this pyramid here . . . what do you think?"

"Should be a dynamic shot. I like it," Don replied.

The two men stood there discussing possible flight paths; the haze of pollution, which was thick in the sky; the angle of the sun, which could hurt or help them.

"The Sphinx looks so small from on top of this thing." Ari zoomed in with his camera on the back of the head of the Sphinx. In the street beyond, he could see the police truck with the blue box. He snapped a last shot of it.

"The whole world looks small from on top of this thing," said Don.

Ari followed Don, traversing after the others, onto to the desert side. They turned the corner and gazed out over a vast expanse of sand. Farouk was speaking to the others.

"Both human and divine, the pharaohs were chosen by the gods to communicate with the people and tell them how to live. After death, the pharaoh actually became Osiris, the god of the dead. In the afterlife, he needed this pyramid. He needed the immense wealth of his treasure buried around him forever."

As Farouk continued, a hint of the supernatural seemed to possess him. He took a sudden step backward toward the edge of the precipice he was standing on, his heels hung out over the edge of the stone. Another three inches and he would have tumbled down the face of the pyramid. Ari and Don leaned forward poised to catch him.

"For you see"—Farouk opened his arms as if receiving some divine energy from inside the pyramid—"in death, the pharaoh grew even more important and powerful than he ever was in life. He had finally become a god."

Chapter 18

Having walked down the quarter of a mile long ramp that carried the stones up to the great Pyramid, the team stood next to the Sphinx.

"Not much of a shot from behind," said Don.

"Nope. You're looking at the city not the desert," agreed Ari.

A documentary crew was setting up a camera, and a tall canvas chair, for an interview in front of the Sphinx. Ari and his own team drifted over to watch. Next to the police truck with the big blue box, a white Range Rover pulled up. An Egyptian got out dressed like Indiana Jones with the wide felt hat and the safari jacket.

"There you see him." Samir pointed. "The second-most famous man in Egypt. Almost a god."

"The minister of antiquities?" guessed Ari.

"Yes, Dr. Nejem. 'His Excellency' is being interviewed."

"So we have to get out of the way?" asked Ari.

"Of course." Samir nodded. "The Sphinx belongs to him. Today it is his film set."

"But tomorrow . . ." Ari left the sentence unfinished.

As Dr. Nejem waited for the interview to start, a small crowd gathered to watch him. Ari got a sudden idea and walked over to the man.

"Dr. Nejem?" Ari stuck out his hand.

"Yes?"

"My name is Ari Basher." Ari shook hands with the famed archaeologist. "I'm here working on an American movie."

"Oh, that's terrific!" Nejem pumped Ari's hand. The ultimate archaeologist had a leathery face and a contagious passion, inspiring and upbeat. His trained eyes darted around Ari's clothes and face making a quick determination. Ari figured he was looking for signs that he was neither a tourist nor crazy. Satisfied, Nejem relaxed.

Ari dove into selling mode. "And the Sphinx will be the signature shot of the movie. In every trailer, poster, and ad. Every movie theater anywhere will have the Sphinx and the pyramids. A seventy-million-dollar marketing campaign; a free gift for the Egyptian tourist industry."

"Wonderful!" Dr. Nejem beamed. "I'm so pleased. You know I went to college in Pennsylvania?"

"Ah, is that right?" Ari basked in the man's charismatic enthusiasm. "I wonder if you couldn't help us. We're having a bit of a problem."

"Anything you need," said Dr. Nejem. "Hollywood has always been a powerful advocate for archaeology."

"We have a special camera for the helicopter shot of the Sphinx, and it seems to be stuck in customs."

The good doctor's smile vanished. His wide twinkling eyes squinted down to narrow slits. "Helicopter shot?"

"You . . ." Suddenly on quicksand, Ari stammered, "You . . . don't know about this?"

"You may not fly a helicopter over the Sphinx." Dr. Nejem made a pronouncement. "I forbid it."

"I thought that . . . you knew," protested Ari.

"Not at all. Excuse me."

Dr. Nejem stepped over to the documentary crew and took his seat on the tall canvas chair. He regained a beneficent expression for the camera. Furious, Ari walked straight back to Samir.

"Samir? What's going on?" demanded Ari. "He doesn't know?"

Samir looked at Ari as if he wanted to slap him across the face. "I do not want to see you again," he said, and walked away.

Ari ran after him. "Why? Because I introduced myself to Dr. Nejem?"

"No, because you do not know what you are doing!" Samir stopped and drilled a question into Ari. "Why did you go over there?"

"Because I thought the minister of antiquities might be able to help us," answered Ari.

"Do you think I do not know how to find the Ministry of Antiquities?" Samir was almost yelling.

"Why are you so angry?" Ari couldn't believe that Samir could get so angry. "Say whatever you want, but don't lose your cool."

"Do you think I have never shot here at the Sphinx?" Samir

pointed at the statue. His finger quivered. His cheeks flushed a light purple color.

"The photos are on your website. What's the big deal?"

"If I had wanted to contact anyone at the ministry, I would have done it by now!"

Ari was incredulous. "You haven't spoken to them at all?"

"Of course not!"

"Samir, please stop yelling at me." Ambling tourists were starting to notice them. Ari tried to diffuse the situation. "In my country it's perfectly normal for me to talk to someone before I fly over their place. Expected even."

"You do not live in a military country!" With that outburst, Samir walked out to the roadway, got into his car, and drove away.

Ari looked up at the weathered and broken face of the Sphinx. What do I do now? he wondered.

Chapter 19

The lights in Samir's office were still on. Ari got out of Hamed's car and looked up at the glowing windows. He had called Samir half a dozen times throughout the evening. No response. He had even tried calling on Hamed's phone, but Samir had hung up on him. Ari had come to the street outside of Samir's office building with the pang of trepidation. What's more, he could even hear Samir's voice on the top floor, shouting.

"Does he always get this angry?" Ari asked Hamed.

Hamed shrugged; the flicker of some past infraction crossed his face. "Cigarette?" was all Hamed would say, taking out his pack.

"No thanks."

The call to prayer sounded, spurring Ari to go up. With any luck prayer would calm Samir. Ari went in and gingerly stepped onto the old elevator.

He felt it bounce a little under his feet as he closed the cage

and pushed the top button. With a scary lurch, Ari rose upward to the distant yelling. It seemed that Samir and his sister
were fighting again. Their loud Arabic, mixed with an occa-
sional phrase of English, grew clearer and more distinct as Ari
ascended above floors full of empty offices closed for the night.

Samir switched over to English. Must be something he
wouldn't want his neighbors to understand, thought Ari.

"Congratulations, Farah! Now that they have fired you, you
know for certain you are on their list." The elevator stopped
and Ari let himself out.

"I'm not your baby sister anymore. You may not scold me
like this!"

"Do you know what they will do to you?"

Ari tiptoed down the corridor and into Samir's anteroom.
Through the open door, Ari saw Samir rolling up his sleeves.
He sat addressing Farah, who stood in front of his desk like
an employee called on the carpet.

"Look!" Samir showed his sister some burn marks like little
circles on his arms. "Look at these!"

"Samir, put your scars away. I've seen them a thousand
times." Farah rolled her eyes at the ceiling.

"Oh, just put them away? Maybe I should drop my pants
and show you the real scars? They will use your body for an
ashtray, if you are lucky! A beautiful girl like you!"

"Samir, don't be disgusting."

He composed himself a little and rolled down his sleeves,
covering the burn marks on his skin. "How long did you work
there?"

"Oh, please, for another job, I could go to Abu Dhabi and
make twice the money, tomorrow—"

"Then go! But don't lead them back to me!" Samir pointed at the door and spotted Ari hovering outside. "What are you doing here? Spying on us?"

"Please," Ari walked in, distracting the two smoldering siblings. "I came to apologize."

"Not accepted." Samir snorted with irritable contempt. "I am finished with you."

"Samir, I'm sorry. I didn't mean to upset you." At this point Ari could only apologize, but he didn't want to. "It's just that everywhere I've gone, all over the world, it always helps to talk to the top guy."

"And did he tell you what you want to hear? Your 'top guy?'"

"No," Ari had to admit.

"If he does, you will regret it. If Dr. Nejem wants money to film, do you know how much he will ask for? Do you know how much that will cost you?"

Ari hadn't expected it to cost him anything. "No."

"Now can you begin to comprehend how unprofessional you are?"

"Unprofessional?" Ari bristled in disbelief and looked at Farah as if she would have some opinion about the matter. No one had ever called him that before.

Samir opened his drawer and slapped some papers down on his desk.

"Here is the permission from the military censor, stamped and signed!" Samir flipped over the next page. "Here is the permission from the head of the crew union, stamped and signed!" He turned over the next. "Here is the approval of the script from the minister of the interior, stamped and signed! And the social censor, who makes sure we are not filming anything against morality, but that is the easiest one, because we pay him not to show up on set. You have waited for one entire day in the back of the airport. Do you now know what is involved in getting all of these permissions?" Samir scooped up all the papers in his hand. "You are only beginning to understand! It takes six weeks, at a minimum! Here, take them and go! Get out of my office! GO!"

Samir tossed the papers down onto his desk, and they slid across the barren glass top toward Ari, who picked them up and looked at the black Arabic words floating around on the pages.

"But, Samir, I can't even read these," he protested.

"And if you could you would read that the permissions may only be given to an Egyptian company, and that these permissions do not even belong to your movie!"

"I can't do this job without you." Ari was getting irritated, coming close to his own boiling point. Samir can't talk to me like this, he thought as he commanded every muscle in his face not to react.

"These are the property of my company." Samir pointed down at the papers. "I could not give them to you even though I want to. They are now worthless, like your empty American smile! Take them and get out!"

Ari slammed his hand down on the desk to anchor himself from Samir's onslaught.

"Do know what's really unprofessional?" Ari's voice started to rise. "A million times more unprofessional than what I did?" Ari scooped up the papers defiantly. "GIVING UP!" He yelled at the top of his lungs. "NOT GETTING THE SHOT!"

Ari had a big voice, very big, which he seldom used. Samir

blinked, surprised by the outburst, never expecting it, his anger incapacitated by an even greater one. Farah smirked, nodding in enjoyment.

There was nothing, short of violence, left for Ari now except to make an exit. So he walked out.

Chapter 20

Ari bounded down the stairs and out into the street clutching the permission papers in his hand. Hamed jumped out of his car and opened the door. Stopping himself, Ari leaned against the car door and looked at the precious and yet potentially worthless papers.

"Give me a minute, Hamed." Ari knew he couldn't drive away and leave. What would he say to Beth? To Frank? To the studio? To the whole crew that was coming over? And the movie stars that would follow them? The whole mess would rest only on Ari's shoulders.

Ari started to pace back and forth in front of the building's entrance. Samir had opened up such fury in him at everything he'd been through since getting off the plane: the customs guards who took the camera, the whispering women from the Press Ministry, the minister of defense, the tourist police.

He knew he had to go back up and say something. He looked at the permits that tied him to Samir. What could he do? Offer Samir more money? No, he wasn't ready to go that far. He kicked the air, muttering to himself, wanting to break something.

"These people are impossible. Can I get my camera? *Inshallah.* Can I fly a helicopter? *Inshallah.* Can I shoot a shot? *Inshallah.*" Ari paced past the front door of the building. Samir's sister stood inside the doorway watching him.

"When does anything happen around here?" Ari sputtered to himself. "When does anybody actually do something? Can I get a cup of coffee?"

"*Inshallah*," they both said simultaneously, she mocking him.

"That was a very dramatic scene. But what are you going to do now? He's very stubborn, my brother. He's not going to come down here to the street to see you, Mr. . . . ?"

"Basher. Ari." He studied her knowing brown eyes. She seemed to understand his predicament better than he did.

"But will you go back upstairs to beg and grovel at his feet?"

"What would you do?" he asked.

"Even Samir can't yell forever." She tilted her face upward toward her brother's office, her long dark hair splaying down behind her shoulders. "He will soon run out of breath."

Ari caught the scent of some wild flower essence in the night air. "Why does he get so angry? It's not smart."

"Well, he was not always that way. He was . . . very sweet as a boy. But that is a question for another time." She stepped out of the doorway. "I will leave you to your predicament. Don't worry yourself too much. I have come to believe that if Samir is *not* yelling at me, I'm doing something wrong."

Ari watched her walk away. Tight jeans; flat, practical boots;

a black leather jacket—she looked less student and more biker chic than she had last time, he thought. She disappeared around the corner.

"Hey, hey, hold on!" Ari started to jog after her. "Maybe you could help me talk to him." Ari rounded the corner to see four men get out of a parked car and surround Farah. She pushed on through them and kept walking. They ran up and started taunting her in Arabic. One of them made a circle around her face with his finger as he spoke, then tapped her on the top of the head. Ari guessed he was mocking her for wearing no hijab. She ducked out from under his touch and spouted an Arabic tirade at him.

The men just laughed. The bold one started to pinch her on the breasts and on the butt, then the others joined in. She swatted their hands away but couldn't repel every grope. This delighted them. They bellowed with laughter.

Ari couldn't comprehend such behavior. It seemed so teenage for men until the bold one, the first to have touched her hair, grabbed her into a headlock. His hand at her throat, he expertly choked off her breath. With dead seriousness, he muttered some sort of threat in her ear.

Ari sprang from his stupor of disbelief and without thinking found himself running toward them.

"Let her go!" he demanded.

The thugs looked at him in amazement for a few seconds. Farah gulped down a great breath of air.

Then Ari yelled indignantly, "Help! Police! Help! Police! Police!" expecting the four thugs to flee into the night. Instead they burst out laughing, unfazed by him in the slightest.

Ari shifted the film permits to his left hand, then reached

in to grab Farah by the wrist. He yanked her away. This made the thugs angry and they grabbed her back. Ari saw a fist with a signet ring on the middle finger coming straight at his head. He felt the ring bite into his temple, and his head bounce sideways. He spun around and down. He saw the permission papers fly up in the air as his vision went gray, becoming two little narrow cones of sight.

To keep from blacking out, he dropped to his knees and put his head down. A car engine roared, coming closer. He looked up. The only thing he could see were two headlights aimed straight at his face. He knew he would be run over, killed in a second. But the tires screeched. The grille stopped a foot from his head.

The thugs jumped out of the way. Hamed's voice yelled in Arabic. Ari could hear the words, "American!" and "Hollywood!" Ari's tunnel vision started to widen. It was Hamed's car.

Ari felt Hamed grab him by the arm and lift him to his feet. Hamed, brandishing an old piece of pipe, swiped at the air with a swoosh. The thugs backed away. Two of them still had a hold of Farah. She screamed when she saw Ari's face.

"What's wrong?" Ari asked, just noticing that there was blood dripping off the tip of his nose. From above came the rhythm of metal clanking. Ari looked up: an old woman was leaning out the window banging two pots together. She was making a cry of alarm. Windows opened up above them. Outraged, women of all ages leaned out banging their pots on their window ledges.

Farah tried to squirm loose. The thugs waved at Ari for him to go away.

"No, not without her!" Ari pointed at Farah.

Hamed banged his pipe on the sidewalk. Men, too, started yelling from balconies above. The entire street seemed to be hanging out the windows. The thugs started to back away from the sheer noise raining down upon them. Across the street, twenty young people ran out of a building following a familiar young man with long hair.

"Rami! Rami!" yelled Farah.

It was the singer and his band of protesters.

"Farah!" Rami yelled back, and his gang dashed across the street, swarming around the thugs, who had to let Farah go. The thugs and protesters exchanged a few kicks and punches. Experienced street fighters, the thugs made a formation, but against twenty they couldn't hold out.

A protester with a camera filmed the fighting.

Farah yelled out in Arabic, pointing at the thugs' faces, "*Kamyra lifa! Kamyra lifa! Kamyra lifa!*" which Ari took to mean "film them." Everyone joined in with her chant, including Ari until he realized that his film permits were underfoot. Ari sank to his knees, trying to gather up the precious papers.

The documentarian stuck the camera in the thugs' faces and shouted questions at them. They tried to grab it. The protesters pushed them away.

Rami stepped forward to speak, and the melee settled down. In the relative lull, Ari crawled around snatching up papers.

"Were you pinching her like this?" Rami said to the camera in English, and he reached out and pinched one of the thugs on the butt. All the protesters joined in, even Farah, pinching the thugs' asses, tweaking them on the chest. The thugs tried to swat the forty hands away, but they were outpinched.

"Hamed, Hamed! Get the permissions!" yelled Ari, desperate to save the permits from this new pandemonium. Still bleeding a little, he had to keep the white papers out from under his bloody nose. Ari crawled through the scrum of protesters snatching up the last of the papers until someone stepped on the back of his hand.

"Ow, Hamed! The permissions! Get them off the ground!"

The thugs had had enough. Their back against the wall, they retreated slowly down the street, yelling menacing threats and punching anyone who got too close. Hamed picked up the remaining few papers. Ari couldn't lift up the last one. His hand was bloody and shaking.

Rami leaned down and picked up the paper, reading it.

"Ministry of Defense?" Rami laughed. "Here you go, man." He handed over the paper and began to sing, joyously, victoriously, and everyone joined in the refrain, even some of the younger people hanging out of the windows:

"Ha, Ha, Ha!"

Chapter 21

"I don't need stitches?" asked Ari. He sat on a stack of cardboard boxes of medical supplies. He cradled the film permits in his arms, his hands and face crusted with drying blood. Farah rummaged through a box and pulled out some packets of gauze, medical tape, and cotton balls.

"It's nothing. Just a quarter of an inch. Head wounds can bleed a lot." She pulled a bottle out of the box. "I'm afraid we only have rubbing alcohol, so this will sting."

She cleaned out the gash, the source of the streaks of dried blood on his temple.

"Ow, ah." Ari flinched.

"It's tiny. Hold still." Farah dabbed the cool alcohol on his forehead with gauze. "You can go to the hospital if you want, but it's a very clean cut, and it's already closed up. I'll put a butterfly on it just in case. Come into the bathroom if you'd like to see yourself in the mirror. You should wash your face, too."

Farah led him through the apartment to a bathroom. It was

a big place with high ceilings and French doors that opened from room to room. The protesters were settling back down to work blogging. Laptops were everywhere, on every surface. The young people had a feverish concentration. The thugs spooked them just enough to fuel their determination with rage. They sprawled over the floor pounding out their stories on their computers, tweeting on their phones.

Farah taped a butterfly bandage over Ari's cut, then rinsed the blood off his face and hands in the bathroom sink. Her fingers lingered on his cheek.

"Thank you," she said, and her eyes welled up for a moment. She tried to control herself, but fell against him shuddering.

"It's all right. It's okay. It's over." He embraced her, feeling the warmth of her breath on his neck. Her hair stuck slightly to his lips.

She choked down a soft sob. "I was so frightened that they would take me into their car and then..."

"Hey, so was I. They're scary guys. I'm still shaking." He held up his quivering hands. With trembling thumbs, he wiped the tears from her face. "What is this place?"

She stepped back and composed herself bravely, but he was happy, almost gleeful that she had leaned against him. "Come, I'll show you."

She led him into a bedroom. Six sleeping protesters lay fully clothed, crashed out across the bed sideways. Piles of rope, tarps, paint, and materials to make signs were everywhere. Three protestors sat in front of a professional video-editing system set up on a dresser. They were already inputting the footage of Farah being abused by the thugs.

"We are spreading the word," she said to Ari. "We are showing everyone that if they beat us down, we bring more people; if they beat them, we bring even more, until one day soon, there will be too many people to beat. If we overwhelm them, you see how easily they give up? Because they don't believe in what they are doing. They are cowards only beating people for government money. Why don't you put that into your Hollywood movie?"

"Well . . ." Ari couldn't think of a less likely subject for Hollywood.

The room lights turned on garishly bright.

The sleeping protesters rolled over, grumbling in Arabic. One opened his eyes and said to Ari in English, "Hey, man, we're trying to sleep. Turn off the lights."

"But it wasn't me." Ari replied.

Samir stood by the door with his hand on the light switch.

"So this is your revolution?" he said to his sister scornfully. "This is how you are going to change Egypt? Everybody sleeps in one bed? Shameful."

"Is this her Muslim brother?" grunted one of the sleepy protesters, annoyed.

"Yes. Quick, film him!" said another. "Put him in tonight's video blast."

The cameraman lying on the bed raised a camcorder that seemed permanently attached to his hand.

"Come with me, Ari." Samir tugged on Ari's arm. "We must get you out of this place." He switched off the lights just as the camera started recording. "Oh, excuse me for disturbing your dreams," Samir said in the dark.

Chapter 22

Down in the street, Samir and Ari walked in silence except for their footfalls scraping on the sidewalk. Ari still held the film permits. Samir noticed that they were wrinkled and dog-eared. Pursing his lips, chewing over words he couldn't say, he frowned down at the pavement. Guilt and rage, thought Ari. Which will be stronger?

Samir finally spoke. "Thank you for saving my sister."

"Don't thank me, *aala wajib*," joked Ari. (It is my duty.)

"Oh no, now you have been in Egypt too long."

"Since I saved your sister's honor"—Ari saw his opening and took it—"doesn't an old Arab custom mean that you owe me some sort of debt of gratitude?"

Samir groaned. "I take it back. You are still a Jew."

"Then I'll collect my pound of flesh, please." Ari held out the film permits to Samir. "So we're back together again? By the way, did the money hit your account, the twenty-five thousand?"

Samir didn't answer.

"You never got the payment?" Now Ari understood the violence of Samir's outburst. "Why didn't you tell me?"

They walked into Samir's building and went up to his office, where he opened his laptop and slid it across the desk. Ari dialed.

"May I borrow your sunglasses?" asked Ari.

Samir took a pair from his pocket and handed them over. Ari put the glasses on over his forehead, hiding his little butterfly bandage.

Beth appeared in bed. "Hel . . . lo?" Her husband did not.

"Beth it's me."

"Oh, Ari . . . what time is it over there?"

Ari ignored her question. "I'm here with Samir."

"Hello, Samir."

"We are so sorry to wake you." Samir was contrite.

Ari was not. "The money did not hit the account."

"What do you need the money for?" asked Beth nonplussed.

"You didn't send it?" asked Ari.

"You can't shoot anything yet."

"Unbelievable!" Ari slammed his fist down on the desk.

"Elizabeth." Samir trained the computer on himself. "If I may speak."

"Of course."

"The day we get the money is an important day," said Samir slowly.

"How so?" asked Beth.

"Then Ari can go back to the airport to get the Space-Cam."

The statement hung in the air. Whether the money was

needed for bribery or some legitimate reason, Beth couldn't ask. She had no choice but to pay. She obviously didn't like it.

"Samir, how are you doing on your budget?" she did ask.

"We will go over."

"Why?" she demanded.

Samir looked over at Ari. "Some occurrences that could not be foreseen."

"Thought so." Beth rubbed her temples. "After this payment, we are not sending any more money until I see a new budget that we both sign off on. We must know how much the rest of the filming is going to cost before we agree to pay." She pressed her point.

"Of course." Samir nodded with a courteous little bow. "That is the way it should be."

"How is it going with permission to fly on another day?"

"I am working on it," admitted Samir.

"Can I speak to Ari?" Beth rubbed her temples again. A headache seemed to be brewing.

"I'm still here." Ari trained the webcam back on himself.

"Alone," said Beth.

"Certainly." Samir put the permits back into his desk drawer, got up, and walked out, closing the door behind him.

"Ari, did we pick the right guy?" She spoke softly, but it wasn't a question.

"Come on." Ari rolled his eyes.

"I'm just asking." Beth was annoyed. "Does Samir have enough juice to handle this? Or is he too small?"

"What are you suggesting? Dump Samir?" If only she knew Samir almost quit, he thought.

"Tell Frank that we can't get the shot legally and that he has to write something else easier to shoot."

"Absolutely not!" Now Ari erupted. After taking the punch, he still had a pent-up fury. "I always get the shot. Always. And whatever you tell Frank, he's not going to believe it unless I say it, too."

They both stared at each other for a moment. Something had snapped between them. They were now in open conflict. "Then good luck tomorrow," said Beth.

"Thank you," said Ari, meaning something else.

"You're welcome," said Beth, meaning anything but, and hung up on him.

"Good . . . ," said Ari to the blank screen, ". . . night."

Chapter 23

Ari sat holding his forms, waiting on a bench in another dark corridor in the bowels of the airport. He didn't know how long he'd been waiting. He didn't care. Samir paced, unable to sit. After a long time, a customs private came to fetch them.

They walked along the dim corridor under each naked light bulb to the end. They entered an outer office, passed several clerks in uniform sitting at their desks, and stopped outside a closed door. The customs private knocked three times. An order to enter came from within. The private opened the door.

Ari and Samir walked into a dark office with windows onto the black void. Behind a big desk, dressed in uniform, sat General Moussa, the head of customs. Slightly chubby, he sported a Saddam-style moustache. A TV was on, playing some sort of Egyptian soap opera.

The private ushered them to take seats by the edge of the desk. The general nodded to them in an amiable way, but said not a word. They were furnished with cups of tea by the private. Samir took the sugar cube and stuck it between his teeth as he drank. Ari copied him.

The general went about his business reading papers, making phone calls, not once looking at the TV, looking over at Ari cheerfully every so often, but with never an invitation to speak, not even an introduction. What is he waiting for? wondered Ari. A bribe? Yet Samir sat on in perfect stillness, waiting.

The soap opera ended. They all had sat there saying nothing for half an hour. An Arabic news program came on with footage of American troops fighting in some war. The private returned and took their glasses.

"*Shukran,*" said Ari, realizing he had spoken the word for "thank you."

The general looked up from his work at Ari.

"*La sukr, aala wajib,*" said the private which, by this time, Ari knew meant: Don't thank me. It's my duty.

An old photo of George W. Bush came on the TV. The general looked at the television for the first time, then at Samir. "Leave us." The general pointed at the door. Slightly humiliated, Samir stood up and walked out.

"Do you like George Bush?" General Moussa asked Ari in halting, heavily accented English.

Ari shifted in his seat. He looked at the empty chair where Samir had been a moment before as if for some sort of clue as to what to say. The chair was vacant. Ari searched his mind for the right answer. Does he want me to praise or to censure? wondered Ari. Probably not praise, but to call an American president a liar, a fool, a puppet of his vice president, seemed unwise, especially to a general in a military dictatorship.

On the wall above the general's head was the omnipresent

portrait of President Mubarak staring directly down at Ari as if to say: "This general facing you between us speaks for me. He is me and I am him." Such is the implication of all such pictures. Wouldn't insulting Bush be insulting myself to such a man? wondered Ari.

There has to be a perfect answer to this question, thought Ari as he fixed upon the man's Saddam moustache.

"I . . . think that . . . Bush made a big . . . mistake going into Iraq." Ari had chosen his words very carefully.

The moustache came alive like two black caterpillars. The general's smile of approval expressed admiration for Ari's chess move.

"You are good man. I give you your camera," said the general in his broken English. He added, "Saddam was great man! No?"

Ari nodded, thinking he could not have imagined himself ever hearing such a question. Let alone answering it, "Yes."

Ari and Samir went back out through the portal into Terminal One, past the customs desk and over to the sixteen SpaceCam cases stacked against the wall. Ari felt unclean. He picked up the closest case. A sergeant ran out of the customs room to stop him.

Ari looked around for help. "Samir?"

Samir had left him. Ari was furious. "You call General Moussa. He gave me my camera! General Moussa, you call him." Ari kept repeating the general's name, but the sergeant wouldn't let go of the case. Ari wanted to lash out, punch the sergeant in the face. Ari had reached his breaking point. He had praised Saddam. What else was left to do?

"Call the general!" Ari yanked hard on the case.

The sergeant grew still. Having seen something over Ari's shoulder, he let go of the heavy black case. It thumped against Ari's legs. Ari turned around to follow the sergeant's mesmerized stare.

Across the terminal, a tall man with a loping stride emerged from the hundreds of travelers. He was such a distinct figure. Very thin, very hip, with a close-cropped gray beard—a cool jazz musician, Ari guessed. The man carried only a newspaper, no luggage. He walked straight toward them, winked at the sergeant with a knowing confidence, and went inside the customs storage room. The sergeant followed him in.

Here was the bag-man, thought Ari, the man who makes all the payoffs at the airport. Without saying a word, the man handed the sergeant his newspaper. The sergeant looked inside, saw something, presumably money, and took the newspaper. The man walked out.

Ari picked up a case, and before he knew it, a team of smiling porters who had been watching everything and knew their cue, wheeled a large wagon underneath the case for him to set it down upon.

"No, mister! We do it," said the porters as they competed with the sergeant over who could stack up the most cases on the wagon.

Ari was elated. He had his cases back. He actually had them. Within a minute, the SpaceCam was rolling out through the terminal. The porters leaned forward pulling the yoke while shooing people out of their path. My own little pyramid crew, thought Ari.

Outside on the curb, Samir stood by a banged-up white five-ton truck.

Ari reached out to shake Samir's hand, but Samir held back. Ari patted him on the back instead. "Well, that's half the battle."

"Not at all," said Samir as the porters started heaving the heaviest cases up onto the back of the truck. Dejected, he turned to go.

"Why so sad? We got our camera! Is everything okay?" asked Ari concerned. "Where are you off to?"

"The Ministry of . . . ," said Samir over his shoulder without looking back, ". . . Defense."

Chapter 24

Back from the airport, Ari walked into the Mena House and over to the front desk in the lobby.

"Anything come for me? Basher, Room 101," asked Ari, expecting nothing.

"Yes, Mr. Basher." The clerk handed over a pink message slip.

I await you in the lobby—Omar el Mansoor, read the paper, written in a florid hand.

Ari looked around. On an easy chair beneath the chandelier sat a large Egyptian man in his late fifties. Dressed in bell-bottomed jeans, a puffy silk shirt, a black velvet vest, and cowboy boots, he had shoulder-length hair, a Van Dyke beard, and a seventies vibe—a chic Egyptian hippie with expensive clothes.

Both men slowly crossed the lobby for that first tentative handshake.

"Mr. Basher?" asked the man with a flawless American accent.

"Yes?" Ari sensed something familiar about this person.

"I'm Omar el Mansoor of Studio Giza."

"Right." Ari remembered the name.

"You called me about working on your movie."

"I know. But we . . . uh . . . hired somebody else." Ari looked around. He didn't want Hamed to walk in and spot him talking to Samir's biggest competitor.

"Whom did you hire? If you don't mind my asking." Omar had a courtly sensitive *politesse*, but it seemed to veil some deeper inner power.

"Pan Egypt Films," said Ari. "Samir Aziz is our fixer."

"Never heard of him," said Omar, nonplussed.

Ari wondered if he was telling the truth. "Well, if you hadn't taken two weeks to call me back . . ." Ari looked at the hotel entrance for any sign of Hamed. "Excuse me, Mr. el . . ."

"Please call me Omar."

"I have a very urgent call I need to make."

Omar was surprised. "But we have a meeting now."

"We do?"

"Elizabeth Vronsky sent an e-mail to both of us."

"Beth did . . . ?" In all the excitement over liberating the SpaceCam, he hadn't bothered to check his e-mail.

Omar continued. "I am about to leave the country in a few hours and this is the only chance I have to meet with you." He pointed to the bar. "May I buy you a drink?"

"Uh . . . someone's coming to drive me over to the university to scout. Do you mind if we go up to my room instead? It's a suite."

"Not at all." Omar followed Ari's glance at the front entrance. "There are no secrets in Cairo."

Upstairs, Ari opened the door and let Omar in.

"*Très élégant!*" Omar admired the view. "You can even see your target, the Sphinx."

"Research," joked Ari. "I had to check out this suite for our star. It was cheaper by the month."

"But of course."

There was something very smooth, very pleasant, very worldly about Omar. College or film school in the States, guessed Ari, and before that he must have gone to some posh boarding school in France or Switzerland.

Ari opened his computer and dialed.

"Hey, Beth." Her face popped up on screen. She was in her office working late. Ari shared his big news: "We got the camera out of customs!"

"Great," she said, unimpressed. "How about permission to use it?"

Deflated by her lack of enthusiasm, he said, "Samir's working on that."

"So I'm paying Don and Charley a thousand dollars a day to sit around on vacation?"

"I don't think they're going to take another pay cut." Ari changed the subject. "Omar's here."

"Did you like him?" Beth perked up.

"He's still with me. In my room. I just bumped into him in the lobby." Ari trained the computer on Omar.

"Oh. Hi, Omar."

"Hello, Elizabeth."

"Should I start?" asked Beth.

Start what? Ari wondered. "Sure," he said.

"Omar," said Beth, "what do you think of Samir Aziz?"

"Who?" asked Omar.

A little annoyed by what he took to be feigned ignorance, Ari said, "Pan Egypt Productions. I mentioned him to you in the lobby."

"Never heard of him."

"Really?" Ari decided that he didn't believe Omar on this point.

"He's a nobody," Omar went on. "How has your experience been with him?"

"So far so good," said Ari. "We just got our camera out of customs."

"Yes. And your budget?"

Beth replied before Ari could. "He says he's going over."

"Uhmmm. Not exactly the right thing to do." Omar frowned.

"It's complicated." Ari defended Samir.

"It always is."

Ari figured he'd better nip off this kind of talk. "Well, Omar, we're committed to Samir. We have a contract with him. So—"

Just then the phone rang. Ari answered.

"Hello . . . ?"

"Mr. Basher, your car is here," said the desk clerk.

"Thank you, I'll be right down." Ari hung up.

"That's my ride. So sorry. This meeting was a total surprise to me. Is there anything else?"

"I want to offer my services, free of charge, as a consultant," said Omar.

"That's very generous." Ari could smell a Trojan horse. "For what purpose?"

"To make sure everything works well for you. That you hire the best crew and you do not get cheated."

"A very, very kind offer." Ari knew it was anything but that. "We'll think it over."

Omar pointed to a spreadsheet on the desk. "Is that Samir's budget?"

"His initial bid. Yes," confirmed Ari.

"Do you mind if I look it over?"

Ari could feel the dynamic of control shifting around him. "Beth?" What would she say?

"I have no problem with that."

Ari picked up the papers, about to hand them over, but he stopped. "Oh, I need this copy."

"Really?"

"It has my notes in it." Ari hadn't written a thing on the pages. "I want to review this on my way to the scout."

"Very well," said Omar cheerfully. "A pleasure to meet you."

He's very charismatic, thought Ari, but underneath lies something reptilian. I like him, but I don't trust him, Ari decided.

Omar stopped with his hand on the antique doorknob. "A suggestion, if I may? Your permission to fly around the Sphinx must be signed by the defense minister himself."

"Tantawi," acknowledged Ari.

"Did you know that the defense ministers of Egypt and Israel talk every week?"

"So?"

"Your production company in Hollywood is owned by one of the richest men in Israel, a former arms dealer on the highest level."

"True," admitted Ari.

"Just a word from one defense minister to another would

solve your problem." Omar's idea to pull strings at the top was undeniably a good one. The sort of thing that only a connected member of the elite would conceive of. "Here is my card. If you need anything . . . ," Omar continued with earnest obsequiousness. "Any complication. Any delay. Anything. Call me anytime. This is my personal cell phone."

"Thank you, Omar." Ari slid the business card into his pocket.

"Good-bye, Beth." Omar waved at her on the laptop. "I'll see you in New York."

"You'll see her in New York?" Ari tried to cover his surprise.

Omar was casually dismissive. "I'm just passing through on my way to the Sundance Film Festival. I go every year. My plane leaves in three hours. So I must say good-bye."

Ari opened the door, relieved to let Omar out.

"Thank you for taking the time to come all the way to Giza to meet me."

"It is nothing." In the doorway, Omar made a polite little bow. "I wanted to shake the hand of the man who will shoot the Sphinx."

Chapter 25

Ari followed the location scout, a talkative, energetic Egyptian with good English, up the stairs of the Geology building of Cairo University. They walked across a marble floor in the large entry hall, their footfalls the only sound. When he stopped to shoot pictures, the snap of his camera echoed in the silence. Ari realized that they were alone in this grand hall. The students must all be in class, he thought. He saw a set of double doors finished in dull green leather with glass portholes in them.

Ari pushed through the swinging doors into a large empty academic theater. He snapped a panorama of the three or four hundred wooden seats with those little half desks for note taking. The huge room had ceiling fans on each suspended light fixture. One was missing a blade and spun around in a wobble out of phase with the others. On the stage was a black slate slab counter with a sink and gas jets. A selection of beakers and test tubes sat in a rack on the counter. On the back wall hung a double row of blackboards, which could slide up or down. The place was a perfect time capsule. Nothing had changed since the 1930s.

"Class is canceled?"

"No, Mr. Ari," said the location scout.

Ari wandered down to the lectern and took some pictures of the empty seats from the stage. He faced the empty chairs.

He had an old college memory of sitting in a large academic theater like this one, as a venerated historian and former national security advisor gave a guest lecture to his Comparative Civilization class.

"In war do you not become your enemy?" the great man asked them. "When one civilization seeks to destroy another, does the victor not consume the vanquished, digest it, assimilate it? Do we not become the very thing we seek to kill?"

Ari walked off the stage. He wandered back out of the lecture hall and up a grand staircase to the second floor. At the top, the landing turned into a square cloistered balcony that looked down on a large courtyard below. Was the style of architecture Spanish? Moorish? Southern Californian? Turkish? Or did all those styles spring from one fountainhead, the assimilation of war?

Ari stopped by a bulletin board laden with notices: APPLY FOR THE HALIBURTON FELLOWSHIP IN GEOLOGY TODAY! FULL TUITION AND STIPEND.

A poster showed young Arab students in hard hats out in the desert with a friendly American engineer, a series of seismic charges blowing up in the background. CONCENTRATIONS IN SEISMOLOGY AND FLUID DYNAMICS WELCOME.

Ari turned around. "Where is everybody?"

"Another student strike," explained the location scout.

They walked along the corridor, which overlooked a courtyard on one side and a row of seminar rooms on the other.
Ari peeked in their open doors as he passed them by.

"Do you want to go in?"

"No," said Ari. "We don't need a classroom. Just a lecture
hall and an office."

There was one door that was almost closed. Ari stopped
next to it. A woman's voice emanated from within, speaking
in both Arabic and English. Ari recognized the voice. It can't
be her, he thought, and he pushed open the door. Farah was
giving a lecture. She finished writing the last line of a large
chunk of computer code on a blackboard. She turned around
and saw Ari. She switched into English.

"If you hack into your operating system and insert this piece
of code . . ."

Ari looked around the small seminar room. A hundred
people were crammed into space for twenty.

". . . then their spyware will cycle into an endless loop. They
will not see anything on your computer until you shut down.
Then it will bypass all of your files and spit their spyware into
your logging off sequence. Any questions before I erase this?"
She put down the chalk and picked up an eraser.

A Lebanese student raised his hand. "Are there digital copies of this code?"

"Yes, but you must only pass this by hand. Never e-mail it
or the Americans will crack it. They have a room at Nilecast,
which I have seen, where they copy every e-mail we send and
give it to Military Intelligence."

Ari raised his camera and snapped a picture. Farah looked at him with a complicated expression of skeptical pleasure.

"This is Ari, everyone. He's come to get an education."

Everyone in the room laughed as she started to erase the blackboard.

Chapter 26

A thousand students hung out on the quad, milling about in clusters, some listening to people making speeches or arguing with each other. Ari and Farah lay on the grass relaxing. Ari raised his camera.

"Smile, Professor Farah. Can you say, 'U.S. Imperialism?'" Ari snapped a picture of her.

"Let me see that thing." She reached for it and he handed it over. "Eh, not my best angle. You can do better. Can you say 'Hollywood movie?'"

She took a picture of him, then both of them looked at it.

"You have a crazy smile." She scrolled back a shot. "You know what it says to the world?"

"Be happy?" he guessed.

"Yes, because I'm smiling you should be smiling, too. Forget everything else. Let's go have fun."

"And what's wrong with that?"

"Someday, maybe, it would be great," she said wistfully. "Where's my brother?"

"At the Ministry of Defense."

"Amazing that he would even set foot inside of that place."

"Why not?"

"You don't know?" Her face darkened.

"Know what?"

"When I was a little girl, he used to have a big smile."

"Samir the Hammer?" Ari couldn't believe it.

"Not hypnotic like yours to cast a spell over people, but a very happy one, yes."

"I don't believe you. He seems like he's angry all the time. Why is he so mad at you?"

"I shouldn't say this, but . . . it's no secret. Everyone knows. Now, he won't touch anything political."

"He doesn't like . . . all of this?" Ari pointed at the students making speeches.

"Well, he fell in with the Muslim Brotherhood as a young man and got religious."

"Were your parents?"

"Not at all. No one was. See all the girls wearing the head scarf?" Farah pointed at the crowd and about 90 percent wore the hijab. "When I started school here, no one wore it. Maybe five percent."

"What happened?"

"You invaded Iraq, then everyone started."

"What's that got to do with—?"

She cut him off. "Everything's political. The scarf on my head is political. The beard on my brother's face—"

"You have no scarf. He has no beard."

"The spot on his forehead . . . was political. On my first day of school here, he dropped me off at that gate over there, and he told me he was coming to pick me up after a meeting at the mosque. 'No, no, I'm an adult now,' I said. 'I don't need you to take me home anymore.' He was the one who disappeared."

"That day?"

"For over a year we didn't know where he was."

"Why?" asked Ari.

Farah sighed heavily. "Eh, I'd better let him tell you."

She scrolled through the pictures on the camera and found the one of her lecturing in the seminar room.

"How do I delete?" she asked him.

"Wait!" He reached for the camera. "That's my only shot of a classroom with students in it."

"They are not students, Ari. They are the brains of the revolution."

She hit DELETE.

Chapter 27

Ari sat in the café at the Necropolis drinking a mango juice. It was dusk, closing time. All across the vast expanse of pyramids and tombs a line of tourist police was shooing the daily exodus of tourists toward the road. Ari was in a misanthropic mood. He looked at the truck with the blue box on the back, with the kids inside. He had never felt so ineffectual.

A cheerful middle-aged Egyptian in an open blue shirt came up to him.

"Mr. Ari?"

"Yes, that's me."

"Welcome to Egypt."

"Thank you."

"You are Ari. I am Ali. I have something very special for you, something special that you will remember for the rest of your life. Come."

"What do you have for me?"

"My family run the light show, take the ticket for forty years."

Ari looked at the man skeptically. Of course, he wants money, thought Ari. Yet the man's effusiveness picked up Ari's spirits a bit.

"Oh, no thank you." Ari shook his head. "I have to meet someone."

"I invite you for a private visit with the Sphinx after closing."

"Alone?"

"By yourself."

"Wow."

Curious, Ari stood and threw some coins on the table. He walked with Ali in the direction of the Sphinx against the flow of departing tourists. Ari pointed out the police truck in the street.

"Tell me, Ali. What do they do with the kids inside that big box?"

"Not to worry, Mr. Ari. They beat them a little on the leg, drive them out of Giza, let them go. Some come back. Many do not."

"Every day?"

"Every night."

"I have a friend who was in that box."

"Do not worry. He will be free."

Ari spotted Samir gesticulating by the Sphinx gate. Samir was hot in argument with a tourist policeman trying to close the area. Ari knew then that his having met Ali was no accident. Samir must have sent him.

They reached the old wrought iron gate. Ali shooed the

policeman away by producing a large old bronze key and unlocking the gate.

"You may want to give Ali a tip," suggested Samir.

"How much?" asked Ari.

"Twenty dollars would make him very happy."

Ari searched his pockets. "Uhm . . . I only have hundreds . . . could I borrow . . . ?"

Samir slipped Ali a bill.

"*Shukran*," Ari thanked him.

"*Fee Kedmehk.*" At your service, said Ali in Arabic as he closed the gate with a clank and left, locking Ari and Samir inside. The two drifted down into the dig that had been excavated around the Sphinx.

"In Egypt miracles happen for twenty dollars," said Ari.

"Sometimes less, sometimes more."

"Sometimes a lot more."

"In America, you have money enough for everyone?"

Ari didn't feel like explaining. "It's just different."

They walked in between the two gigantic front paws of the Sphinx and stared up. If it were alive, the creature could have crushed them. They weren't even as tall as its paws, but it looked straight ahead, over them, unconcerned with their fate.

Ari began to speak, slowly, deliberately. "Samir, did you know that the Israeli defense minister has a conference call with the Egyptian defense minister every week?"

A grim look came across Samir's face. "Tantawi."

"Yes, Field Marshal Tantawi. Out of respect, I'm asking you for your permission for the defense minister of Israel to speak with Field Marshal Tantawi about our film—."

"No," insisted Samir.

Ari tried to stay calm, to keep emotion out of the moment. He'd already had Samir quit on him once. "Why not?"

"It is not necessary."

"Is it because he's Israeli? Is that why you don't want to do it?"

Samir looked up at the face of the Sphinx. "At the airport, when you were alone with the head of customs, what happened?"

"He asked me if I liked George Bush."

"A tricky question."

"I didn't what know what to say," admitted Ari. "What was the right answer? But I didn't want to make a mistake and say the wrong thing. I thought, does he want me to say 'I hate George Bush.' Or, 'He's a war criminal.' That kind of thing? Was that what he wanted?"

"No, that would not be an Egyptian answer."

"I thought so, but why?"

"It would be giving away too much, and he would have thought you were a coward, just saying something to please him that you might not believe. What did you say to answer him?"

"I said, 'I think George Bush made a mistake, a big mistake going into Iraq.'"

"And he said?"

"'You are good man. I give you your camera. Saddam is great man!'"

"Really? He said Saddam?" Samir chuckled softly.

"Yes, Samir." Ari turned to face him. "I'm so afraid."

"Of what?"

"I think this whole . . ." Ari's voice choked up for a second as he reflected, wondering why he felt such strong emotion. "That . . . everything here is a test." He patted the immense dry dusty paw with his hand. Heat still radiated out of the limestone. "I'm on some path through the desert and if I take one step in the wrong direction, I'm lost."

"Now, you are starting to think like an Egyptian." Samir reached into his pocket and pulled out a letter.

"Read it," said Samir.

Ari took the letter and squinted at it in the blue twilight. "I can't. It's in Arabic."

"Would you like me to translate?"

"Please."

"'Your request to fly a helicopter around the Sphinx has been approved.'"

Elation flowed into Ari's breath, into his chest. Lustful for this turn of fortune, Ari grabbed Samir by the arms and shook him. "Oh you, you crazy son of a . . . ! You've been holding out on me!" Samir must have had that letter for at least an hour. "That's great! Great news! If I didn't get that shot then . . . then . . . I don't know what." Ari leaned back against the massive lion's paw. His tremendous relief was delicious. What could Beth say now? "How much did this cost?" he asked Samir.

"Ask the Sphinx." Samir pointed up at the broken stone face, scarred by the sands of time. "Only he knows."

PART FOUR

What is the creature that walks on four legs in
the morning, two legs at noon, and three in the
evening?

—Sophocles, *Oedipus Rex*,
The Riddle of the Sphinx

Tomorrow was the big day. Ari couldn't sleep. He'd had several beers in the hotel bar with Don and Charley to talk about the flight, but the alcohol had just energized, not calmed him. He flopped around in the huge bed. He craved Beth, but he didn't want to call her. Samir still owed her a budget for the overage and he didn't want to hear her gripe about it.

He remembered Farah sitting on the grass on the quad at Cairo U. He wondered, if he set his intention to it, could he get her to fall in love with him? The dangerous thought shuddered his body as if he had lain on a bed of ice. Why did he crave people to love him so much? What an insane mess that would make. Did he need some sort of self-sabotage to complicate things, to give him an ever-increasing problem to solve? What would Samir do if he even thought Ari was attracted to her? Not that she could ever see him in a serious light. She was a true believer, a real revolutionary.

She made Ari remember his own radical college days back

in the States. Sitting on the grass with a cute redhead from his Macro Econ class on the quad in the midst of a peaceful yet rowdy mob. Some students had chained the front doors of the administration building closed, demanding that the university sell all its investments in South Africa.

"What do we want?" went the chant.

"Divestment!"

"When do we want it?"

"Now!"

Then there was a lull. The microphone was open.

"Why don't you speak?" the redhead from Econ class challenged him.

"Yeah, why don't I?" Ari had jumped up, stepped over everybody sitting on the lawn, walked up the steps of the building, and grabbed the mic. He didn't know what he was going to say, but he stared out at the cute redhead and six or seven hundred other students looking up at him and thought, what does she want me to say? What do they want? The question kept repeating over and over in his head. I've got to give them what they came here for. I've got to, if I can only figure out what that is.

"You know you're going to win, don't you?" he asked the crowd while he looked straight at her. "In a matter of days, this university is going to announce that it's selling all its stocks in South Africa. How do I know this?"

Everyone sat up. They didn't know how he knew. Even he didn't know how he knew. He just knew it. "If the University of California is going to dump three billion in investments, so will we. If Harvard is talking about it publicly, you can bet that our administration is talking about it privately right now."

Everyone nodded vigorously. The redhead was beaming. Ari looked at the student organizers. They were all spellbound, nodding, smiling. She—no—they all love me, he thought. I can feel it washing over me brighter than sunshine and it feels so good, better than sex.

"But why stop at South Africa? Why stop with one thing? We know we can do this now. We can vote with our money. Why don't we organize a list of all the biggest corporations in the world and pass this list to every college everywhere? Why don't we figure out who is the best and who is the worst on human rights, labor, the environment, and lobbying the government? We find out who is the best, or really, who is the least worst, and spend our money with that corporation, and ask every college to do the same.

"A corporation has no morality. Its only morality is profit. People have morality, and people buying things make those things profitable. If we have the power to end apartheid in South Africa, we have the same power to tell Exxon and General Motors and McDonald's and AT&T what to do and what not to do. We are just getting started!"

Ari went on and on about building a new society based on voting with your dollars and trying to make every decision a moral one. He spoke far longer than anyone else. After he finished, everyone cheered, mostly from the break in the monotony of days of divestment talk.

He went back to his redhead, who squeezed him in a big hug. He felt her breasts press against him. With adoration in her eyes, she told him that his was the best speech, and he felt as if a messianic vista has opened before him. They left, went back to his room, and made love. Ah college!

She invited him to her folks' house for the weekend. When he got there, he realized they were rich.

"What does your dad do?" he asked.

"He's a diamond merchant," she answered.

"What?" He was shocked. "Apartheid paid for this house. The price of diamonds is controlled by the De Beers cartel in Johannesburg."

"I know," she said. "I've heard the speeches."

At dinner, in front of her parents, she kept prompting him to talk about divestment. This is too weird, he thought. There was some kind of father/daughter rebellion thing going on here, and Ari didn't go for it. She was mad at them both, he could tell. She argued divestment with her dad, but Ari kept silent. Did I even believe what I said at the rally? he wondered, or was I just carried away with the adulation of the crowd?

Later, when she sneaked into his room, they argued. "I'm not going to eat the man's food, stay under his roof, and insult him. If I'm going to insult him, I'm going to have to leave here. And you can't take his money for tuition or whatever and say you're anti-apartheid. You're saying one thing and doing the opposite. He wants you to stay in school, so he's not calling you on it, but I'll bet you he's thinking exactly that." They made love that night, but it wasn't the same.

On Monday, back at school, he didn't see her at the rally. Mid-week the university issued a statement from the board of trustees recommending divestment. He saw her at finals.

"Thank you, we did it," she had said as they were filing out their Macro exam. "Do you want to go study together?"

"I can't; I've got a review group for my History of the Middle Ages test."

They lost touch over the summer. The next spring he got a postcard from Cape Town. She was going to school there, spring semester abroad. About exam time, there was a story in the school paper, then in the news, that she'd been arrested for hiding fugitive members of the ANC in her room at night. She was sentenced to ten years in prison. He thought of writing her in prison, but he never did. He felt responsible in some way, that he had made her face some inevitable conclusion from which she could not turn back and resume her previous life.

After graduation, Mandela was freed, and so, presumably, was she, but he knew that if he ever saw her again, he would be embarrassed. He had talked the talk, but she had hidden revolutionaries under her bed.

Chapter 29

Ari was staring at himself upside down in the giant pol-ished brass headboard of his bed when his computer rang. He dreaded answering it.

He hit a button. "Hello, Beth."

"Hey, buddy," said his old friend's voice.

"Frank?" Ari sat up in bed. "How you doing?"

"I hear you're flying tomorrow."

"That's right," said Ari, proud he could tell Frank himself. "*Inshallah*, as they say around here."

"Good work, be safe." They had both seen men get hurt and even die filming. "If anything seems out of whack, don't fly."

"Don't worry Frank, we'll get a great shot for you." Ari was touched that in all the maelstrom of trying to finish the filming in New York, Frank had found time to call him. "I'm told that the Air Force is giving me the best pilot in the best squadron."

"Right." Frank didn't speak for a moment. Their private con-versations were short, but often had long pauses. They had known each other since they both were kids just starting out in the business. They had developed some tacit way of communicating. "Ari, why'd you think I was Beth? Were you expecting her to call you?"

"She's waiting on a budget and . . . we haven't sent it yet."

"Are you two uh . . . ?" Frank let the question peter out. He already seemed to know the answer.

Ari was evasive. "Why do you ask?" Then an idea dawned on him. Could it be that Frank wanted her? "Frank, look I didn't know that you . . ."

"That I what . . . ? Me and Beth? Are you nuts?"

"If I knew, I mean if I had the slightest idea that you and Beth were . . . then I wouldn't be . . . You do know that, don't you?"

"Of course, of course. Don't worry about it." Frank reassured Ari, then added, "Be careful. She's never going to leave Glenn. He gives her exactly what she wants."

"Which is?"

"Masochism. Be safe tomorrow."

"I will."

They hung up.

Ari flopped around in bed a few times, then kicked off the sheets and turned on the light. He paced the huge suite like a caged animal.

"What am I doing?" he said to his reflection in the polished bronze headboard with Arabic etchings all over it. Sleep was impossible. He stepped on a shirt on the floor and noticed that he had amassed quite a bit of dirty laundry. Time to clean house. He grabbed the Mena Hotel laundry bag from the closet and violently snatched up his pile of discarded clothes, stuffing them into the bag, committing a kind of reverse purge.

As he hung the fat bag on the doorknob to his suite, he noticed the laundry price list clipped on to it.

"Four dollars a shirt!" he said to himself.

Outrageous, he decided, and grabbed up the bag. He walked out of the hotel and down into the dark streets of Giza. He knew he had to leave the tourist quarter, so he put the pyramids to his back and kept walking.

Every woman he passed wore the hijab. At every corner, he asked another woman: "Laundry?" He pantomimed washing clothes. They pointed him further into Giza on the big street until he saw the laundry, with steamy windows. A man was ironing at incredible speed with a big heavy metal iron, which had a gas flame inside of it. The man had a big powerful right arm holding the iron and a scrawny little left arm moving the clothes around.

Ari liked this. It was real. He wanted to vote with his money, to spend it, give it to someone who did the work, not the hotel chain owned by some giant corporation somewhere else. He liked the laundry man, who was happy to see him and take his clothes. Armed with his ticket and a sense of satisfaction, Ari strolled out on the street and meandered his way back toward the hotel. He had found what he was looking for, a simple pleasant human interaction with an ordinary Egyptian.

It was past midnight and the street was teeming. He strolled in front of a storefront mosque packed with thin men who had long beards and very short hair. An imam was making a passionate speech. Ari stopped to watch, and thought, he's a true believer. Ari found himself nodding along with the group, entranced by the imam's intensity and hypnotic rhythm. Even though Ari knew nothing of what was said, he felt a sense of agreement.

The imam spotted him and stopped talking instantly. All the men turned to look at him. Ari nodded to them, smiled, and waved. All of them wore dishdashas and sandals. They stared at him, their eyes unfriendly.

Ari smiled harder, but it didn't work. They hate me, he realized, because I'm an American.

Chapter **30**

Ari, Samir, Don, Charley, and the location scout all stood outside the guardhouse at the entrance to the Air Force base, which coincidentally was on the far side of Cairo International Airport. They had been standing there for over an hour.

Ari was pacing and muttering to himself, looking at his watch, holding his model Sphinx, pyramids, and helicopter. Everyone gave him a wide berth. His eyes were bloodshot. He had not slept. He had the distinct look of urgency that had reached the point of pain like that of a child forbidden to go to the bathroom. He had contained himself, repressing the urge to start yelling. He needed to get that helicopter off the ground before Beth called to stop it.

Samir was arguing with a tall, wiry sergeant of the guard, who smirked at anyone without a uniform, then looked past them as if they didn't matter. Samir's sheer volume of Arabic increased, driving the sergeant backward. The angry outburst calmed Ari a bit. He walked over to Don and Charley, who leaned against the airforce base wall.

"What's he saying?" asked Ari. The sergeant of the guard retreated from Samir's wrath all the way inside the guard booth, and he was now yelling back, gesticulating defensively.

"The sergeant is pointing at the fax machine," said Don.

"Fax machine? Don't tell me a written order has to get here from some other place." Ari started to hyperventilate. There goes the day, he thought. He wanted to punch the brick wall with his fist.

"Looks like the camera just arrived." Charley pointed out toward the road.

The dilapidated white truck pulled up on the road with the camera cases in the back. The driver jumped down out of the cab and walked over, all smiles, his sandals slapping on the road.

"Finally," said Ari, and he walked over to the guardhouse. "Samir, what's going on? We're losing the morning light."

"Just one second." Samir held up his hand and continued his Arabic rant.

Ari was pissed off by the gesture, but he said as calmly as he could, "The camera's here."

A jeep pulled up inside the wall and a lanky young lieutenant stepped out. He had a face pocked from acne scars. He walked directly up to Ari. This must be a good sign, thought Ari. Someone's expecting us.

"I am the military censor," said the lieutenant.

"Can you help us?" Ari changed in his anger for supplication. "We can't seem to get permission to go inside."

"No, I am the military censor. I must see every shot."

"Do you know how to reach the base commander?"

"No base. No aircraft," insisted the censor.

"Right." Ari looked at his team with mock seriousness. "Don, Charley, no base. No aircraft. Only Sphinx. Only pyramids."

Don and Charley both said "Yes, sir!" simultaneously, with the same tone of mock seriousness.

The military censor looked at them, suspicious that he was the butt of a joke, which he was. Ari turned his back on the censor and walked over to the guard booth.

"Samir, what is taking so long? At this rate, it'll be dark before we get the camera mounted."

Samir looked down. Ari knew he would get angry at what Samir was about to say. "The authorization for us to enter must be faxed to the guard."

"Faxed? Really? So?"

"The fax is out of paper."

"Oh my god!" Ari couldn't believe that a country could run this way. "Send someone to get some paper."

"That is already happening," said Samir.

"Who uses a fax anymore?" lamented Ari. "Samir, I need a word with you." Ari took him aside. "What do we have to do if we don't get the shot today? Apply again?"

Before Samir could answer, Hamed's car zoomed up and screeched to a halt on the road surrounding the base. Hamed held a roll of thermal fax paper out the window like a runner's baton. The truck driver grabbed it and ran it over to the sergeant in the guardhouse.

"Okay." Ari turned around to face his crew. "Let's get that camera in here."

Beyond them, Ari saw something that he simply couldn't comprehend. The camera truck was driving away. Ari looked at the truck driver beside him, then back at the truck. The cab was empty. No one was in the driver's seat.

"Not possible," said Ari. "That's impossible."

Slowly, but picking up speed, the truck rolled straight along the road, which dipped down to a long hill.

Ari started to jog. As the truck accelerated, so did he. Everyone else watched for a moment in disbelief, then ran after Ari, who was now sprinting as fast as he could. He sprinted alongside, then in front of the truck, put his hand on the grille and planted his feet like Superman stopping a train. The truck would have easily run him over, but on that stretch of road was a fine, sandy dust, a slight incursion of the desert into the city, and Ari's sneakers skated along the surface of the asphalt gaining no traction at all. Samir ran up next to him.

"Ari, get out of the way!" he yelled.

"No!" Ari would not let go.

"Please, you will be crushed!" begged Samir.

Ari looked down at his white sneakers skimming over the black gray asphalt, the tiny tan rivulets of a dust cloud sweeping behind them. "I didn't come all the way here just to have the camera roll down a hill and crash!" yelled Ari.

Samir grabbed hold of the truck and tried to slow it, to no avail. Don, Charley, Hamed, the guards, and the censor all ran up and grabbed hold of the truck while yelling at Ari.

"Ari . . . ! Let go . . . ! You will be killed . . . ! Mr. Ari, stop . . . ! There is no way!" they all shouted.

The truck driver ran up last. His sandals prevented him from closing the gap. They broke or flew off as he put on one final burst of speed. He reached the cab in his bare feet, jumped up on the running board, and opened the door just as the truck was about to go through the intersection of the busy road that wrapped around the base to the airport.

"Stop! Damn you, stop!" Ari commanded the truck with every last shred of his will.

The driver hit the brakes. The truck screeched to a halt, stopping at the stop sign. Everyone doubled over exhausted, sweating, red faced, smiling, gasping down great gulps of air, relieved. All of them except for Ari, whose face had a maniacal wrath. He had skated on the dust under his sneakers most of the way.

"Why didn't you put on the emergency brake?" Ari demanded from the relieved truck driver.

"I did, Mr. Ari! I swear it! I swear I put it on!" the truck driver protested innocently as he reached in and pulled on the brake handle. With a metallic clicking, grinding sound the whole emergency brake came off in his hand. He held up the useless lever out the truck window to Ari as proof.

Chapter 31

"That's not a chopper." Ari shook his head as they drove across the tarmac to the old Soviet Mi-17. "That's a bus with a rotor on top."

"An old bus," added Don.

The crew chief and ground crew stood by, milling around as if they'd been waiting there for hours. The camera truck, the censor's jeep, Samir and Hamed's cars all pulled up. Then Ari, Don, and Charley jumped out and went into overdrive pulling the cases off the back of the truck, laying them out and opening them up, their frustrated energy exploding into a frenzy of work.

The Egyptian crew stood by watching, ready to lend a hand. The crew chief and Charley seemed to recognize each other instantly as the men who made things work. In a minute they had developed their own sign language.

"Oh my god." Ari opened the last case and slid it next to the cargo bay door. "This helicopter has got to be fifty years old!"

"At least." Charley strapped on a tool belt.

"I hope it doesn't fall apart on us. Charley? How long do you think before we're ready to fly?"

Charley pulled out a tape measure and checked the distance from the short wing with rocket launchers on it to the ground.

"We're in luck. See this hole in the wing? This is a military camera mount." Charley pointed at what looked like a big aluminum grommet through the wing close to the fuselage. "We can just screw in the ball right here underneath."

"Is there enough clearance for it under there?"

Charley looked at the tape measure. "Three feet, one inch. Just barely."

Samir's phone rang. Ari flinched.

Samir looked at the number. "It's from the United States."

"Don't answer it," commanded Ari with a tinge of panic.

"But . . . did you look at the new budget?" Samir drew a sheaf of papers out of a plastic folder. "I finished it at dawn. Here."

Samir handed Ari the spreadsheet with every line item in it. Ari flipped straight to the last page for the total.

"Oh no, Samir. This is double the bid. This is a quarter of a million dollars?" Ari imagined Beth's face seeing the number on her computer, probably just a minute before she placed that call.

"Yes, it is very thorough." Samir showed Ari the level of detail on the other pages.

"She'll freak out." Ari closed up the pages and handed them back. "How am I going to justify this?"

"Everything has taken twice as long," protested Samir. "Everything costs double."

"Not really, Samir. It's not twice the work. They won't pay this. They'll say you're cheating us."

"Look at it line by line. You will see."

"It can't be double. Beth will punish us for this."

"Punish us? How?"

A jeep pulled up next to them on the tarmac to take them to the squadron commander's office.

"We've got to get airborne before anyone in LA wakes up," Ari said emphatically, half to himself. "Where'd I put my Sphinx and pyramids?" Ari gathered his props from off of one of the cases. As he stepped into the jeep, he barked out a question. "How long, Charley?"

Charley emerged from the ground crew hovering around him waiting for some little piece of the equipment puzzle to carry into place. "Ninety minutes," said Charley.

"You've got one hour."

Ari and Samir clambered into the jeep, which drove away from the ramp along taxiways through the sand. The Air Force base was one vast rectangle of desert with runways in the middle. Off in the distance behind a long low dune was a plane graveyard with commercial airliners that looked like they would never fly again. Some were missing engines. Their paint had been sandblasted off the sides from years of desert sandstorms. They had faded names on the side of coup-ridden nations like Air Mozambique or Libya Air. Beyond them was the civilian half of the airport that Ari knew so well.

The jeep pulled up in front of a low long building of simple military construction. The jeep driver, a corporal, led them into the squadron commander's office.

There was the big desk, and in front of it, the customary two lines of chairs facing inward filled with the pilots of the entire squadron in a staff meeting. Ari looked at the Egyptian pilots, and like pilots in every air force, he knew they were not really military men. In fact, the urge to fly is such an act of freedom that military discipline is diametrically opposed to it. Most infantry don't even consider pilots soldiers at all.

The squadron commander, a compact, slightly bald major, was smoking. He rose to shake their hands, introduced them to two lanky pilots, both captains in flight suits, and invited them all to sit. Mint tea was served.

After a respectful three sips, Ari held up his pyramids and gestured for permission to set them up. The major nodded, and Ari set out his mini Necropolis on the desk.

Ari "flew" his toy helicopter very low around the Sphinx. The two pilots nodded. The squadron commander shook his head.

"What's the problem now?" asked Ari.

"Major Horus says that the pattern is too low," translated Samir.

Major Horus raised Ari's hand with the helicopter.

Ari turned to Samir. "That won't work. It's too high."

Major Horus and Samir exchanged a few words in Arabic. "He says it will frighten the tourists."

"The Sphinx will be open?" Ari couldn't believe that. The statue could be easily cordoned off as it actually had a wall around it and a gate. Ari and Samir had been there. They had been locked inside it for their private audience with the creature.

Samir gave a look of warning to Ari to let the matter drop and said, "The Sphinx never closes."

Chapter 32

The three-foot-round SpaceCam ball hung under the wing with barely an inch to spare off the tarmac. Charley gave the ball a hard tug. It seemed solidly mounted, so he grabbed his fist, giving the ready sign to Don. The lens in the ball turned left, right, then up and down.

"Good to go," said Charley.

One of the ground crew offered the military censor a cigarette, then held out a lighter. At the exact moment the censor was distracted by lighting it, the crew chief put his arm around Charley's shoulder, and another ground crew member pulled out a digital camera and snapped a picture of them both next to the SpaceCam. The censor spun around suspiciously, but the crew chief had already relaxed his pose and nothing looked amiss.

Then in an almost choreographed ballet of picture taking, half a dozen cameras appeared in the hands of the ground crew, Samir, and even Charley. Every time the censor spun around, another camera appeared behind his back, snapping away. This game delighted everyone. Ari had to admire the skill with which these men could run circles around their own censor.

Ari enjoyed a good practical joke as much as anyone, but he distrusted too much horsing around on set. That's when things go wrong, he thought. Fights erupt, things get broken, or people get hurt. He made a spinning motion with his finger to the pilots. Once the jet engines started to spool up, all the cameras disappeared into pockets.

"Don?" asked Ari.

Don sat on the deck of the cargo bay behind the camera control console.

"I'm set." Don gave Ari the thumbs-up.

Samir's cell phone rang again. Ari froze.

"It's Beth," said Samir, examining his phone.

"Don't answer," insisted Ari.

"But she must approve this budget." Samir held up his copy in the clear plastic folder.

"Don't answer the phone! I'm telling you, she'll hold us up. She'll stop us."

"But without her approval, how can I know if I will get the payment for this flight?" asked Samir.

"I'll get you your money," Ari promised. "But I can't talk to her now."

"Why not?" Samir was mystified. "This is not the correct way. I gave her my word."

"I need to believe what I'm saying, don't you understand? I need to have confidence when I talk to her."

"Confidence?" asked Samir. "Confidence in what?"

"That we got the shot. Then I can sell it. Then I can sell anyone on anything, as long as I know that the shot's in the can. Hang up!"

Samir shook his head in a tremor of resentful tics. He could not serve two masters. "I do not like this."

"Trust me." Ari pointed at the ringing phone. "I know what I'm doing."

Samir denied the call. Ari reached into a case and pulled out two sets of aviation headphones. He put one around his neck and passed the other to Samir.

"So you can hear the pilot over the engines and the rotor going round."

Ari walked to the chopper. He had a mercurial look in his eyes, a hyperawareness that subdued Samir.

"Let's get in," commanded Ari.

Ari and Samir climbed into the cargo bay next to Don. The crew chief ran over to Samir, speaking into his ear over the rotor sound.

"What's wrong?" asked Ari.

"The pilot says that the camera ball is too big. It is only one inch above the runway. As we taxi it will hit the ground and break."

"No, no, it'll be fine." Ari got in and plugged his headset into a jack.

"Tell him that once the rotor spools up the aircraft will rise on the landing gear about five or six inches off the ground. That will be enough to taxi."

The crew chief shook his head.

"He says no."

"Tell him it's my personal camera. Tell him I own it. If we break it it's my responsibility."

Samir balked. "But that is not the truth."

"So what? Tell him!" insisted Ari.

Samir shouted a few words over the growing rotor noise and pointed at Ari. The crew chief nodded, then hopped into the cargo bay, taking his position in front of the bay door. The military censor climbed in and found a place behind Don where he could watch the screen. Ari looked at the censor, then jumped up.

"I'll be back in a second."

Ari hopped off the chopper. Ran to his bag and grabbed his own little digital camera. He slipped it into his pocket.

"We have a clearance to fly!" Samir yelled at him from the chopper as it started to roll forward onto the taxiway.

"I'm coming! I'm coming! Don't wait for me!" Ari ran back and jumped aboard as the chopper lifted off the ground. The rotors made a heavier thwacking sound, biting more air. The black tarmac on the sand dropped away under them.

Ari looked at his crew. "Samir, I think you're blushing."

"You were right," Samir admitted. "This is the coolest."

"Now, it's my turn to give you a date with the Sphinx you will always remember," said Ari, panting hard from the run to get his camera.

Chapter 33

From up in the air, Egypt makes geographical sense. The Nile runs north within a narrow band of green stretching down into the desert. However, Cairo is the place where the longest river in the world fans out into an enormous delta. Some twenty million people live on that vast triangle, starting with Giza, then the city of Cairo, as the river grows wider and wider, into a verdant martini glass shape.

"Look down there." Samir pointed out of the cargo bay door. "That fast boat on the Nile."

Ari craned his neck out into the downdraft from the thwacking rotors above. On the broad river across their path was one of the most incongruous sights he had ever seen. A speedboat splayed out a white vector behind it. Within and without the V, a water-skier slalomed back and forth, expertly jumping the wake. Never would Ari have expected to see waterskiing on the Nile, let alone find that the skier was a woman in a full black burka with a veil and gloves.

"Don, roll a few feet on that woman waterskiing. That'll wake them up in the editing room."

Don zoomed in on her with his three-hundred-millimeter lens and turned on the camera for a few seconds.

"Have you ever seen that before?" Ari asked Samir.

"No."

With the water and the wind, the black fabric clung, wet, to every curve of her body.

"Man, she's an excellent skier. That wet burka, that's not hiding her figure at all. She looks really . . ." Ari caught himself.

"Go ahead," urged Samir. "You can say it."

"Sexy. She knows what she's doing to all the men for miles. She's got to know."

"She must be a Saudi," said Samir.

"A Saudi feminist. Cut! Cut the camera, Don. That's enough film of that. Look, all the cars on the bridge are slowing down to watch her. If she doesn't keep going upstream, there's going to be a traffic jam."

"If she doesn't disappear down the Nile," said Samir, "all the men in Cairo will go swimming."

"Samir the Hammer, you made a joke!"

"Look." Samir grew serious and pointed toward the pyramids out the cargo bay door. "The Necropolis. Are we ready to shoot?"

"Yup," said Ari.

The military censor was busy watching the woman skiing, so Ari pulled out his camera and snapped a picture of Samir behind the censor's back. Samir's smile had emerged. It was as if he'd become a different person, boyish, excited; his smoldering had vanished somehow. Ari felt a warm sentimental wave of affection for him. The pyramids on the plateau of Giza loomed in the distance.

"Look." Samir pointed excitedly. "The Necropolis. Should I tell the pilots to start?"

"We're set," said Don.

"Remember, Don, we shouldn't know it's the Sphinx until we pull back," said Ari.

"Right, boss."

The pilot banked around past the top of the Great Pyramid and dropped down into the little valley underneath the Plateau of Giza. The ship lined up abeam to the Sphinx.

"Ready and . . . roll camera," said Ari.

The pilot flew in a perfect arc around the Sphinx's head, corkscrewing back up and past the top of the Great Pyramid. Don zoomed in tight on the top of the head of the massive statue, but not tight enough. Ari could still tell it was the Sphinx, even from the beginning of the shot. That was not what he wanted.

"Cut, cut, cut!" said Ari. "Reset."

"How was that?" asked Samir.

"No good. We're up too high. We've got to fly lower."

Samir translated into his headset.

Ari looked out the back of the banking helicopter as the horizon of the desert tilted vertically to one side and then all the way to the other. He could see over the ramp that made a tailgate at the back of the aircraft; it was like the back of a pickup truck, the only difference was size. You could drive a pickup truck up that ramp inside this helicopter, he thought. The horizon leveled off. Then the chopper started on its course again.

"Roll camera," said Ari.

"How is it?" asked Samir.

"Not great." Don started the shot again, but it was already too late in the flight pattern to salvage the shot. "I can do better."

"What about all the tourists staring up at us?" asked Samir.

"We don't care about them," said Ari. "We can erase them digitally after we edit the film. Cut, cut, let's go again."

"Still too high?" asked Samir.

"Yuh, reset," said Ari with a blasé look of disappointment on his face.

Samir told the pilot, and he cut his pattern short, banking hard, pulling three Gs. Everyone grimaced as the horizon went vertical out the back. Ari could feel the strain on the rotors as their every thwack became a shake. The helicopter leveled off to descend to its starting point.

Samir argued with the pilot as he banked around to reset. The helicopter started the pattern again. Ari didn't bother to speak.

"Aren't you going to roll?" asked Don.

"There's no point." Ari leaned back against a machine gun mount in the side of the ship. He was on strike. He wasn't going to look at the screen unless he thought it was worth it. "We're just wasting film. We've got to get low, really low, right down next to it, or the shot'll never get into the movie."

"The pilot says he won't fly any lower." Samir pointed at his headset.

Ari lashed out. "Did we come all the way here, go through everything that we went through, just to film something that's okay?" Ari was yelling now. "No, it's got to be great! It's got to be the best, or there's no point! We'll just wind up on the cutting room floor!"

Samir gazed back at Ari, furious, humiliated, for he internalized failure, blamed himself. This is the breaking point, thought Ari. Either he's going to push through to the other side or he's going to give up.

"*Inshallah?*" asked Ari sarcasticly.

Then something welled up inside of Samir—some determination to reverse the force of compromise, of moderation, of playing it safe and keeping to the rules. Ari knew he had cracked Samir open, cleaved off the lid on his mind.

Samir ripped into the pilot in Arabic. Arguing, then screaming at him. A lifetime of pent-up rage at the rusty machine of post-British colonial pan-Arab Socialist police state bureaucracy poured out of him.

"Yeah, yeah, that's right!" Ari goaded Samir on like a demon on his shoulder. "Tell him the whole world will see this shot! And that we will put his name in the credits at the end of the movie in every theater as the pilot who flew around the head of the Sphinx!"

Samir yelled and then yanked his headset plugs out of the jack on the bulkhead and pulled himself forward through the banking aircraft toward the cockpit. The censor and the crew chief tried to stop him, but they could only use one arm each to keep from tumbling over in the banking chopper. Samir plugged into a jack in the cockpit and resumed yelling. The pilots looked behind themselves at the maniac at their shoulders. More afraid of Samir than the consequences, the pilot pushed the stick forward and dove. They came in low, way down low by the head of the Sphinx.

"Oh yeah!" cried Ari. "That's what I'm talking about! Roll camera!"

Don started the shot as tight as possible, then pulled out. The head of the Sphinx filled the frame. They were right down beside it.

"Perfect . . . perfect. Steady on the Sphinx, now wider, wider. That's good, good."

The shot was locked on the face of the Sphinx, as the helicopter arced, the background of stone and sand twirled behind the massive head. Ari knew that on a giant screen the effect would be dizzying, spellbinding, movie magic.

"Those people are running," said Samir.

"Shhh!" Ari lashed out. "I need to focus. Okay, okay now . . . pull back, wider, wider. Right over the top of the pyramid, right over the top, tell him to fly right over the top!"

Samir yelled at the pilot, who flew right next to the top of the Great Pyramid.

"Awesome! Cut! That was perfect!" Ari high-fived Don and looked out the cargo bay door. Below, they had just hovered over fifty or sixty buses parked in rows by the entrance to the pyramids. Trapped between the buses, hundreds of tourists were running away from the rotor wash, an inverted mushroom cloud of dust that gushed down between the buses and shot little wind tunnels of sandstorm through each parked row, engulfing the tourists like escaping insects.

"Ari, look at those tourists down there!" cried Don.

"They're running away!" realized Ari. "From us. Oh, they're

getting sandblasted. Tell the pilot to climb once we get near the pyramids or we'll ruin those people's day."

"That is what I was trying to tell you," said Samir. "Reset?"

Ari looked out the back of the ship. A tan cloud described their path.

"Uh, we kicked up too much dust all over the place," Ari admitted. "You can't even see the head of the Sphinx anymore. It looks like a sandstorm hit."

Samir talked on the headset with the pilot.

"He wants to know should we fly over the desert for a few minutes to let the dust settle down?"

"No, let's go back to base and reload. We got it. We got the shot. Whatever happens now is just gravy."

"Just gravy?" asked Samir.

"Extra. A bonus."

The helicopter leveled out and headed back over the city, back to base.

Chapter **34**

The ride back from the Sphinx in the helicopter held a sublime satisfaction. The engine noise, the thwack of the rotors faded away into a quiet that only comes when you touch the face of the impossible and the extraordinary. The team basked silently in the achievement borne of their own determination until Ari noticed Samir muttering to himself.

"What is it?" Ari prompted him.

"I was looking right into the eyes of the Sphinx."

"Yeah?"

"You do not know what that means to an Egyptian."

Don looked at his monitor at something in the city below. "What's that?"

On the screen, a mass of people was moving down a boulevard beneath them. Ari looked out the bay door. Protesters marched along the avenue into a large circular square from every direction, some holding signs and banners. Ari looked back at the protesters on the screen, thousands of little dots all moving in unison.

"Don, roll me a few seconds of that." Don turned on the camera, but Ari thought better of giving the studio something else to worry about. "No, wait. Cut. Don, that's a lot of . . . how many people would you say that is?"

"It's got to be four, maybe five thousand."

"Five thousand, as many as that?"

Ari was spooked by the size of the crowd. This wasn't just a few college kids anymore. This was something to pay attention to. I've got to go and see this for myself, he thought, as soon as possible.

The chopper landed and taxied onto the ramp. Charley met them and opened the ball, downloading the film, threading a new magazine into the camera. The fuel truck pulled up as the jet engines wound down.

Samir and Ari hopped off. The crew chief snapped a photo of them behind the censor's back.

"Going up again?" asked Charley.

"Sure, but we got it," said Don.

"We got it good!" Ari high-fived Charley and Don, and he lifted Samir's hand and high-fived him as well. Samir's cell phone rang.

"It's Elizabeth." Samir looked at the screen. "Should I . . . ?"

"Sure," said Ari with ease. "I'm ready now. Answer it."

"Hello, Elizabeth," said Samir into his cell before passing the phone. "He's right here."

"Hey, babe!" said Ari cheerfully.

Beth's voice came through the line with a slight delay.

"Did you see the budget—?"

Ari overwhelmed her with a joyful tirade. "We got it! It's amazing, fantastic, perfect! Frank's going to love it! Did I see what . . . ?"

"That budget!" She was almost yelling over the phone.

"Yes, I saw the budget. So what . . . ?"

"Are you high?"

Ari laughed—high on life, he thought. "The studio doesn't understand it yet. They don't know what I know. Look, this is going to be the signature shot of the movie! It'll be the poster! It'll be the commercial! It'll be the trailer! It will be why people go to buy a ticket in the first place. . . !"

"But it's a quarter of a million dollars!" She was yelling now. "Twice the bid!"

"I know it's double, but what are you going to do?" He didn't care. He wore a manic set of armor impervious to her anger. "You've got to come here to shoot the end of the movie. We've got to get the SpaceCam back out of Egypt. We've got to get the film out. You've just got to pay. What choice do you have?"

"You fucked me, Ari!"

"Babe, babe, calm down, we're reloaded here." He had fucked her in the way that she meant, and he had to admit to himself that he enjoyed it. He had broken with her in the way a child keeps testing and testing adults until one day he sees that their real power over him is really quite limited by his own resolve.

The pilots jumped out of the cockpit and embraced Samir, kissing him on the cheek, Samir who had been screaming at them barely minutes ago.

"Wait till you see the shot," Ari told Beth. "It was worth it."

The ground crew hooked up the fuel hose from the truck

and started refueling the aircraft. Beth lashed into him. She knew that something had changed. He had lost his fear of her and this enraged her even more.

"Ari, you're going to write me an e-mail right now, that you went ahead without my approval—"

"Beth, I've got to go flying again. You're just wasting your breath. Are you on set?"

"Yes, but you're going to put it in writing that you went around behind my back—"

"Are you near camera. Are you near Frank . . . ?"

She breathed heavily for a moment. "Yes."

"Then pass him the phone."

Ari heard some whispering on the line, then Frank's voice.

"Hey, buddy," said Frank. "Did you get it?"

"I shot the Sphinx! It's *awesome*! You're going to love it!"

"Good job," said Frank. "Got to get back to work here."

"Hey, Frank, are you still on schedule to arrive on Friday. . . ?"

"Yes, Ari, we'll be wrapped in New York by the end of tomorrow."

"See you when you get here. . . ." Ari heard the phone jostle as it was passed back over to Beth.

"I'm totally serious about that e-mail, Ari!" she whisper-yelled at him.

"Beth, Beth, calm down! Didn't you hear me? I shot the Sphinx! I just shot the Sphinx!"

Ari hung up the phone and handed it to Samir, who embraced him and kissed Ari three times on the cheeks.

"Whoa!" said Ari surprised.

Ari laughed, giddy with glee. He kissed Samir back, and

then the pilots were there and he kissed them on the cheeks, too. A jeep zoomed right up to them with a screeching halt. The squadron commander, Major Horus, hopped out spitting mad.

"Oh-oh." Ari backed away. The two pilots sheepishly walked over to their commander, who started yelling at them for flying too low.

"Hamed?" Ari looked around. "Where's Hamed? I've got to go."

Don was stunned. "We're not flying another mission?"

"Of course," said Ari. "You guys do it." Ari pointed to Major Horus chewing out his pilots. "Look, they're going to have no asses left in a minute. You'll never get that low again." Ari started to walk off toward Hamed's car.

"Where the hell are you going?" demanded Don.

"Yes," added Samir, offended. "Where are you going?"

"We got the shot, guys. We got the shot," said Ari over his shoulder to a very confused Samir, Don, and Charley. Ari jumped in Hamed's car and drove away.

PART FIVE

The black and white days are coming, there is no grey.

—Tweeted by Gsquare86, Gigi Ibrahim,
Tahrir Square, Cairo

Chapter 35

Traffic snarled to a standstill near Tahrir, so Ari grabbed his camera and hopped out of the car. He made his way through the traffic onto the sidewalk. A lot of young people were out, but there were older people, too. Everyone wandered around aware of everyone else. They glanced around at each other with searching looks, for what? Permission to simply be there together? Excited curiosity flickered about from young face to old face to shopkeeper to taxi driver to those who ambled toward the growing din or walked there with purpose. Ari snapped their photos.

They even glanced at Ari for answers. Could this really be happening, such an improbable thing, an unnameable thing? Dare I look upon this greatest of obscenity in my own personal dictatorship, in the police state inside my mind? were the questions on everyone's faces as Ari caught them looking into his camera lens.

Ari could hear music and singing echoing in the square

ahead. Singing in unison, clapping in rhythm, thousands in angry jubilation.

When he entered the square, it was a party, and Ari took its smiling picture: people milling about in groups sharing bread and hummus, some clustered around happy impromptu leaders chanting, some with paint, paper, and bedsheets making banners and signs; others stood off alone, confused or embarrassed by the collective transgression all around them.

Ari could see a small stage at one side with a band on it setting up their instruments and Rami with his acoustic guitar waiting to sing. Ari scanned the densely packed crowd near the stage for sight of Farah.

A very handsome man with strong chiseled features, surveying the scene as if he had just arrived, walked in front of Ari.

"Khaled Nahkti?" asked Ari in disbelief.

"Yes?" said one of Egypt's biggest movie stars, wondering at the Westerner who had hailed him.

"I'm Ari Basher. We'll be shooting together in a couple weeks. I've been talking with your agent."

"Of course, of course!" Nahkti embraced him. "I am with you on such an honorable place! To meet with you in such a glorious time of all the Egyptians for all of us to achieve our goal, which is the democracy, which is the change." Men started to cluster around him, touching him on the shoulders or the arms as if he were a religious relic or an icon vestment of deliverance.

"Take our picture on our birthday of the new Egypt!" Kahled Nahkti threw his arms around his brethren and as if on cue

Rami and the band struck up a song, which echoed out around the square through large amps and speakers beside the stage.

Ari snapped away as Rami's simple rhythmic words rang out, a song meant to be repeated by the crowd—and they absorbed it, listening at first; then it spread through their number, the crowd clapping a sharp clap at the end of each line until it was a rhythmic thunder. Then the words grew in everyone's mouth as they learned them, and even Ari could almost sing them. He certainly recognized two words: "Hosni Mubarak."

"What's it mean?" Ari asked Khaled Nahkti, who was singing away. He switched into English, translating for Ari's camera.

"All of us . . ." He clapped. ". . . standing together," *clap,* ". . . asking for one simple thing." *Clap.* "Leave . . ." *clap,* ". . . leave . . ." *clap,* ". . . leave . . ." *clap,* ". . . leave." *Clap.* "Down, down with Hosni Mubarak." *Clap.* "Down, down with Hosni Mubarak." *Clap.* "He will leave," *clap,* ". . . cuz we won't leave." *Clap.* "He will leave," *clap,* ". . . cuz we won't leave." *Clap.* And on and on it went for several minutes, building to a frenzied crescendo.

Ari zoomed his lens in, picking out interesting faces: a man with a small half-open turban and owlish glasses; a woman covered head to toe in a black chador, dancing, with flowers stuck out of her hijab making her face look like a flower, the flower petals encircling her face like a wreath. Many danced with their hands, making autonomous flicking movements, snapping, or making circles in the air in the Arabic style. No more were these faces timidly looking for permission. They had the answer. They gave themselves permission. They took it.

The group around Khaled Nahkti grew so big and crushing that Ari lost him in the melee. Individuality raged, newborn, from all the clusters within the large crowd, like a thousand wedding parties careening into each other.

Ari fell in with a gaggle of pretty young women in western clothes, their heads uncovered. They pushed their way forward toward the stage to join another gaggle of girls upfront. Ari took pictures of them, and then he saw Farah, dancing and bouncing above the crowd, pumping her fist in the air.

"Farah!" Ari yelled, but it was impossible for anyone more than a few feet away to hear him amid the crosscurrents of sound and motion. He pushed on with the girls toward Farah by the stage. Rami finished singing the song, and Ari lost sight of her when she stopped bouncing up in the rousing ovation of clapping and rising fists.

"Farah? Farah!"

Ari pushed through to the spot where she had been dancing. He scanned the faces of each one of the smiling, ecstatic young women.

Yet amid all the bustling joy he couldn't find her.

Chapter **36**

The next day, Samir invited Ari to his home for the first time to watch the dailies of the shot of the Sphinx. Hamed smoked out front, leaning against his car in the street. The neighborhood had large trees and three- or four-story buildings mostly built in the 1960s and later. A lot of children, clean and well cared for, ran around squealing, playing soccer with a red rubber ball.

Samir and Ari sat on a low modern sectional couch watching the first series of helicopter shots, which were the only ones low enough to use. The furniture in Samir's home struck Ari as brand new and extremely clean. Persian carpets lay in every room over polished tile floors. In the dining room, Samir's wife, Leela, was setting the table for dinner. She wore the hijab.

"That is the best take," said Samir after the shot that ended with the tourists getting sandblasted between the buses by the pyramids.

"Frank's going to love it," said Ari, pleased with himself.

The Sphinx shot ended and a few seconds of protesters marching to Tahrir Square came up. The film rolled out on the image. Ari picked up the DVD remote and pushed pause. The last frame of the helicopter shot of the crowd froze up on the flat screen.

"Samir, Ari," called Leela. "The food is on the table!"

"We're almost done," Samir called back.

"These demonstrations are getting big." Ari pointed at the crowd.

"They can grow as big as all Cairo, and in the end, the streets will be empty."

"Empty?" Ari didn't believe it. He hadn't slept well thinking of yesterday's demonstration.

"The government will crack down any day now"—Samir slapped his hand with his fist—"and everyone will go home. You will see. There is a line you cannot cross or you are dead, or in jail." Samir gave a look like he had lived those words.

Ari was uncomfortable. He knew he had to broach the subject of what to do about the demonstrations with Samir, but he was afraid of a temperamental reaction. "Let's talk about scouting."

Samir's face brightened. "I want to get you out on the road every day until Frank gets here. First we must find the locations that are supposed to double for Iraq."

"Tomorrow afternoon I'm going to go to Jordan." Ari dropped the bomb.

"Jordan?" Samir suppressed his surprise. "Why? Are you thinking of shooting the Iraqi scenes in Jordan?"

"I got some photos from their Film Commission." Ari had

spent a great deal of the night on the Internet thinking about the demonstration and trying to come up with a plan B. "The pictures of Jordan look a lot like Iraq."

"Jordan is nothing like Iraq." Samir started to get that dark look in his eyes, a brewing fury. "It is covered with hills."

"It's on the border of Iraq," said Ari.

"Yes, but that is the desert part way out toward the border, not in the city." Samir's eyes widened. He took on a jilted look. "There is a week's worth of filming set in Iraq. That is half our work."

Ari didn't want to argue with Samir in his home about cutting his job in half, not in front of his wife. "Look, Samir, nothing is decided yet. I just have to go and see for myself. You can understand that. We both have to do what's best for the movie. Right?" Ari stood up.

"You will see." Samir ushered him into the dining room. "It is more expensive than here."

"A little more"—they came to the dinner table—"but it looks more like Iraq."

"How are you doing on casting?" Samir moved on to a different topic. "I will need the actors' passports to get them work permissions with the union."

"They like Khaled Nahkti. I saw him in Tahrir Square yesterday."

Leela walked in holding their two-month-old daughter.

"Khaled Nahkti? Khaled Nahkti? He's so handsome," teased Leela.

"And what am I?" asked Samir.

"You are my beautiful husband, but he's Khaled Nahkti! Will I get a chance to meet him?"

"Yes," said Ari.

"No," said Samir, and they all laughed.

Ari hovered over the round tiny face of the baby, her expression so curious, so trusting. "And this must be . . ."

"Yasmine," said Leela.

"She's beautiful. Hello, little Yasmine. I'm Ari."

"Say hello." Samir put his finger under her tiny toes, and she clutched it the way baby toes do.

"How old is she?" Ari asked Leela.

"Two months."

"Oh my god," exclaimed Ari. "I'm really stealing your husband."

"Stealing him?" she asked perplexed.

"It's a joke," Samir explained. "He means taking me away from you."

A lot of Samir's anger made sense to Ari now. He was under the pressure of a big job and a new baby.

"Now, she is 'stealing' my daughter away from me," said Samir.

"I wish you wouldn't use that word," said Leela with disapproval.

"Yasmine will visit her grandparents during the shoot," explained Samir, "in Palestine."

"Palestine?" Ari realized Leela wasn't Egyptian, but Palestinian. "Gaza or . . . ?"

"My wife is from the West Bank. Her parents were—"

She corrected him forcefully. "Are from Jerusalem."

"So I'm lucky to meet Yasmine," said Ari as warmly as he could, but there was now a charge in the air.

"Sit, sit." Samir sat after Ari. "Leela will bring us some

coffee. And who will play Nahkti's sister? Have they picked an actress yet?"

"I think they like, uh . . ." Ari searched his mind for the name of the actress. "Afareen . . . Afreen . . . somebody."

"A Persian name?" asked Samir.

Then Ari remembered. ". . . Ben Jakob."

"Israeli?" asked Leela, surprised.

"She's an Iranian Jew," said Ari. "She moved to Israel when she was fourteen. She has an Israeli passport."

Leela and Samir looked at each other.

"What's wrong?" asked Ari.

Samir gazed back at Ari without anger, devoid of anything but disappointment. "You don't see a problem with an Israeli playing an Arab?"

"Well, find me someone better," said Ari, knowing that was almost impossible in the next few days.

Samir forced himself to smile. He dished a heap of rice and lamb onto Ari's plate and let the matter drop, for the moment.

Chapter 37

Ari spotted Khaled Nahkti in the café. He was impossible to miss. Twenty people surrounded him, shaking his hand and asking for an autograph. Ari waited at a respectful distance, watching for a sign of exasperation, but Nahkti patiently shook every hand and signed every piece of paper. Good, thought Ari. He's a pro. He's a real star. He understands that without the fans he would be nowhere. Ari stepped behind the last fan on line.

"Can I have your autograph?" asked Ari, holding out a pen and a manila envelope he was carrying.

"Oh, it's you!" Nahkti laughed. "Let us go inside. They have a table for us at the back."

Nahkti led Ari in, and the effusive maître d' seated them. The energy in the room seemed to rise up and conversations buzzed as people turned to notice the movie star passing among them. As Ari and Nahkti sat, immediately a shy young woman came over and held out a scrap of paper. Khaled asked for her name and signed a little note to her.

Finally, Nahkti turned to Ari, focusing on him completely as if the room were empty of anyone else. Ari felt sucked into a vortex of charisma.

"My heart is overjoyed to meet with you," said Nahkti, clapping his chest.

"My heart is happy to meet with you, too," replied Ari.

"Please tell Frank how honored I am to be acting in so important a movie."

"And Frank is also honored." Ari bowed his head.

"To tell the truth about war is the most important movie there can be."

"Thank you. I agree completely, and I know that Frank is very happy that you think so." Ari felt that they needed to make some more small talk before coming to the real question. "Have the costume people been to see you yet?"

"Yes, there are some clothings that are okay." Nahkti spoke English boldly with a few malapropisms. "When Frank will come to Cairo so I can wear them for him to choose?"

"Soon. In a week, when he finishes shooting in New York. Khaled, if we had to move all of your Iraqi scenes to Jordan, would you have any objection to going there for a week?"

"I shoot anywhere. Jordan is closer to Iraq."

"Can you drive a car?"

Nahkti puffed up his chest. "An Egyptian man is not a man, until he drives a car in Cairo."

Ari laughed. "I know what you mean. We have some stunt driving if you're comfortable with it. You know the scene where you have to drive away from the American soldiers while they're shooting at you?"

"Do not worry. Any taxi driver in my country is ready for Formula One. I am better than the best American stunt driver. Trust me."

Then a thought popped into Ari's head. "Do you know Omar el Mansoor?"

"From Studio Giza? Yes, very well. Why do you ask?"

"Do you trust him?" asked Ari.

Nahkti took a moment to measure his words. "Get your money up front."

Ari nodded. "Tell me, would you be free to do a costume fitting on Friday?"

"Friday is tough. I will be in the Square."

"You're going to the Square all day?"

"Why don't you come with me?" Nahkti was excited by the idea. "You must tell your friends in the American media what is happening."

As much as he'd like to hang out with Nahkti, he had a lot of prep work to do for the crew's arrival from New York. "Uh . . . I'll have to call you about that."

Ari opened his manila envelope and put a glossy headshot of a beautiful actress, who bore a resemblance to Nahkti himself, on the table between them.

"Who is she? I do not know her." Nahkti picked up the photo. "She will play my sister? She is not from Egypt."

"Her name is Afareen Resavi . . ."

"An Iranian?"

". . . Ben Jakob. She grew up in Iran and then moved to

Israel." Ari held up her picture and asked the question he had come to ask. "Will you work with her?"

"Of course," said Nahkti without hesitation.

"No problem?" Ari had to be sure.

"The Actors Guild might fine me or throw me out for working with an Israeli," said Nahkti flippantly.

"Oh, we can't ask you to get in trouble with the union." This was no trivial matter. In America, the union could shut down a production.

"So what?" said Nahkti. "Let them throw me. They are small-minded."

"Will they block you from working in Egypt?"

"So I will work outside of Egypt until they forget," said Nahkti confidently. "Before that day, they can go and fuck themselves."

PART SIX

The desert is an ocean in which no oar is dipped.

—Robert Bolt, *Lawrence of Arabia*

Chapter 38

The flight from Cairo to Amman, Jordan, takes twenty-five minutes on an American plane. On EgyptAir it's closer to forty because you have to divert to the south around Israeli airspace.

Ari took the window seat whenever he could. As a pilot, he liked to watch the takeoffs and landings. In a perfect landing the touchdown is so smooth that you don't even feel it; rare in a commercial airliner, but that is the holy grail for all pilots. The landing in Amman was smooth, perfect.

The airport was small, fifteen or twenty gates. Ari walked off the plane, and a minute later he was standing on the line at passport control. A Jordanian man dressed in a blue blazer and tie came up to him.

"Mr. Basher?" the man asked in a slight British/Arabic accent.

"Yes," said Ari, surprised that he had been identified in a planeload of people half full of Western tourists.

"Let me have your passport please," said the man in the blazer.

Ari studied the man. His affect was too polite to be that of a policeman. Ari handed over his passport. "Follow me please." Ari followed the man over to the diplomatic desk. The customs official stamped Ari's passport immediately without checking it and handed it back to Ari. In less than sixty seconds, he was through passport control.

"Do you have any baggage, Mr. Basher?" asked the man as they walked past the baggage carousels.

"No," said Ari, "just my knapsack." They walked outside to a waiting black car, the door already open. Ari got in.

"I will tell them you are on your way," said the man.

"Thank you," said Ari, perplexed by such VIP treatment. What was behind it? He had never entered a foreign country so fast. From stepping off the plane to getting in the car was less than five minutes.

Ari opened the window. The outside was about ten degrees cooler than in Cairo. The altitude is higher, remembered Ari. Green farm fields rolled by in the desert with sprinklers shooting out of giant water pipes on large wagon wheels that would roll through the rows of vegetables. Unlike the chaos of Cairo, everything was orderly, save the hills of Amman.

The city was full of hills. This will never pass for Baghdad, thought Ari. I might as well turn around and go back to Cairo. I'm wasting my time here. The central road into the hotel district was like a reverse roller coaster where the land rose and fell in valleys and hills below the roadway with traffic circles overhead. The driver pulled off onto one of those overhead exits and then turned into the driveway of the Sheraton.

Ari left the car to a bomb-sniffing German shepherd. At

the front desk, the clerk handed him a pink message slip, which read:

We are in the lounge and you have already been checked in. Sharif.

The desk clerk handed him his key cards. He said, in yet another slight British accent, "You are on the top floor, Mr. Basher. Your guests have arrived."

Ari was puzzled. "They checked me in? They're allowed to do that?"

"Oh yes, Mr. Basher." The clerk gave him a knowing smile and pointed. "They are waiting for you. The lounge is right across the lobby."

Ari made his way past the elevator bank. The lobby was full of little clusters of Americans having furtive and urgent meetings, some in military uniform, others in civilian clothes but with military haircuts. This is the American gateway to Iraq, Ari realized.

Out of an elevator stepped two hulking Arab bodyguards in black suits and sunglasses. They surveyed Ari, decided he was harmless, and nodded to someone inside the elevator. Out stepped Mahmoud Abbas, the president of the Palestinian Authority. Ari stopped to watch Abbas and his entourage pass by on their way to a waiting car.

Ari walked into the lounge and saw his reception party, six men in suits and ties and two women in business attire. Sharif, the oldest and most dignified, rose to greet Ari, who felt naked in his polo shirt, chinos, and white tennis shoes. They looked like a bunch of bankers.

"Mr. Basher, welcome to Jordan." Sharif introduced the

circle of people: a production manager, his assistant, three people from the Film Commission including the commissioner himself, a location scout, his assistant, an accountant—everyone needed to start working on a film immediately.

"Well, we have a week's worth of shooting that's supposed to take place in Iraq during the American invasion." Ari pulled a file from his knapsack with the Iraqi sequence script pages, Samir's budget, and location photos from Egypt. He handed them to Sharif.

"We've already copied these pages from the script you sent us last night," said Sharif as his assistant passed out a copy to each person in the circle. Sharif handed the budget to the accountant and the location photographs to the location scout.

"We had planned to shoot these scenes in Egypt," said Ari, "but with everything that's going on there it might be . . . safer to move that material over to Jordan." The Jordanians nodded almost in unison.

Ari took a few minutes to run through the details of each scene. Everyone listened attentively, taking notes, and when he finished he concluded, "so what I need as quickly as possible is the difference in cost between Egypt and Jordan."

"You will find labor more expensive here," said Sharif, "but there are other savings."

"Such as?" asked Ari.

"Things are very direct here," said Sharif, "not so . . . Byzantine."

Did he mean bribery? wondered Ari. "Who . . ." Ari corrected himself. "Whom do I have to thank for my speedy trip through the airport?"

"That is nothing," said Sharif modestly.

"No, really," pressed Ari. "I've never experienced anything like it."

"Sharif is too modest," explained the film commissioner. "In addition to owning the production company, he owns the largest travel agency in Jordan and serves as the minister of tourism as well."

"Ahh." Ari nodded. That made sense.

Their meeting seemed to have come to a pause. No one moved or said a word. There was a hint of something unsaid in the air.

Just then the film commissioner received a text. He handed his phone to Sharif, who looked at the message.

"His Royal Highness, Prince Amir, invites you to join him for dinner at his home."

"But—but," Ari stammered looking down at his dusty tennis shoes. "I wasn't expecting to . . . I didn't bring any other clothes." Ari shifted anxiously in his chair.

"Don't worry." Sharif flashed Ari a reassuring smile. "His Royal Highness will not mind. He will be happy to see you exactly as you are."

Chapter 39

Ari sat next to Sharif in the back of a black SUV on a road that wound up a hill. They came to a checkpoint with a guard-house and giant bollards in the road. A friendly Jordanian soldier with a small submachine gun strapped around his chest poked his head in the window and carefully looked around the inside of the vehicle. They passed through two more checkpoints on the way up the hill. As the eldest brother of the king, Prince Amir was next in line to the throne.

Now the day made sense except for one thing, thought Ari. The speed with which he had been ushered through the airport was obviously to finish the meeting in time to get to dinner with Prince Amir, but why? Ari was only in Jordan to make a movie. Or was he?

At the top of the hill, they reached a large spacious house; built in the fifties, guessed Ari. Not ornate, but secluded on its own private hilltop overlooking the city. The citadel of the palace was visible miles away. Ari and Sharif stepped out into the cool night air. They walked past a number of cars in the driveway. Sharif and Ari seemed to be the last to arrive.

"I've never met a prince before," admitted Ari nervously. "What do I call him?"

"May I suggest, Your Royal Highness," said Sharif.

Without a knock, the large front door opened before them, held by a very tall Nubian servant. They walked inside a large foyer, then stepped into a large living room with about twenty people in it. Ari froze.

"Everyone is in a suit and tie except for me," Ari whispered to Sharif. "Does he know that this is a complete surprise? Or I would have dressed."

"He has been told," said Sharif.

"I would have gone out and bought some clothes."

"He knows that you had no time to shop."

Sharif instantly and very publicly pulled off his tie and jacket, then unbuttoned his shirt collar to put Ari at ease.

Up on a second-floor landing, a door opened. Prince Amir walked out. He was a small man, and very fit. Ari couldn't believe what he was wearing: a polo shirt, chinos, and white tennis shoes. He had dressed exactly like Ari.

The guests parted between Ari and Prince Amir, who came down the stairs, walked directly to Ari, and shook his hand.

"Mr. Basher."

Ari relaxed. "Your Royal Highness is . . . unbelievably thoughtful."

"You are too kind," said the prince with a British accent. "I do know, when one is traveling away from home, the impossibility of preparing for every circumstance. Please meet Jala, my wife."

A pretty, bright-eyed woman stepped forward and offered Ari her hand, which he shook.

"We are told that you just arrived from Cairo?" asked Princess Jala.

"Yes, except for a meeting with Sharif and his team."

"You will find them all extremely good and competent men," said Prince Amir. "Sharif is our minister of tourism, and Duad, his location scout, knows every corner of this kingdom. They are both at your disposal while you are here."

"Thank you, Your Royal Highness. That is . . . fantastic."

"Tell us," asked Princess Jala. "How do you find Cairo?"

"Oh, it is a magical place," said Ari.

"Yes," she agreed knowing that that was not a complete answer.

Ari continued. "And yet . . ."

"Yet?" asked Prince Amir.

"It is sometimes a little difficult to get things done," said Ari. "Particularly, with the military."

"I am a military man," said the prince. "I was educated at Sandhurst, and I know that all militaries everywhere have a certain . . . inflexibility. Yet, if one can establish a relationship with the commander . . ." He let the suggestion hang in the air.

"Yes?" asked Ari.

"Anything can be made to happen," said the prince.

"You must be quite hungry after your journey," said Princess Jala.

"Shall we go in to dine?" Prince Amir asked Ari, who nodded trying not to betray his own hunger.

In the dining room, a sumptuous Middle-Eastern dinner

was served. Ari marveled at the sheer variety of food, as if every known Arab dish was placed upon the table. The popular ones were replenished and those untouched were removed. Ari had a chance to study the other guests. They were young, stylish, sophisticated, and yet modesty seemed important within this contained circle of friends in this small country. They all spoke English, perhaps for Ari's benefit. A hush fell over the table as everyone realized the meal had finished.

Princess Jala turned to Ari. "What is your movie about?"

Ari rattled off his stock answer to the question: "It's the true story of a CIA agent who comes to the Middle East to find out if Saddam Hussein can make a nuclear bomb. Her husband, an ex-ambassador, is sent to Africa to find out if Iraq has been getting nuclear fuel."

"We remember this story well," said Prince Amir.

"As you know, they find out that the Iraq war is based on . . . an untruth." Ari didn't want to use the word lie. "The story takes place in Washington, Egypt, and Baghdad."

"Controversial?" asked Princess Jala.

"I imagine that it will be," said Ari.

"My wife is not afraid of controversy." Prince Amir raised his glass to her. "She was a journalist for the BBC. She was working in Baghdad when the bombs started to fall."

"Really?" asked Ari. "How did you two meet?"

"The first time I saw her was on television with explosions behind her head," said Prince Amir. "I soon found myself paying equal attention to the message and the messenger."

So Princess Jala had been a serious journalist, and once a reporter always a reporter. My movie could be more than just a movie to them, Ari realized. It's a story, a scoop, the second draft of history. The table broke up when the royal couple rose and led everyone back into the living room for coffee.

"There are over a million Iraqis living in Jordan now." Princess Jala steered Ari through French doors into a smaller sitting room off the living room with two red velvet armchairs side by side. This room was meant for more private conversation in the midst of a party.

"You let them stay?" asked Ari.

Prince Amir joined them. "The Iraqis are our neighbors. They can walk across the desert. There is no fence."

The prince sat in one armchair and motioned for Ari to take the other.

Then Ari asked, "Do you think it would be possible to shoot in Baghdad?"

"You would like to go there?" asked Princess Jala.

"Do you think shooting there could be safe?"

Prince Amir considered it. "You could be protected. We will speak to the right people."

"That would be amazing." Ari beamed; the possibility of telling Frank that they could shoot in Baghdad excited him.

"Would you like to meet George Tenet?" offered Prince Amir.

Ari didn't quite believe his ears. "The former head of the CIA George Tenet?"

"He will be here tomorrow night," said Prince Amir. "He is a personal friend and I could introduce you."

Ari tried to comprehend exactly what was happening. On a gut level, he found the prospect unappetizing. "I don't know if he would approve of the movie I'm making. You might want to check with him to see. He might not even want me to shoot in Jordan. Is this a problem?"

"Why would it be?" asked Prince Amir.

"In Egypt, you have to give your script, translated into Arabic, to the Ministry of Defense to approve," explained Ari.

"There is no censorship in Jordan." The prince said it quite firmly.

"And film permits take an enormous amount of . . ." Ari raised his fingers and rubbed them together.

"Permits here are instantaneous and free of charge. There is no bribery here. It is not tolerated."

"Excellent." Ari was pleased. "If an actor from Israel wanted to . . ." Again Ari tried to read the answer before he finished the question.

"Any artist may work in Jordan," said the prince.

"With an Israeli passport?" Ari pressed the point.

"Anyone," said Prince Amir.

Princess Jala asked, "How do you find the Egyptians to work with?"

"Very strong willed," admitted Ari. "They can be a little bit . . ."

"As if their way is the only way?" suggested the prince.

Ari agreed. "Exactly . . . stubborn. But I suppose Americans are worse."

"Not at all."

"The Iraq War?"

Prince Amir leaned back in his armchair to parse his own words. "We were constantly asked for advice. We gave it freely. We predicted everything that would happen. We could have

prevented all of the tragedy, almost all. Americans are perfectly rational people, but they don't listen. They listen but
they hear only what they want."

"And George Tenet?" asked Ari.

"His job was to hear only what he was supposed to hear."
The prince seemed both sad and amused. "But that is the story
of your movie, is it not?"

The next day Ari visited every flat street in Amman.
He took many pictures. On the way to the airport, he was
brought to a military base. Duad, the location scout, showed
Ari a line of Humvees that could each be used in the movie
for three hundred dollars a day, including driver. M1 tanks
were a thousand dollars a day, delivered. In a hangar was a
brand-new Black Hawk helicopter.

"I'm going to find a way to use this." Ari walked up to the
chopper and ran his hand along the cargo bay door. "We'll
think up a shot for it. What will the military charge us?"

"The same as the Egyptians."

"How low can we fly?" asked Ari.

"There is no limit."

Of course, thought Ari, why would there be a limit for a
prince?

Chapter 40

A day later, Ari was back in Cairo scouting places that were supposed to double for Iraq. He saw several houses that would play well, but he couldn't stop his mind from circling back to the rows of the Jordanian tanks and Humvees and, of course, the Black Hawk helicopter. Wistfully, Ari imagined it swooping overhead, a shot impossible to get in Cairo, but easy in Amman. In the afternoon, he scouted several mosques, and Samir came to join him in the courtyard of the last one.

"Doesn't it look like an Iraqi mosque to you?" Samir asked.

"In Hollywood, a mosque is a mosque is a mosque," said Ari, snapping a single photo of the intricate floor of ancient tile mosaic where the men would soon come to pray.

"And all Arabs look alike?"

Ari shrugged. "Maybe late at night."

"*Alahu Akbar. Alahu Akbar.*" The call to prayer sounded from the minaret above.

"And night approaches," Samir said. "Tomorrow we will pick you up at six in the morning."

"Why so early?" asked Ari.

"In order to drive out to Wadi al Jadid." Samir pulled out a cigarette.

"Wadi al what?"

"The Western Desert." Samir took a drag and let the smoke drift out of his mouth.

"Sand dunes?" asked Ari. A whole day lost driving out into the desert with no phone, no Internet, no chance to do any work. He mused over the idea of asking for the location scout to take pictures and bring them back, but Samir didn't give him the chance to back out.

"Sand of such a quantity that you will not find in Jordan." A fierce pride curled the corners of Samir's mouth, the journey now a matter of honor.

What could Ari say? So he found himself outside the Mena House at 6:02 A.M. the next morning, where he met Samir. A red Toyota Land Cruiser waited with two Egyptians in the front seat, the location manager, and a fellow named Wael, who owned the SUV. They were both eager and wired on Egyptian coffee. Ari pet the bomb-sniffing German shepherd and stepped around the security guard holding the proverbial mirror on a stick checking the bottom of the car for explosives. The moment a Westerner entered a vehicle, the search was over.

Ari had taken a pillow from his room. He'd spent enough of his life driving around in vans and four-by-fours to lose any sleep on a scout. Ari could feel Samir's eyes watch him closely, looking for any hint or clue that Ari would send his job to

Jordan. Ari had no thoughts one way or the other, so he screwed his head into his pillow and closed his eyes.

At first, Ari feigned sleep. He could hear the chatter of Arabic from the front seat until the silences between phrases began to grow. It wouldn't be long now. Ari knew from many a car journey with film crews all over the world, the small talk always peters out, and then even thoughts, until a vacant meditative stare takes over, but not for the man in charge, no, never for him. No, Ari's eyes stayed closed.

For an hour or two, Ari would doze and wake. If the car jolted or slowed, he would lift an eyelid and catch a glimpse of a water buffalo ploughing a field, or a scrawny dray mule dragging a cart, or an old 1960's truck coughing black smoke, its bed piled up impossibly high with bales of cotton.

On his side of the road, a green swathe of cultivated land followed the bank of the Nile. They drove south, following the river toward its distant glacial Ugandan source. An ancient tractor, its sun-baked red paint faded to a rusty pink, chugged along tilling under plucked beanstalks and bare chickpea plants. Children picked cotton. Men dressed in dishdashas moved among them with sacks to collect the white puffy little balls. Half a mile beyond that, the lush greenery of the crops ended.

The Nile fed a mile-wide oasis, a river of green in an ocean of sand. Every possible hectare at the edge of the desert had been cultivated for thousands of years. An ancient system of irrigation ditches, occasionally watered by an odd diesel pump chugging away, spilled the river up its banks to flood then dribble through those narrow farms.

The red Toyota slowed to a crawl at a military checkpoint

that looked like a tollbooth. A soldier wearing sunglasses waved them over to the side of the road with his rifle.

"What's up?" Ari looked at Samir for the first time since getting into the car.

"We are about to enter a restricted zone. There is little reason to come. Very few people live out here. We are almost at the Sahara."

The soldier asked some questions of Wael and pointed at Ari.

"He wants to see your passport," said Samir.

Ari pulled out his well-worn little blue book and passed it up front. He was always nervous whenever any soldier took hold of his passport. He couldn't help himself. He'd had to buy it back from underpaid sergeants on roadsides a few times in other countries. He looked at Samir, who seemed to enjoy Ari's discomfort. The soldier found the big tourist visa and started to argue with the location manager.

"Why doesn't he just give him the two bucks?" asked Ari.

Samir didn't answer. Ari finally pulled out a couple of bills and handed them out his own window. The soldier took them, closed the passport, and handed it back.

"Do you think we like paying baksheesh to any soldier or policeman who thinks it's his right?" asked Samir.

This wouldn't happen in Jordan, Ari almost said, but kept quiet.

Again they passed the towering cotton bales on the rickety truck. The Toyota left the highway, veering off onto a road straight out into the desert dust as far as the eye could see. They drove for an hour without passing another car. Strange shapes emerged in the road casting long shadows. Giant sandstone pillars rose up one hundred feet high, some shaped like jagged mushrooms, their shade like beach umbrellas, their bases cut away from beneath them by millennia of shifting sands.

The tan pillars gave way to flat rocks; polished black pebbles polka-dotted the desert floor. A shimmering speck of green materialized down the road, a distant oasis; then it disappeared into heat waves on the horizon. At first, Ari thought it was a mirage, but the green speck returned several times, then grew into date palms rising up slowly above the sand. As the Toyota approached, Ari saw a few very dark-complected men wearing turbans up in the trees pruning dead palm fronds or lowering flat baskets of red dates on long ropes from treetops forty feet up in the air.

Almost lunchtime, they stopped for gas, and bought water and tan beans, which they scooped out of small metal dishes with flat hot bread pulled right out of a roadside oven fed by dried palm ribs. Boys sold them dusty brown dates on the vine, a large cluster for half an Egyptian pound. They were meltingly sweet and so cheap. Ari and Samir bought much more than they wanted. Their hunger sated, they piled back into the red Toyota and drove off away from the shade of the green fronds out into the noonday glare.

Another half hour and Ari saw what they had come for. The horizon undulated. Dunes swelled around the car as it drove among them—first five, then ten, then twenty feet high, some massive as beached whales.

"The Bedou call this The Sea of Sand," said Samir. "The end of the Sahara desert. There is nothing for two thousand miles to the West, but . . ."

"Emptiness," Ari said.

Samir said something in Arabic to Wael, the driver. Wael nodded, took his foot off the gas, came to a stop, and shifted the Land Cruiser into four-wheel drive. With a lurch, they turned off the road onto the sand.

They drove fast along a row of small dunes, a stream of dust kicking up behind them. When they hit a dip in the dune line, Wael swerved over the crest and cut over to the next line of dunes a few feet taller than the ones before. Like surfers, they raced sideways along the static waves until they found a gap that would not flip them and crossed and climbed up the faces of bigger and bigger swells, each crest revealing a more enormous one on an elusive, tantalizing horizon. Sometimes the vehicle would fly over the top of a crest and drop airborne down the face of the next dune.

The effect was as if the car were shrinking down to the size of a tiny toy. The dunes rose up to at least three or four hundred feet tall—almost as tall as the Great Pyramid at Giza. Elated, Ari wanted to go higher. If Samir had pointed Wael straight across the desert, Ari would not have objected.

"Happy?" Samir shouted over the roar of the engine when the wheels left the ground.

"Yes!" Ari shouted back.

Summit fever overcame them. They were now on a quest for the largest, twisting around one towering dune after another. The Land Cruiser surged up on top of a plateau before an abyss.

"STOP!" screamed Ari then Samir in Arabic.

Wael slammed on the brakes, throwing them all forward. They could not see the sand below, the face of the dune was too steep, at least a five-hundred-foot drop.

Wael put the Toyota in reverse and backed down the face of the dune, but too slowly. The sand slid down around them. Wael tried to go forward. The wheels spun. He tried to reverse. They spun again.

"Doesn't he know that he's just digging the car down deeper when he spins the wheels?" asked Ari.

"The car is his," Samir snapped as he opened his door. Wael jumped out and immediately started digging away the sand in front of the wheels with his bare hands.

Ari watched for a minute, thinking that digging would lead nowhere, but he said nothing. Wael finished scooping out craters in the soft sand in front of his wheels, jumped back into the driver's seat, and gunned the engine. The car rolled down into the holes he had dug and almost up the other side until the wheels spun again. Wael dug new holes and repeated the process, gunning the engine with the same result. Impatiently, Ari took his camera case and a bottle of water out of the car.

"What are you doing?" asked Samir, alarmed.

"I'm going to snap some pictures of dunes."

"The desert is a dangerous place." Samir walked over the soft sand to Ari. "I'll come with you."

"Don't worry. Once you get the car out, follow my footprints and find me."

Ari turned his back on Samir and started to walk away.

"Wait, take a walkie-talkie." Samir handed him a radio from the car. "If the wind gets strong, you must come back quickly or you will lose your way. Your footsteps will be covered and we will not be able to locate you."

"Okay," said Ari, taking the radio and pushing the key to talk. "Radio check." He heard his own voice on the other walkies in the car. Then he turned and left them. He walked along the ridge where it dipped. As he descended, he started little sand avalanches with his feet. The fine grit worked its way down around his socks into his sneakers.

This isn't the beach, he thought grimly. The powdery sensation between his toes was annoying but not uncomfortable. He resigned himself to the dry powdered grit and climbed up the next ridge, trying to follow the firmest sand and find the easiest path to walk. When Ari reached the top of the next dune, his radio crackled.

"Ari?"

Ari pulled the walkie off his belt. "Yes, Samir?"

"How are you? Are you thirsty?"

"Not yet."

"Do not drink all your water at once."

"Don't worry. I'm good about that kind of thing."

"I can see you."

Ari turned around. Samir waved at him from a thousand feet away, the top of the neighboring dune. Ari waved back. A white speck rolled over the top of a dune and descended down into the bottom of the valley between them, slow and weightless.

"What is that?" asked Ari.

"It looks like a plastic bag for shopping."

It was exactly that, but it must have rolled in from a thousand miles away. Faded to translucence and sandblasted to the consistency of tissue paper, the thing was hardly a bag, but a ghost of one, a tumbleweed from a distant city.

"Where did it come from?" asked Ari.

"Libya."

"All the way across the Sahara?" Ari marveled that garbage could penetrate the emptiest place on earth.

"Yes, the wind is from Libya."

"The west?"

"Yes."

"The plastic wind." Ari heard Samir's laughter as he turned and descended down the far side of the dune, out of sight. When Ari reached the bottom of the next valley, he put the wind at his back. Knowing that the road was to the east, Ari walked and walked a serpentine path through the harder sand of the valleys beneath the dunes. Samir called him on the radio, but Ari did not answer.

The radios could only transmit line of sight, so Ari soon lost contact. He stopped every so often and snapped a few pictures of the most magnificent dunes, but try as he might, the camera didn't convey the scope and power of the tidal waves of sand.

He began to hum, then sing, a tune he had heard once in a movie.

"As he walked along the Bois de Bologne
With an independent air,
You could hear the girls declare,
'He must be a millionaire.'
I'm the man who broke the bank at Monte Car-arlo!"

After an hour of walking, he continued east. They had not come for him, so they were still stuck, reasoned Ari. The sun was already halfway from high noon to the horizon. He had only one objective now—to find the road before dark. The wind died down, giving him no direction, but as the sun set in the sky, Ari walked away from it. He walked for another hour in the twilight. The dunes diminished in size as darkness closed in. There was no moon, only starlight. He scanned the sky for the North Star or the Southern Cross, but the stars seemed scrambled and unfamiliar. Stumbling over a ground that he could barely see, Ari hoped that he was moving in the right direction.

He crossed over the top of one dune and saw headlights illuminating the black road at high speed from miles away. To intercept them, Ari would have to run. He tried to find the hard-packed places. He ran around the dunes and not over their soft tops. He picked up his pace until the dunes shrank back down to ripples lapping at the black ribbon of asphalt. Ari ran out into the middle of the road waving his hands.

"Stop! Stop!" he yelled.

A white pickup truck approached at high speed. Ari had to step out of the road to avoid getting hit. The truck came to a halt and reversed back to him.

A tall thin young man with very dark skin and a pointy beard stared bewildered at Ari as if at some alien from another planet. The man said something in Arabic. Ari shook his head.

"I . . ." Ari pointed at his own mouth. ". . . show . . ." Then he pointed ahead down the road. ". . . you?" Ari asked, pointing at the empty passenger seat. Comprehending, the man opened the door, which had a Governmental seal and some Arabic writing on the side. Ari got in. Ari pointed down the road and nodded. The man began to drive slowly.

Ari sized him up. He wore a white shirt with breast pockets

that had flaps on them. He had boots on and khaki trousers. He was not a city person, but very much of the desert. Ari read him as some sort of park ranger-type of a Bedou tribe.

After about a mile, they both spotted the Toyota's tire tracks in the sand on the roadside.

"There! Right there!" cried Ari, but he didn't have to. The ranger nodded. He put the truck into four-wheel drive and set out at about twenty miles an hour through the black desert night. The ranger drove expertly, much lower on the dunes than Wael had driven before. They followed the twin snakes of tire tracks back across the most giant dunes.

Cones of headlight illuminated the sand in the night until, slowing, they came upon a great mess of sand and footprints. The red Toyota Land Cruiser sat in the middle of a large hole. Wael and the location manager were both sweaty and shirtless in the cool chill of the desert night. Their skin was plastered with dust as if they wore tan makeup on their faces. They had been digging the sand from under the car with their bare hands. They peered up out of their giant foxhole, blinded by the headlights.

The Bedou ranger got out of the cab of his truck and walked over to the two heads sticking up. Ari followed.

"Where is Samir?" asked Ari.

"He went to find you," said the location manager. "When he could not hear you on the radio, he became frightened."

"Ugh." Ari should have expected Samir to worry and come after him.

The ranger waved for the two men to get out. Sheepishly, they climbed up the side. The ranger began to kick sand down into the hole around the car. Ari thought for a moment that they would tackle him, as he was undoing what they had spent hours on with their bare hands, but the ranger's confidence gave them pause. He piled sand around the wheels, then gestured for all three of them to join him and put their shoulders to the car. Ari jumped down into the hole. Under the ranger's command, the four of them rocked the vehicle back and forth. With each sway, the car raised up a quarter of an inch as the sand spilled under its tires. The Toyota slowly rose up out of the hole as if lifted by an invisible string. They rocked some more, and the ranger kept plying the wheels with more sand. In a matter of twenty minutes the car was back up on top of the dune. Sheepishly, they got into the Toyota and followed the ranger back out of the dunes along their tracks.

They found Samir sitting in the sand by the side of the road surrounded by cigarette butts. He had seen the second set of tracks and realized that another car had come to their aid, so he had waited.

On the drive back to Cairo, he did not speak or look at Ari. Ari wanted to make small talk, say something of the day, but Samir was humiliated. They reached Giza as dawn was breaking behind the Sphinx. Samir hadn't said a word.

PART SEVEN

Love and doubt have never been on speaking terms.

—Khalil Gibran

Chapter 41

The following morning, Ari headed to the airport to meet Beth, who was arriving on the overnight flight from New York. He grew more excited to see her the closer the moment of reunion. He had a bounce in his step walking through the terminal. Even the sight of the dreaded customs desk didn't kill his mood. He did notice several wealthy Egyptian families with school-aged children rushing to make flights. Shouldn't they be in school? he thought.

He stopped behind the customs desk and looked up at the portrait of President Mubarak in a gilded frame. Lighthearted, Ari started humming the song from the protest. "Leave, leave, Hosni Mubarak." One of the customs officials recognized the tune and gave him a dirty look. Ari quit humming, but savored the moment and the power of little bit of song.

When he saw Beth rolling her suitcase toward customs, his heart quickened. Despite her anger over the cost overrun on the Sphinx, he had missed her. He hadn't realized how much

until that moment. He felt the urge to run to her and em-
brace her like long lost lovers in a movie. But for the customs
officers between them, he might have done so until he noticed her talking to somebody. She wasn't alone. Omar el
Mansoor from Studio Giza, dressed in his bell-bottom jeans,
was rolling his own suitcase right next to hers. He had a pair
of ski boots slung over his shoulders.

"What the . . . ?"

They both waved at Ari and walked past the customs desk
without being stopped. Ari and Beth reached out to each other
to shake hands, very businesslike, concealing their relationship from Omar. Ari felt a strange energy from her, sexual yet
searching, as though she wondered if they were still lovers.

"Same flight?" asked Ari with as much nonchalance as he
could fake.

"Same row," said Beth.

Ari turned to Omar. "I thought you were going to Sundance?"

"I felt I had to come back," said Omar. "The press of
business."

"Omar came to visit our set, Ari," said Beth. "He met Frank."

"Oh?"

Omar gestured at the exit. "Shall we take my car?"

"Thank you, no." Ari craved a few minutes alone with Beth.
"We have our own driver."

"Send them away, Ari." She cast a meaningful glance at
him. "We're going with Omar."

In the back of Omar's car, Beth sat between the two men.

"How was the film festival?" Ari asked.

"Sundance was fantastic." Omar gave Ari a thumbs-up. "Awesome snow."

"Did you see any movies?" asked Ari.

"Nope," admitted Omar, "but I did catch a few great parties."

"That so?" Ari spotted the *Cairo Times* English Edition in a pocket behind the front seat. He pulled it out and began to read the lead story.

After a minute, Beth asked, "What's your take on Jordan, Ari?"

Ari didn't answer. He was lost in the newspaper.

"Ari?"

"What?"

"You seem so . . . distracted. I just asked you a question."

Ari pointed at the newpaper. "This story I'm reading. It's so . . . I can't believe it."

"Oh yes, very sad," agreed Omar. "An old story. It's been all over the news."

"What happened?" asked Beth.

Ari described the article. "Says here that this guy was driving in downtown Cairo. He gets stopped by a couple of cops. They take his cell phone and 163 Egyptian pounds."

"How much is that?" she asked.

"Thirty-five dollars," said Omar, "a little less."

Ari continued. "So the next day the guy goes to the police station, fills out a complaint. The day after that the two cops come over to his apartment . . ." Ari stopped scanning the page. ". . . and throw him out the window."

"What?" Beth was aghast. "How horrible."

"For thirty-five dollars and a cell phone. The cops just got sentenced to two years in jail."

"Two years? That's it?" Beth looked at the newspaper.

"That's the headline." Ari pointed at it. "ONLY TWO YEARS."

"Very sad, very sad," said Omar, "but I wouldn't take it at face value."

"What? They didn't kill him?" asked Ari.

"No, no, I'm not saying that he jumped out the window from depression. It's just that in Egypt you get an ear for when the news is too simple and everything's tied up in a nice little bow." Omar made a dainty little knot in the air. "He might have been Muslim Brotherhood, he might have been involved in something shady, the cops could have been paid to kill him—"

"Paid?" asked Beth.

"Or someone who did kill him could be paying the cops to go to jail instead."

"What?" That made no sense to Ari. "Cops volunteering to go to jail?"

"If someone confesses to a murder," explained Omar, "there's no trial, no investigation. If someone's poor enough, you could pay them to confess in place of you."

Beth was curious. "How much?"

"I've never done it, but . . ." Omar looked out the car window at some poor kids playing football barefoot in the street. "Maybe . . . ten thousand dollars for each year in prison, I'd imagine."

Ari folded the paper back up gingerly as if it were unclean and slipped it back into the pouch behind the driver's seat.

Chapter 42

"I was allowed to purchase Studio Giza from the government a few years ago," Omar told Beth and Ari as they drove through the front gate of Omar's facility. "The studio was built in the 1930s along the Hollywood model."

Now comes the seduction process, thought Ari. It was all very familiar. Just like in LA, there was a front gate in the tall white walls and a guard who checked them in. They pulled up in Omar's personalized studio chief parking space closest to the head office bungalow.

"Hundreds of movies have been made here," continued Omar as they got out of his car. "We might not be on the same scale as a Paramount or a Universal, but we're still very Hollywood. I ask you, what's the difference between the Spanish Moorish LA style of architecture and the Arabic Egyptian style?"

"This place is cute," said Beth.

She's drinking the Kool-Aid, thought Ari as Omar led them through his campus of art deco buildings.

"We have about a dozen soundstages, a scene shop, lights, equipment, cameras, a mixing stage, everything you need to make a movie. The government has always understood that Egypt's image was crucial to its economic development—see, we have a movie and three TV shows shooting right now."

Omar laid it on thick. How the studio had been built by the government in the 1930s and the Egyptian film industry was created. He elaborated on the history of the studio, showing them through a dark soundstage where a film crew was shooting on a set. He took them outside onto the studio street lined with building façades of every style from Venetian to Wild West. Two more film crews were working at either end of the street.

"And you?" asked Ari. "What's your interest in all this?"

"Me?" Omar stopped and put his hand on his heart. "I'm on a one-man crusade to modernize Egypt's film industry."

"Tell Ari how you want American productions . . . ?" Beth prompted him.

"When American studios come to Egypt, they have a bad experience with inefficiency, corruption, delays, you name it, and they never come back."

"I will," said Ari.

"You are almost an Egyptian." Omar patted him on the back. "You are the talk of the town. In fact, because of you the Supreme Military Council has forbidden the photography of the Sphinx from a helicopter."

Beth's face sharpened up. "What happened?"

Ari shrugged sheepishly. "We sandblasted a few tourists."

She seemed to suffer a momentary migraine at the thought, but let the matter drop. "Omar, Ari thinks we should move half the shoot to Jordan."

"Why? Because of these demonstrations?" Omar brushed aside the air with his hand. "Listen, there is a line the Army won't let them cross, then . . . wham." He clapped his hand with his fist. "This is all just a bunch of kids on the Internet who never felt an Army boot on their asses yet. It happens to every generation. It happened to mine. See this?" Omar stopped and lifted his hair. Behind his ear, he had an old scar. "Nineteen stitches from a police baton in the side of my head."

Ari shivered, remembering how that fist hit him in the temple. Farah's face spinning away from his own as he almost blacked out, almost lost his vision. He stepped away from Omar and Beth absentmindedly.

"Ari!" Beth called to him.

He turned around. "What?"

"You're in the shot." She pointed at a movie camera aimed back down the studio street at them.

Ari froze, embarrassed, mortified. He'd broken a take for the first time in his professional life. The movie's director laughed and walked over to them.

"Take five!" the director said to the film crew. "Omar my brother." He and Omar kissed.

Omar clowned around, making a big show for the crew. "Don't stop the camera! Keep rolling! Do you know who this is?" Omar pointed at Ari. "The man who shot the Sphinx!"

The actors and everyone on the crew applauded Ari.

"Take a bow!" demanded Omar.

Ari winced and shook his head as he walked away.

"What's wrong?" asked Beth as she followed him.

"He did that on purpose," said Ari tersely. "Samir's going to hit the roof when he finds out we've been here."

"We have every right to get a tour of this facility," she shot back. "And how's he going to know?"

Ari stopped, turned to her, and said, "There are no secrets in Cairo."

Chapter 43

Beth picked up the framed photograph of Samir's wife, Leela, and his daughter, Yasmine, from the glass top of his desk. Samir was nervously fondling a cigarette as he watched his computer, waiting for it to ring.

"Your daughter?" asked Beth. "She's beautiful. Oh, I miss my kids." She sighed wistfully. Ari shifted in his seat. She had never mentioned them before, not to him.

"One thing quickly," said Samir. "I did not get the latest wire transfer."

"Oh?" said Beth a little too innocently.

Ari looked at her, trying to figure out if this was an accident on her part or some sort of deliberate maneuver. "The money didn't hit the account, again," he said.

"I'll look into it," she told Ari, then turned to Samir. "How are we doing on the budget?"

"I will have it finished by dawn at the latest."

"I don't need it that fast," Beth told him. "You can do it to-morrow."

"No, I need to think. There are too many people around when the sun is up," said Samir. "Too much distraction."

"Great," said Beth, and then a tense silence settled into the room for a few moments. Each waited for the other to say something.

Finally Ari spoke. "We need eighty-five thousand dollars to start paying the crew or nothing is going to happen."

Beth locked eyes with Ari and pointed at the computer screen. Just then the computer rang and Samir answered it. The group of producers popped up on the screen on set in New York.

"Hey, Ari," said one of the producers. "What's this I hear about the King of Jordan in tennis shoes?"

"King Abdullah?" Surprised, Samir turned to Ari.

"Prince, Prince Amir." Ari corrected him. "I flew in for the day to scout, so I just had the clothes on my back, tennis shoes and a polo shirt." Ari pointed at his own clothes. "When I got to his house I was embarrassed, so he changed into exactly the same thing I was wearing."

"Why?" asked another producer.

"To make me feel welcome," said Ari. "They had told him I was nervous about my clothes."

The producers each marveled. "Wow . . . That's manners . . . Considerate . . . Do you think he would buy Paramount?"

"While we're waiting for Frank . . ." Ari got down to business. "The Jordanian military has a uniform price list for equip-ment. It's very cheap. Humvees are three hundred dollars a day. Tanks are a thousand. Tanks come with a crew and a truck that drops it off and picks it up."

"What kind of tank?" someone asked.

"An M1," said Ari. "It's all American. Everything's American. The same stuff used in Iraq."

"And the paint? Do we have to paint them to look American?" asked another producer.

"No, they do that. There's a military paint shop. They paint everything except for aircraft. There's a Black Hawk that—"

Frank walked over from a distant movie camera behind them.

"Hi, Frank!" said Beth with forced cheerfulness.

"Hi, buddy." Frank spoke only to Ari. "What did I miss?"

"Hey, Frank, I was just talking about equipment in Jordan," said Ari.

"Did you say Black Hawk?" asked Frank.

"Yes, there's a Black Hawk that doesn't have any markings on it. It belongs to an elite commando unit, so we don't have to paint it."

"How low can we fly?"

"No limit. We can fly it right down the main street in Amman, between the buildings."

"I want that shot," said Frank.

"You got it boss."

"I saw the Sphinx shot."

"And?"

"Good." Frank nodded slightly. "Very."

Frank and Ari smiled at each other, a tight, contained,

knowing smile. There must have been a lot of talk about the cost among the producers, thought Ari.

Then they all chimed in. "It was amazing! . . . Great work! . . . Fantastic! . . . The studio wants to make it the poster!"

"Okay, okay." Frank hated any unbridled compliments that flew around a set and always quashed them. "I'm trying to finish up our last day here, so let's get to it. Are we going to have a problem with these demonstrations? Ari?"

"Well, I haven't seen anything that would stop us from shooting yet. The university seems to empty out whenever there's a rally."

Everyone laughed.

"And the airport, Samir?" Ari turned to him.

"It will never be affected," said Samir. "It is well guarded and attached to the Air Force base where we flew to the Sphinx."

"The museum?" asked Frank.

"There was a rally that completely surrounded it," said Ari, "but that was announced well in advance."

"Beth, should we be thinking about moving more of the shoot to Jordan?" asked Frank. "What's your opinion?"

Everyone waited for her answer as she shifted the webcam to focus on her.

"Well, the insurance won't cover an act of war," said Beth. "Civil unrest, maybe. Samir, do you think the protests will get bigger?"

"The government will crush . . . I mean stop them," said Samir.

"What does the other guy think?" asked Frank.

"Omar?" asked Beth. "He says the same as Samir. Plus we've already started spending money to prep Cairo. We shouldn't throw that away."

"Omar?" asked Samir.

"So we stick with Egypt?" asked Frank. There was a moment of silence for anyone to make an objection. "What do you guys think?" Frank prompted the producers.

"Yes . . . Yeah . . . It's the right choice," they all agreed.

"I do like the airport in Cairo," Frank mused. "It's scary. It's also from the same period as Saddam International."

"So we would have to bring the actress . . . ?" asked Ari.

"What's her name?" Frank turned to the producers.

"Afareen?" Samir dropped his cigarette. It rolled off the desk onto the floor. His hands patted his shirt pocket for another. He could find none.

"We'll have to bring her from Israel," said Ari.

Samir erupted. "No!"

Beth and Ari look at each other, and Ari said, "Samir, whoa . . ."

"An Israeli actress cannot work in Egypt!" Samir insisted, glaring at Frank on the computer screen.

"Why not?" Frank asked Samir simply, without emotion. "Is there a law against it?"

"It is not done. I'm telling you. It will not be allowed! Permissions will be taken away!" Samir's rage flared up. He tried to control himself with great difficulty. "No actor will act opposite her. If they do, they will be thrown out of the Actors Guild."

"Why? Because she's Jewish?" probed Frank.

"No, because she's Israeli," insisted Samir.

"Ari, what do you think?"

"It's probably true," said Ari. "There's some cultural thing that we don't understand. They really fetishize the wars against Israel here."

"You will lose Khaled Nahkti," insisted Samir. "He will refuse to be in your movie."

Frank became very calm. "Ari, go ask Khaled."

"I will call his agent right now," offered Samir.

"No," said Frank. "I want you to go see him, Ari, look him in the eye and ask him. Got me?"

"Actually, I had dinner with Nahkti." Ari turned to Samir. "He said he would do it."

Samir stiffened, blushing a little, humiliated.

"When?"

"Who's Khaled Nahkti?" asked one of the producers.

"He's the Brad Pitt of Egypt," said Ari.

Another producer spoke. "Omar said—"

Samir cut him off. "Who is Omar . . . ? Who is Omar?"

No one answered the question. It was as if Samir no longer existed.

"Frank, the Jordanians will work with an Israeli," said Ari. "We can just use the airport in Jordan—"

"I don't like it." Frank silenced Ari. "It's wrong. It's too small and new. I like Cairo International. And I'm not going to blacklist somebody because they're Jewish or anything else."

"I will call the Actors Guild right now to ask permission, and you will see the answer," said Samir almost as a threat.

"No," said Beth. "Don't call anyone."

The producers seemed to close ranks and cluster around Frank.

"Hey, Frank, they need you on set," called out an assistant director in the distance.

"I've got to go back to camera," said Frank. "So we're done?"

"Yes," said Beth.

"Bye, buddy." Frank waved to Ari. "Take care of yourself."

Ari pushed a button and hung up the computer closing the screen for good measure.

"Samir, Samir, Samir . . ." Ari shook his head. "You can't yell at the director."

"He is wrong," insisted Samir, reaching for the cigarette on the floor.

Ari wanted to say, the director is never wrong. My job is to make him feel like Superman. If he thinks the sky is pink or two plus two equals five, we have to figure out how to make it that way. Every time he talks to us he has to feel empowered, not distracted, not diminished. Ari didn't say a thing.

Beth spoke before he could. "It doesn't matter if he's wrong. There are ways of telling him no. You just don't do it to his face."

"You ease him into it," agreed Ari. "You should know that, Samir the Hammer."

Samir lit the cigarette he had been toying with and took a long calming drag. "So you dined with the prince? You did not mention it."

"I didn't want to rub it in," said Ari.

"Rub it in?"

"I thought I might make you feel . . ." Ari didn't want to say the word inadequate. "I just thought it was bad manners to talk about."

"No," Samir took another drag and let the smoke drift out of his mouth. "In manners it was quite the opposite."

Chapter 44

Ari took Beth to the café around the corner from Samir's office where he had dined on his first night in Egypt. They both wanted to get the bad taste of the meeting out their mouths, and Ari thought he'd show off his local knowledge of Cairo cafés.

The waiter set down a small plate of hummus. Beth tore off a piece of bread, scooped some of the creamy paste, and wolfed it down. Suddenly her chewing slowed and she started to savor what was in her mouth.

Beth swallowed. "This is . . ."

"Yes?" said Ari, proud of his little magic trick.

"The garlic was just—"

"Crushed, exactly." He picked up a piece of bread for himself.

"Crushed just now?" She pointed back toward the kitchen.

"The minute you ordered it."

"Wow, it's powerful."

"Yes, like it's alive, almost."

Beth picked up another piece of bread. "Now, I get hummus. I mean I finally get it."

"Ah, you're starting to think like an Egyptian," said Ari with mock sagacity. "Let me have some of that. If you're going to do garlic, I'd better do garlic, too."

As Ari scooped up a dollup of hummus, Beth saw something over Ari's shoulder and grabbed her handbag. "Ari look!"

A young Egyptian man sprinted, full speed, around the corner then halfway down the street.

"Who was that man?" asked Beth. "A thief?"

Before Ari could answer her, another three young men ran around the corner looking over their shoulders. Then a government thug turned the corner chasing them and taunting them as cowards. Everyone in the café stopped eating to watch, their heads turning in unison.

Suddenly the three protesters came to a halt and turned around. The government thug pulled up short. They stared at each other for a moment, then they all realized it was three against one. At this the protesters lunged backward and the chase reversed. The thug dropped his bravura, turned tail, and fled. The reversed chase disappeared back around the corner.

"What the hell just happened?" asked Beth.

Everyone in the café burst into spontaneous applause, including Ari.

After dinner Beth and Ari rode back to Mena House in Hamed's car. Ari sat up stiff in his seat, giving off no hint that he and Beth were lovers. Beth was busy texting.

"Important?" asked Ari.

"He yelled at Frank." She meant Samir. "Everyone's pissed."

Ari waited until Hamed was distracted while making a turn. Ari let the momentum lean him over to whisper in her ear.

"We're not alone."

Ari pointed secretly at Hamed, meaning not to say anything sensitive, then he slid his hand in between Beth's legs. She stifled a gasp.

They managed to make it to the hotel with only furtive touches in the backseat, but once they got into the elevator, they clinched into their viper kiss.

They burst through the door of the suite. Ari and Beth careened violently against the walls and into the furniture. They kissed a rough spastic waltz all the way into the bedroom.

An hour later, the sheet and pillows were on the floor. Ari lay with his head resting in the small of her back, sprawled naked across the heavy antique bigger-than-king-sized bed, which had somehow migrated a foot from the wall.

He remembered the first time he saw her naked back. She was turning around to get dressed on the night their affair started in her office, months ago. It was the sexiest back he'd ever seen. He could have entire conversations with her staring only at her back. It always told the truth. Her shoulder blades, her spine recessed into a channel of soft white skin— her ribs would falter with her breathing, and he would know when there was an untruth or a half trust coming out the other side of her body.

He turned over and kissed down along her spine and nibbled her buttocks.

"Are you kissing my ass?" she murmured.

"Yes, boss." And he went back to it.

She laughed and turned over, holding his head against her soft creamy white tummy.

"What am I going to do with you, Ari?" With one finger she started to align his errant locks of sex-tousled hair.

"You seem to know that pretty well."

"Should I blow up my home?" She grew serious. "Ask Glenn for a divorce?"

Both scared and excited, Ari turned and looked up between her breasts into her eyes. "Would you . . . divorce him?"

"Do you want me to? Do you? Really? Deep down?" A glimmer of hope, a memory of some first love, fluttered up in her for a brief breath. "Or . . ."

"I love you," he said. He knew from a lifetime of throwing his heart around that if you fall in love with careless people who betray you or forget you, it is possible to wear out the heart, and finally use up its capacity for love. That wellspring can grind down from misuse until it becomes only a pump.

"Or . . . ," Beth continued, her gray eyes searching his, ". . . or is that your worst nightmare? Normalcy? Normality?"

He didn't answer. In the silence, they both knew that all he was and all he could ever promise to be was one of these movie men. She had worked with hundreds, all of them ever drawn back into a perpetual adolescence, wandering the world, catching little dreamlets on film. And she was the one who cleaned up after them.

Beth didn't wait for her answer. She dropped his head and got out of bed.

"Hey, where are you going?" Ari pretended he didn't understand what had just evaporated between them.

"It's morning in America." Beth started getting dressed with a hardened, war-weary resolve. "I'm going to have to order a wire transfer for a lot of money."

She threw Ari's clothes off the floor at him.

"Hey! What the . . . ?"

"We have a meeting."

"Now? It's the middle of the night." Women, he thought to himself as he pulled on his underwear. What did I say?

PART EIGHT

All things truly wicked start from innocence.

—Ernest Hemingway

Chapter 45

Ari wandered out onto his terrace, putting on his shirt and looking at the black outline of the Sphinx, the light show extinguished for the night. The pyramids were dark black triangles up on the Giza plateau. A sharp knock sounded. Ari poked his head back in.

"Somebody's at my door."

"It's Omar," Beth said, in the bathroom tying her hair back.

"Oh no." Ari felt that vertigo sensation again of spinning, losing control.

"I've asked him to join us," she called from the bathroom.

"You are making such a mistake."

"Open the door, Ari."

"You don't know what you're doing." He shook his head. "You have no idea."

"Open the door!" she ordered him.

"I can't open this door, Beth."

"Why not?"

"There are no secrets in Cairo!"

"Do you want me to tell people that you're losing it?" Beth charged out of the bathroom.

"I'm not losing it. I am crystal clear about what is happening here."

Ari opened the door. Omar stood there in the hallway holding Samir's budget.

"Come in," said Beth.

Omar walked in with respect. He made a little half bow, half nod to each of them. Ari couldn't conceal his own incensed frustration at being set up this way, at this time of night, without a word from Beth.

"Omar," Beth began. "Just a couple of questions. Would you be able to shoot at Cairo International Airport with an Israeli citizen?"

"Yes."

"Really?" Ari challenged him. "That's not what we've been told."

"There is no law against it," said Omar pleasantly, patiently.

"But the Actors Guild forbids it." Ari went into a hostile cross-examination.

"We don't tell them," said Omar.

"Not tell the union?" asked Beth, surprised.

"Hey," said Omar, "she doesn't look like an Israeli. We just slip her into the scene on a tourist visa."

"What about the censor who follows us around on set?" asked Ari. "Won't he check her passport?"

"We pay him not to show up. Censors are like mosquitoes. We shoo them away with money. Why don't you check with Khaled Nahkti? Ask him if he will he act with an Israeli?"

"He will," admitted Ari.

"See, a real artist knows no borders," said Omar without gloating, without smugness, simply instructing Ari.

"What about Samir's crew?" Ari pressed. "Will they stay and work for you?"

"Crew?" Omar seemed nonplussed. "If you pay them, they will come. Is it not the same in your country? Besides, I have a whole studio full of crew."

Ari searched his mind for another issue. "What about the permits?"

"That is nothing." On that point, Omar looked away and seemed insincere.

"What about the permits?" pressed Beth. "We have them, don't we?"

"As Omar knows"—Ari jumped at his opening—"our film needs permits signed by the minister of defense, the Ministry of the Interior, the Actors Guild, the Crew Guild, and the social censor. Samir already got all those permits. The process takes six weeks."

"But they're our permits," protested Beth. "We paid for them."

"In Egypt, the permits don't belong to the film." Ari quoted from his fight with Samir on the night Samir gave the permits to him, the night he got hit in the head for rescuing Farah. "They belong to the local Egyptian production company. Those permits are Samir's property. How do you propose to get them from him?"

"Give him five or ten thousand dollars," said Omar dismissively, "to go away."

"Absolutely not." Beth shook her head.

Omar made a fist and clenched it tight. A deep reptilian violence flashed through his eyes. "Then we crush him."

Ari didn't quite understand. "Crush Samir?"

"In a manner of speaking."

"Can you please not crush somebody I consider a personal friend?"

"We squeeze him," said Omar. "We accuse him of stealing money from us. There are special police for foreigners, to protect foreigners. We use that complaint to justify taking the permits."

"Brilliant." Ari couldn't hide his distaste for this tactic. "We call the cops on him? He hasn't stolen any money from us."

"We don't intend to prosecute him," explained Omar, "only to go to the various ministries and guilds to take his permits away."

Ari pressed. "And why would they want to favor us?"

"Because I do so much more business with them. He is nothing." Omar opened his arms as if he held the world in his hands. "I am Studio Giza."

And what could Ari say to that?

"Have you read Samir's budget, Omar?" asked Beth, pointing at the papers in his hand.

"Yes, it's a little tight." Omar thumbed through the pages, looking at his notes in the margins. "Some of the salaries are low, but I will commit to doing the shoot for exactly the same money as Samir."

"The same, not less?" asked Beth.

"I don't think you can cut this budget," said Omar.

"If we're getting it for the same money, why switch?" Ari asked Beth.

Omar spoke up. "You're getting the Israeli actress at Cairo International Airport. Exactly what the director wants."

"For the same money?" Beth looked Omar in the eye.

"You have my word," said Omar, solemnly raising his right hand.

"You could easily get us halfway through the shoot and then raise the price," said Ari.

"So could Samir, if he hasn't already," countered Omar.

"Why should we trust you?" said Ari, unable to mask his distrust.

"Because I want your poster on the wall of my studio. I want you to have a good experience, to tell everyone in LA, all the studio heads, and then come back with more and more films." Omar kept his amiable disposition, but Ari felt as if he were facing a crocodile who could devour him without warning. "Don't you think that bringing movies to Egypt is in my own interest?"

Beth cut in before Ari could answer the question. "Okay, okay, I don't think we should impugn anyone's motives here. Omar, can you give us a minute?"

"Of course." Omar walked over to the door and let himself out into the hallway.

Ari didn't wait for the door to close. "You are out of your mind."

"Ari, all the producers have taken a vote."

Ari was stunned. "Without me?"

"Everyone wants to dump Samir."

"How are we equal on this? I've been here. They've been on a computer."

"Maybe you've let yourself get too close to Samir? You just called him your friend."

"Omar is just telling you exactly what you want to hear. You Americans, you're not listening!" Ari started pacing around the room, then pointed out at the Sphinx for what seemed like no reason. "Beth, nothing goes in a straight line here, nothing."

"Ari, you're not making sense."

"Even if Omar could pull this off and get the permits away from Samir, which I doubt—don't forget every government ministry is swamped with all these demonstrations going on— it's not going to be easy because Samir's not just going to go away." Ari started to speak quickly, almost maniacally. "This will soak up all of my time, and the film won't get prepared properly because I'll be running all over Cairo in some crazy bureaucratic game of chess with Samir and police and lawyers and judges and ministers and guilds, stuck in traffic, sitting in dusty, dark Kafkaesque hallways waiting to see somebody and drink another cup of tea!"

"That's your job," said Beth.

"Where I won't be is at the studio making sure things get organized for Frank when he gets here!" A fleck of foamy spittle flew from Ari's mouth and landed on the arm of Beth's blouse. She looked down at it.

"It's decided, Ari."

"You're not hearing me."

"No, you're not hearing me," she said firmly. "He yelled at Frank. We can talk to Omar. He's one of us."

Beth walked straight to the door and reached for the antique doorknob.

"Beth, wait a second! Take a breath."

She stopped.

He continued. "Before we go down one path or another just try to ask yourself: Is this personal? Are you mad because we shot the Sphinx before you approved the cost?"

"Yes, I am mad at that. Yes."

Ari softened and went over to her. "So is this between you and Samir, or . . . between you and me?" He reached out and touched between her shoulder blades.

She stiffened under his fingers. "It's business, Ari. It's always business with me. Omar's our man. Do you want to tell him or should I?"

Ari knew he had lost. He reached around her and opened the door. Omar was standing there with a big smile on his face. Ari still thought he looked like a crocodile, even more than before.

Chapter 46

Ari sat next to Omar in the back of his car. Omar's driver pulled out of the Mena House driveway into the dark empty Giza streets.

Omar broke the silence. "You should offer him ten thousand."

Ari looked down at his belt where his secret pocket held the bundle of cash. "Beth won't go for it."

"It will happen in the end, might as well get it out of the way," said Omar.

Ari folded his arms and looked out the window. He made it clear he didn't want to speak. They rode in silence all the way to Samir's office, where Ari knew Samir was working on his budget.

When they turned onto Samir's street, Ari looked up and saw Samir's light was off.

"He's gone," said Ari contemptuously. "Looks like we took this whole ride for nothing."

Omar's car pulled up in the dark quiet street. Ari got out and jogged to the building. He was going to go up to the office in the elevator and check. At that moment, Samir walked out of the front door holding a clean, new budget. They ran smack into each other.

Ari didn't know what to say to fire Samir. He hadn't planned his words. He just said, "That's the new budget?"

Samir started to hand it over, but didn't let go.

"You were at Studio Giza today."

"Yes."

"Why? Are you negotiating with me to lower my price?"

"No, Samir. We . . . they . . . when you yelled at Frank in front of everybody . . ." Ari didn't finish his words.

"Do you think Frank is right?" asked Samir.

"It doesn't matter what I think."

"But what do you believe? You? By yourself?"

"Blacklist an actor?" Ari felt he was being asked to choose and he had to choose his own kind right or wrong. "Of course he's right. The director is always right. He has to be, or you'll never finish the film."

"Here is my budget for your shit movie," sneered Samir. "Give it to Studio Giza for them to copy."

"It's not shit." Ari was deeply offended. Why that word should bother him at this moment, he could not understand, but the film and its message had become a kind of crusade to him.

"I'm finished with you." Samir let go of the budget and started to walk away. Ari followed him and walked up beside him.

"You've got to be professional about this. These things happen. No one is any good until they've been fired."

Samir stopped and turned to face him. "I'm no good? You should fire yourselves."

"Samir, it's happened to me, when I first started out, and so I learned how to go with the flow. That's how you learn it."

"And our contract?"

"Samir."

"So your word, your bond is toilet paper to you? Did you get the shot?"

"What shot?"

"Of the Sphinx?"

"At twice the budget. How much of that money did you really spend and how much did you keep?" They both knew that Samir had overcharged for that shot. "Let's get real, Samir, I need the permits."

"Never." Samir started to walk away again, his shadow from the streetlight sweeping around on the sidewalk behind him.

"But you already gave them to me?" Ari ran up beside him again. "Threw them at me."

"That was my choice," said Samir defiantly.

"Then I saved Farah from being . . . raped . . . right here, right here on this street."

Samir stopped again. He could not disagree. He wavered there for a moment, staring at his shadow on the sidewalk.

"I'm begging you, as a friend. Think about your future. If we can't shoot because you gave us a problem, the insurance companies will make sure you never work again on an international production."

"You are threatening me." Samir looked at Ari, surprised, and a little sad. His anger was melting into sadness.

"No, no, Samir. It's just the reality of what will happen." Ari realized that, more than business, more than anything else, Samir felt rejected, and Ari had to show that he cared. "If I don't tell you now, you'll never know why you never worked again. You don't want to get on the blacklist, do you? That guy, Omar, wants to call in the police."

Samir suddenly shivered and recoiled in horror. He started to back away from Ari.

"To . . . to . . . do what?"

"To investigate you."

Samir was shaking as if the temperature around them had dropped below freezing. "On what grounds?"

Samir saw headlights erasing his shadow on the pavement. Omar's car was inching along in the street toward them. Samir noticed. He saw Omar in the backseat. Samir started backing away in fear, staring at Ari as if he held a knife in his hand.

"Samir? Why are you looking at me like that?" Ari couldn't understand it. "Let's go back to your office and get the permits . . . wait!"

Samir turned and walked away faster and faster. Ari jogged after him, trying to keep up. The faster Samir walked, the faster Ari jogged, and the faster the car picked up speed.

"Where are you going? Samir—Samir!" Ari called after him. Samir was jogging. "Wait a second! I'm not going to hurt you! Let's talk about this!"

Soon they were running through the streets full speed. Samir dodged down a narrow alley between two closed-up shops. Ari chased him into the darkness. The car couldn't follow.

"Samir," Ari called after him, "this is crazy!"

Ari lost sight of him in the shadows, and slowed to a walk,

thinking that Samir had hidden or got away. Turn around, thought Ari. A back alley in Cairo? But he couldn't leave it like this, not with Samir so afraid of—what? Of him?

"Samir?" Ari called out softly. "Samir? Where are you? Come out. I have money."

Ari had second thoughts, but he reached under his belt, into his secret pocket, and pulled out the ten thousand dollars. He held it out like a gun or a flashlight as if it would guide him or protect him. Ari came to a little dogleg where he could not see around the corner and the canyon of the alley narrowed overhead. The very walls seemed to close in upon him. Ari stopped in his tracks. He could smell fear in the shadows around him. Slowly, he looked over his shoulder. There in the black crevice between two buildings, Samir hid, flattened up against the wall.

"Samir, what are you scared of?" asked Ari softly. "I can't hurt you."

"Oh yes, you will." Samir's two black eyes peered out of the darkness terrified. "You are an American!"

"What?" Ari was perlexed, then insulted, then angry. He lashed out. "What the hell is that supposed to mean?"

Samir lunged out of his hiding place and barged past Ari to run away. Ari stumbled back against the other wall and caught his balance, too confused to chase after him.

Chapter 47

Ari squinted in the noon glare as he rode in the backseat squeezed in between Beth and Omar. Omar's car pulled up in front of a fortresslike old Moorish building made of red brick walls and tan corner stones. This was an old police station.

"Here we are," said Omar.

They got out. Parked on the street were a couple of police cars with freshly broken windows, and vans with police hustling in and out of them. A scrawny little porter stretched a hose toward the water tank of an armored personnel carrier with a water cannon on top. Everything seemed to have an air of preparation about it.

Omar ushered Beth and Ari inside past the desk sergeant with a quick question. The sergeant pointed down a hallway. Omar led the way. The number of police bustling through the station, both uniformed and plainclothed, seemed excessive for the narrow hall. The walls were painted a dull light green running up to very high ceilings. In each room was an old ceiling fan on high speed creating little drafts of wind past each door, stirring the hair and the papers of the police in the rooms.

On a bench at the end of the hall sat several clusters of people who looked like crime victims waiting to make complaints. No one was paying any attention to them. They seemed like they had been there for hours.

Omar found a particular door, peeked inside, then waved at Ari and Beth to follow him in.

The room had only a table and several wooden chairs scattered around. A sergeant sat at a table with a stack of several forms and a couple of pens. Behind him, by the window, stood a very short, very powerfully built man in a suit, who was bald and looked like a human bullet.

"Beth and Ari, this is Detective Kek," said Omar. "He will be expediting our case."

The detective nodded, then sat on the windowsill, splitting his attention between what was happening inside the room and what was going on down below in the street.

The sergeant took a form and picked up a pen, poised to write.

Omar started to dictate a story in Arabic. Several times Ari heard his own name mentioned and Samir's. Omar worked himself up from fairly calm into a tone of righteous indignation. At some point, Detective Kek barked an order to a passing porter in the hall, and a few minutes later, cups of mint tea appeared. Detective Kek watched with an air of attentive boredom. Every time a vehicle pulled up, he would look out the window.

The sergeant wrote everything down word for word, stopping Omar every so often to catch up with his narrative until, finally, Omar had finished. The sergeant spun the form around and slid it across the table to Ari.

"Okay, now sign it," said Omar.

Ari looked down at the form on the table. "What's it say?"

"It tells the story," said Omar. "The history of your dealings with Samir."

"It says that he stole our money?" asked Ari.

"In order to strip the permissions away from him, we need to accuse him of theft."

Ari slid the paper across the wooden table over to Beth.

"You sign it."

She looked back at him poker faced for the benefit of the police, but Ari knew her well enough to know that she was seething inside.

"Ari, that won't work," said Omar.

"Why not?"

"She just got here yesterday, and besides, she's a woman," explained Omar. "It's already filled out in your name all the way through."

"But it's bullshit," said Ari.

Detective Kek stood up from the windowsill and stepped over to Omar, saying something in Arabic and pointing at the paper.

"No, no," said Omar, shaking his head at the detective emphatically. Then Omar turned to Beth and uttered with forced jollity, "This does not look good, arguing in front of them."

Beth turned to Ari. "When we walk out of here, do you want to call Frank and tell your old friend not to come and finish his movie? And the twenty-nine other crew who are booked on a plane here the day after tomorrow? Is that what you want?"

Ari was seething, but he had to admit, "Of course not."

"Then strap on a pair of balls and get the shot." She threw his favorite justification for any behavior right back in his face.

Ari picked up the pen. He tried to read the Arabic for a moment.

"This is too fast." Ari shook his head and signed. Omar and Beth stood up to go. Ari didn't move.

Outside the window, a familiar truck pulled up, the police truck from the Sphinx with the navy blue box on the back.

Then a policeman walked into the room with two injured protesters in handcuffs. One had a head wound and looked like he'd been dipped facedown in blood, like a red ghost with two white eyes that seemed alert. The other clutched his stomach where his shirt had boot prints on it. He looked like he had been walked on. He had no other visible signs of injury. Detective Kek pointed to the bloody one, said something in Arabic, presumably that he was fine, then picked up a statement form and handed it to the policeman.

Detective Kek then lifted the eyelid of the protester holding his stomach and checked his pupil dilation by turning him to face the window and passing his hand over the light several times. The bored detective's eyes came alive for the first time with urgency. The detective pointed out to the street to an ambulance standing by, and spoke a torrent of Arabic. The policeman quickly grabbed the protester holding his stomach and took him away. The bloody protester stood there forgotten.

"I think I made a mistake," said Ari breathlessly. "Tell him

I want to take it back. Tell him . . . Tell him . . ." Ari couldn't catch his breath.

"Tell him what?" demanded Beth.

"That it's too quick. That I didn't have a chance to think it over."

"Look, Ari . . ." Omar spoke softly, sympathetically, to Ari. "When you're done shooting, we'll just come right back here and withdraw the complaint. Nothing will happen to Samir. We just need the accusation to take away his permissions. It's just a bureaucratic move."

Beth was impatient. "Ari, let's go." She pulled him up out of his chair by the shirt.

As they walked out and down the front steps of the police station, a line of protesters was jumping down out of the big blue box on the truck from the Sphinx. They were all daisy-chained together, zip-tied hand to hand with white plastic flex-cuffs. The last one was filming the whole scene with his cell phone. When he hopped down, the policemen wrestled the phone out of his grasp and stomped on it, crushing the phone on the asphalt with their boots like a bug.

Ari knew that he had made a mistake.

Chapter **48**

Ari stood on his terrace at the Mena House watching the
Sphinx fade slowly into the night at the end of the light show.

"I saw Anthony and Cleopatra pass," boomed out the British voice through the loudspeakers. "Alexander, Caesar, and
Napoleon paused at my feet. I saw the ambitious dreams of
conquerors whirling like dead leaves. Tomorrow, once more,
the rising sun will give me his first caress . . ." The plummy
British voice droned on, and Ari could feel Beth's arms slide
around his waist from behind.

He felt the downy white hotel bathrobe against his back,
then her lips on his neck. She turned him around. Her robe
fell open. She was naked underneath. The perfume of jasmine
and bath salts wafted up off her skin. She nuzzled him and
her lips came up to his, but he turned slightly and she missed
his lips, kissing him only on the cheek.

"Honey, what's wrong?"

"Nothing," he lied.

She said softly, "We had to do it."

"Of course, we . . . did," said Ari sardonically.

"We had to cut Samir loose. Had to."

"But how about a little warning?"

Beth closed her robe and tied the belt. "Why do you think I came early, before the rest of the crew? To make sure you did what had to be done."

"You should have told me first."

"Sweetie, you're a coward." She took his hands and interlaced their fingers. "You have a hard time telling people what they don't want to hear. You need everybody to love you all the time, but they can't. Besides, you were going to lose anyway, so what difference would it have made?"

"Didn't you once tell me, 'Surprises give you cancer?'" He pulled his fingers out of hers.

"Ari." She tried to grasp his hands, but he broke free, went inside, then straight to the door. "Ari!" she called again, surprised, as he walked out.

He hopped in a taxi, a dented black Fiat belonging to a mad driver. They careened across Giza to the highway toward downtown Cairo. They found the apartment around the corner from Samir's office where Rami, Farah, and the other revolutionaries hung out.

Ari paid the cabdriver and got out of the cab just as a bunch of protesters came out of the building.

"Hey, Ari!" some of them called out in English. "Ari, my brother!" They raised their fists to him.

Ari didn't recognize most of them and wondered how they knew him. "Hi, guys," he said as he passed through the group and went inside the building.

The door was open, so Ari let himself into the apartment. Just like at the police station earlier, the place was a beehive of fervent preparation. Ari passed through the rooms of the grand old Parisian-style apartment searching for Farah. He didn't see her in the living room where people lay all over the floor or sat on couches banging away on their laptops. In the kitchen, big pots of beans and chickpeas were on the boil. A team of women was busy cooking, but Farah wasn't one of them.

Ari found the master bedroom, which was dark, just lit by the screens of the editing system. Rami and five others hovered over the editor's shoulders watching a shot of a bloody unconscious protester being dragged to safety away from some thugs.

"Ugh." Rami shook his head. "Let's post it on YouTube."

"Rami?" Ari called him.

Rami turned and squinted. "Ari, the movie star? Do we have a great shot of you."

"Is Farah around?"

"She's out with Rami's Angels," said a protester on the bed, and the others laughed.

Rami explained. "She's passing out flyers with the girls."

"Where?" asked Ari.

"By the museum. Hey, Jameel—" Rami tapped the editor on the shoulder. "Show Ari his close-up."

The editor clicked open a shot of Ari getting punched in the head by a thug. Ari saw the fist fly at him, his head snap back like a boxer getting KOed, and the permits fly up in the air.

Everyone in the room moaned, "Owwahh!"

"One more time," said Rami, "in slow motion."

The editor played the clip again in slow motion. The thug wound up. His fist came around—a metal ring on his middle finger—and connected with Ari's temple. A painful grimace splashed across Ari's face as it sank down in the frame. The papers floated up in the air, a perfectly composed action.

"How did you get that shot?" Ari asked, mesmerized.

"We were following Farah to film her for our documentary," said Rami. "And those dumb government thugs didn't notice our camera. Now we will put it on the Internet for the world to see."

"Please don't," begged Ari.

"Why not?" Rami didn't understand. "You're part of the struggle, man."

"I don't want to get in trouble with my job."

"Really?" Rami gave an ironic look. "Don't you have freedom of speech in America?"

"Yeah." Ari nodded. "You can say anything you want as long as nothing changes. Catch you later." Ari walked out of the bedroom heading for the front door.

"Hey, Ari, wait a sec." Rami ran out of the bedroom and caught him in the vestibule. "Would you bring Farah this box of fliers?" Rami picked up a heavy cardboard box off the floor. A sample flier was pasted to the top. "She just texted me that they're running low."

Ari looked down at the flier on the box top. It was a picture of Farah and three very fine-looking Egyptian girls passing out fliers on the street.

"What's it say?" asked Ari.

"Come to Rami's concert in the Square," translated Rami.

"Nothing revolutionary, right? I can't get involved in that," insisted Ari.

"Only a concert, come on, man."

Ari looked at it. Every time Rami sang a song, it was a revolution. "Okay," said Ari, and he took the heavy box out of Rami's hands.

"Woof," Ari grunted. "How many is this?"

"It's only five thousand."

"Five thousand!" exclaimed Ari. "Who are you, Bob Dylan?"

Chapter 49

Ari heard footsteps coming up behind him. He shifted the heavy box of fliers from one hip to the other to look over his shoulder. Six thugs were walking half a block behind him along the walkway in front of the museum. Don't look again, he told himself as he heard their footsteps and started to get nervous. He picked up the pace, walking a little faster. They walked a little faster, too. He heard them closing the distance, and he walked even faster, which was difficult on account of the heavy cardboard box.

He thought of dropping the fliers and running, fleeing. He looked at the box top and saw Farah's picture. I've got to find her no matter what, he thought. He kept walking, the box slipping down in his sweating hands.

The thugs started to jog up behind him. They pulled out knives and blackjacks. Ari felt an extra rogue heartbeat of adrenaline surge the blood out to his fingertips. He was overwhelmed. He stopped and put the box down on the pavement panting with terror, cold sweat chilling his brow.

The thugs jogged right past him. They were after someone else. Ari sank sitting down on the box for a minute to catch his breath. What am I doing here? he asked himself as he closed his eyes and breathed deeply until he felt ready to stand. When he opened them again he realized he was sitting in front of a miniature statue of the Sphinx beside a long rectangular reflecting pool.

"Ari?"

He thought he heard his name. He looked around. Farah and Rami's three gorgeous groupies approached flirting and handing out concert fliers to passing men. Ari stood slowly and heaved up the heavy box as the girls came toward him.

"Ari, you joined the revolution just in time." Farah was happy to see him. "We only had three fliers left."

Farah broke open the top of the box in Ari's arms.

"This is crazy." Ari wiped his brow. "I didn't come to join the revolu—"

The girls clustered around him. "*Shukran*, Ari!"

The girls each took a handful of fliers, which lightened his load a little, and he followed them around looking for people in cafés, shops, or just out on the street. People took the leaflets warmly, gratefully. Ari resupplied the xeroxed papers when they ran low. The girls chatted excitedly in Arabic about the concert on Friday. Ari hung back a little to let them flirt. When will I get a chance to see Farah alone? he wondered.

After another half an hour of wandering the streets, one of the girls said good night. Ari followed Farah and the two other girls, walking a little slower, not so energized, chatting a little less. The girls were tall, but Farah was the tallest. She had a long confident stride. Ari told himself to stop staring at her, but it did keep him moving forward.

He pulled out the last thousand fliers and left the empty cardboard box on the corner. Passing out the fliers became harder as fewer people were out walking on the street. Some people already had fliers from before on their way back from wherever their evening had taken them. Another of the girls said good night.

Ari, Farah, and the last of Rami's harem walked even slower, even more tired. Ready to finish their chore, they gave out fliers twenty at a time to anyone who would promise to pass them on until, to their surprise, they had no more fliers. The final groupie yawned and said good night. Farah and Ari stood there facing each other. Dawn started to break in the sky.

"Here's the last one." Ari held it up. The street was deserted, no one to give it to.

"Keep it, so you remember this night."

Ari stuffed it in his back pocket and pointed. "The sun is coming up."

Farah took his arm. "Let's go get some breakfast." She put a scarf over her head, and they walked up the hill toward Al-Hussein Square outside the ancient mosque.

They bought a few *ataif,* stuffed pancakes; yogurt with saffron; coffee; and a pastry to split. They rinsed their hands in a big star-shaped fountain and lay down on its walls, their heads coming to a point. They ate until the remains of their breakfast lay on the star wall between them.

"Farah?"

"Yes, Ari?"

"I have to tell you something."

"You have fallen deeply, passionately, madly in love with me?"

"I might have . . ." Ari found it almost impossible to speak. ". . . to fire your brother." Ari veered away from telling her that it had already happened.

Farah laughed.

"What's so funny?" asked Ari.

"And I thought you were nervous from seeing me."

"You're not angry at me?" Why didn't I just tell her the truth? He berated himself in his mind.

"Fired from a stupid American movie, why should I be angry?"

"It's not stupid." Ari took offense.

"It's a blessing."

"It's a very important film . . . about the truth," he insisted.

"In a few days, you won't think so. Nor will Samir. Don't you get it? You are like two flies on the back of a camel walking into a sandstorm. Everything will be turned upside down. Everything."

Ari stared at her, furious that she had called his movie stupid, mad at himself for telling a half truth, afraid she would hate him for hurting her brother, needing her to absolve him when she didn't even care. She looked so beautiful, her brown eyes so wise. If I kiss her maybe she won't hate me when I tell her about the police. He leaned over and felt her breath on his lips, sweet. He kissed her, barely, softly. Her lips trembled. She pushed him away gently.

"Stop. Ari. Where do you think you are? This is Cairo."

"Sorry, sorry." He withdrew, crushed.

She caught his hand and squeezed it. "After the revolution, if you still feel this way, if you still remember me even, come find me and we can do this for real, but not now. You mustn't kiss me because you feel badly about hurting Samir."

She knows, thought Ari. She knows everything. Tell her what you came to tell her. Don't be a coward.

"I might have to . . ."

"Yes?" she prompted him gently.

"Call the police on him."

"What? Police?" She recoiled trembling with revulsion. "No, no, you can't do that. And think of yourself; don't call in the police. It is so . . . unnecessary. It will be the end of him."

"Why? They say it's just a bureaucratic thing."

Farah took a deep breath, then spoke. "Remember how I told you he had disappeared for a year?"

"The day he dropped you off at college, yes?"

"When he finally came home, he was a walking skeleton. His clothes hung on him like a wire hanger. His back had skin that looked like scrambled eggs, even the soles of his feet had scars on them. He could not control where he went to the bathroom."

Ari understood. "The Muslim Brotherhood raped him?"

"No, no, not the Brotherhood, the government, Ari. He was locked up for a year in a secret prison."

Chapter 50

Omar's office was a big art deco affair with high ceilings, metal moldings, and cone-shaped sconces on the walls. He had a big mahogany desk, which had probably been there since the beginning. It looked like a movie set of a studio chief's office from the 1930s.

Ari was daydreamy from no sleep. He half expected a lion to roar, trumpets to sound, and little spotlights to cut up through the air from out of the brass inkwells attached to the antique desk blotter. A black-and-white movie might start any second, and the three of them would morph into Boris Karloff, Sydney Greenstreet, and Peter Lorre hatching some plot.

Beth and Omar sat at the desk pouring over Samir's budget. Ari couldn't focus on it anymore over their shoulders. He had passed out Rami's fliers until dawn. His mood had collapsed into exhaustion and gone sour. He pulled his chair over to the window and looked out through wooden Venetian blinds at some electricians pushing big old arc lights on battered rolling stands down the street toward a soundstage. The round housing fell off an arc light and clattered onto the street. Ari wondered if those spotlights were from the 1930s, too.

He reached into his pocket and pulled out the last flier from the night before. He sneaked a peek at Farah's picture with the other girls.

"Samir has two drivers in here for every vehicle." Beth pointed at the numbers with her red pen. "Should we cut them?"

"They are cheap," said Omar, "a few dollars a day. It's not like teamsters in New York." He rubbed his face wearily. "Is anyone hungry?"

"I could eat," said Beth. "Should we take a break?"

"The meal is ready. They will bring it." Omar called out to his secretary in Arabic.

Ari stood up and stretched. He didn't want to make small talk with them, so he picked the *Cairo Times* from Omar's desk and leafed through the Arabic pages not understanding a word. He just looked at the pictures, mostly of police looking heroic and some of the protesters looking guilty and suspicious.

A porter carried in a big tray with a lot of little dishes on it.

"Do they have hummus?" asked Beth.

"Always," answered Omar as he offered the bread basket to her.

Ari picked up a spoon and scooped up some rice and lamb onto a plate. With his other hand he turned the page of the newspaper.

"What the . . . ?" said Ari. He dropped the spoon with a clatter and picked up the newspaper. He held up his own picture in black and white.

"Ari? What's wrong?" asked Beth.

"That's me! That's my picture!" Ari handed the paper to her.

She turned to Omar. "What's it say?"

"Uh, uh, uh, 'American Producer to Film Israeli Actress' at Cairo International . . .'"

"Airport?" Beth finished the sentence.

Incensed, Omar scanned the text. "Samir planted this story."

"Of course he did. Brilliant. Just brilliant!" Ari raged. "Once we bring in the cops . . . of course he has to defend himself. His back is up against the wall! You guys are geniuses. Now we're in a war with Samir." Ari leaned over the desk and glared at them. "What's the endgame?"

An hour later, Ari was riding with Omar in the back of his car toward downtown Cairo. Past a certain point the traffic thinned to almost nothing, then just simply disappeared. They went round a traffic circle. In the middle stood a bronze statue of a man wearing a fez.

"That is Talaat Harb," muttered Omar. "He built my studio."

"A film distributor with a statue?" asked Ari.

"No, he was a great man, an economist. A visionary of the future." Omar sighed. "If only such people still existed."

"What happened to all the taxis?" said Ari, noticing that they were the only car going around the circle in the middle of the day. "Where is everybody?"

Omar didn't answer. He had a grim look.

They turned off the traffic circle onto a big boulevard. Halfway down to the next square, a line of police in khaki uniforms with truncheons stretched across the street blocking their path. Omar pulled out his cell phone and made a call, speaking a few urgent words in Arabic.

A police sergeant stepped out of the line and flagged them down. Omar's car stopped. The driver opened his window. Speaking Arabic, the sergeant pointed back the way they came and gestured that they should turn around.

Omar said a few words, then passed the phone up out the window to the sergeant, who took it with some annoyance. When he heard the voice on the other end, his entire demeanor changed to one of crisp obedience. He ordered the policemen out of the way and motioned Omar's car through the police cordon.

They drove to the next square, around another traffic circle, down another avenue, this time closed off by a cluster of police in riot gear and armored personnel carriers. Another sergeant stepped forward, this one angry, more insistent, yelling and waving them away. Again, Omar handed his cell phone out the window. Again, the sergeant waved them through.

They came to a crowd of two hundred thugs milling about in the middle of the street who held sticks, broom handles, and homemade weapons. Omar's driver leaned on the horn. Slowly the thugs moved out of the way like wild animals in a game park and let the car inch forward. Curious, they all looked inside suspiciously at Ari.

Detective Kek, from the police station, was directly in front of them talking to a group of thug bosses while he had the phone pressed to his ear. He turned to face the car, saw Omar, and they both hung up with a little wave of recognition. Evidently, they had been on the phone together. Detective Kek told the thug bosses to wait and walked around the side to Omar's window.

Shaking his head, Detective Kek said something disapproving in Arabic.

"I know, I know," said Omar. "Once we get this done, we'll get out of here."

Detective Kek waved at the thugs, but they were less disciplined than police, so he had to yell at them to get their attention. He even slapped one thug on the back of the head who was busy goofing around. Tension was high.

Omar's driver honked and pulled carefully through the rest of the thugs, then sped down the avenue until he turned onto Samir's street.

They stopped right in front of Samir's office. Ari and Omar got out of the car, each clutching a copy of the newspaper. They ran inside.

Chapter 51

Samir fed the last of the stack of permits into the shredder. He slid his computer into its case and packed it into his satchel. His desk, in fact his entire office, was completely clear of not just papers, but everything except for the baby picture of his daughter, Yasmine.

"*Habibti*," he said as he kissed the picture.

The call to prayer sounded. Samir did the standing portion of the prayer, then got down on his knees and prostrated himself. The door opened, and Ari and Omar walked in holding their newspapers.

"So this is Studio Samir?" Omar looked around contemptuously. "A one-room office. He's more of a nobody than I thought."

"Omar, please," said Ari.

Samir froze for a second. Then continued to pray.

"I don't know why he's making so much trouble," Omar continued. "We're just going to win in the end anyway."

"Can you just let him finish?" asked Ari.

"Why? He's praying for our destruction, but will God lift a finger to help you?" Omar asked rhetorically.

"Please, can we leave God out of this?" asked Ari.

"No!" Samir jumped to his feet breaking off in mid-prayer; something that is not done. Samir pointed at Omar. "His god is money!"

Omar sneered. "That's very funny coming from you."

"Samir, as a friend . . ." Ari stood between them trying to put as much sincerity into his words as he could. "I'm asking you, please just give us the permits."

"A friend? Did you go to the police and sign a paper that I am a thief?"

Ari couldn't answer the question. What was there to say except yes? "Samir."

"Did you do that against me?" Samir pressed. "Admit it!"

"It's just business." The words tasted like chalk in Ari's mouth.

"When you know that I am not a thief?"

"It's not that simple, Samir. You know it's not. I'm just following Omar. I have to take his lead."

"So you signed a lie. Admit it. You are a liar." Samir smiled a pained smile.

"Oh?" Ari was annoyed with the pleasure on Samir's face. He slapped his own picture in the newspaper down on Samir's desk. "Why did you plant this story? That we're filming an Israeli actress?"

"Is this untrue?" asked Samir, still amused.

"It will be," said Omar.

Ari turned on Omar. "What do you mean 'It will be?'"

"Aha!" Samir jeered at Omar in triumph. "He knows that now everyone will be watching you."

"What?" asked Ari, dumbfounded. "Omar?"

Omar held up his newspaper. "Only because he planted this story."

"And God wills it," said Samir.

"Fuck!" exclaimed Ari as he realized the whole move against Samir had backfired. Ari could never get the shot.

"Did he promise you that you would film an Israeli at the airport?" asked Samir.

"Yes," said Ari blankly.

"Of course, that is how he seduced you and got the job away from me. Then he is a liar, too. Do you like him because he says nice lies to you?"

"Samir." I've got to calm this down, thought Ari. Take emotion out of it.

"Do you like him better than me?" asked Samir, the pain of rejection so plain on his face.

"He's very smooth." Ari studied Omar. "He's a pro. He's made a lot of movies."

"Do you know who he is? He is from an old military family. His grandfather was chief of staff of the Air Force, before Mubarak, before Nasser even, under the time of the British Interference! How do you think he is so rich? How do you think the government just gives him the oldest and largest movie studio in the country?"

Now Omar took offense. "What is this? I have a mortgage."

"Guys, guys—" Ari tried to stop the argument before it veered off into useless acrimony.

"A mortgage from the bank of your uncle?"

"And who are you?" Omar shot back. "You are Muslim Brotherhood. You are nothing! You give money to your friends in Hamas!"

"Okay! okay!" Ari yelled and silenced them, then said, "Samir, we need the permits."

"Impossible." Samir shook his head.

"Give us the permits and I'll go straight back to the police station right now and tear up the paper I signed."

Ari reached under his belt and pulled out a bundle of hundred-dollar bills.

"Here's ten thousand."

Ari broke the band and fanned the money out on the desk like a deck of cards. Samir picked up the bills, looked at them for a very long time. With vehement contempt, he hurled the bills into Ari's face with the force of a slap. Shocked, Ari recoiled. The bills flew around his head and floated down onto the floor.

A perfect stillness settled for a moment after they came to rest.

"You should not have done that," said Omar almost without emotion. He took out his cell phone and sent a text message as Ari dropped to his hands and knees. He crawled around picking up the money off the floor. Samir laughed.

"You people are crazy . . ." muttered Ari to himself, snatching up the hundreds.

"Go on, pray to your god." Samir kicked a few stray bills toward Ari.

Just then, a strange and distant sound wafted in through the open terrace door, an entomic buzzing. Ari thought it might be a swarm of thousands of bees until he realized it was the roar of human voices, a quarter of a million, maybe more. The sound started to organize into one chant. Ari recognized the spoken words from Rami's song.

"We won't go until you go! We won't go until you go!" over and over again in Arabic.

The three of them looked out toward the open balcony. The distant words became louder and clearer.

"What is that?" asked Ari.

"Ha! The Day of Rage," exclaimed Samir.

Muffled shots or explosions popped in the distance like tear gas fired from grenade launchers. The sound of the crowd devolved from a chant into an angry roar. The three men paused again for a moment to listen.

"It's getting closer," said Ari.

Omar got a text on his phone. He walked over to the door and opened it. "Ari, leave the money on the floor."

"But that's ten thousand dollars! Beth'll tell the studio that I lost ten grand!"

"Ari, stand up," said Omar.

Ari noticed Detective Kek in the doorway smoking a cigarette.

Scooping up what last money he could, Ari got on his feet.

"Kek?" said Samir as he recognized the detective.

"You know him?" asked Ari.

"Samir, Samir, Samir." Detective Kek wagged his finger at Samir and closed the door. He walked over to Samir's desk and pulled out the chair, beckoning Samir to sit. Samir obediently went and sat down. He seemed to shrink in size before the short detective, whose force and prowess made him seem bigger, enormous.

Detective Kek took off his jacket. He had thick biceps that bulged against his shirtsleeves, a broad chest, and the narrow waist of a body builder. He wore a shoulder holster and a gun under his arm.

Detective Kek took a blank confession form from his pocket, showed it to Omar, and placed it down in front of Samir.

"No," said Samir.

The detective then drew a pen from his shirt pocket and slapped it down on the glass desktop with the flat of his hand. Samir flinched. He shook his head.

"No," said Samir again.

Detective Kek took a puff of his cigarette. He picked up the framed photograph of Samir's wife and child, studied it for a second, then put it away in a desk drawer.

"What's he going to do?" asked Ari.

"Don't worry," said Omar. "It'll be over soon."

Detective Kek then took his cigarette and tapped the ash off directly over Samir's head. The tiny ember dropped onto Samir's scalp. Samir shook it off with a sudden convulsion, his whole body shivering from fear.

The detective produced a pair of handcuffs.

"Ari," said Samir.

"Omar, you've got to stop this," said Ari. "It's not . . . I'm not down for this."

Detective Kek turned to Omar, gave a sharp order in Arabic, and jerked his thumb toward the door.

"I know, I know," said Omar as he grabbed Ari's arm. "Let's go. We've got to get you out of here." Omar opened the door and dragged Ari out into the hall then quickly down the stairs.

"Ari!" he heard Samir cry.

Ari grabbed the banister and stopped himself. Omar tugged him down another step.

"What's he going to do?" Ari stopped again and turned around.

"Don't go back up there," warned Omar. "You will only confuse things."

"But . . ." Above him were only a few stairs, below the staircase spiraled downward out of sight.

"Don't worry," Omar coaxed soothing and smooth. "Samir has the money."

Omar peeled Ari's fingers off the banister and led him down another step. Ari stopped and reached under his belt and pulled out another two packets of bills. "We should go back and offer him another twenty thousand."

Omar shook his head. "It's a waste of cash, really. Not necessary, not at all."

Ari pointed upstairs. "They seem to know each other."

"Ari, he's Muslim Brotherhood, hard core. He's been in prison. Of course the police know him."

Upstairs there was a sudden crash and sound of breaking glass.

"Help! Help me!" cried Samir. Ari broke free from Omar and raced back up the stairs and into the office. The desk had been knocked over on its side, the glasstop in pieces all over the floor. Detetive Kek was in front of the overturned desk. Samir was cornered behind it. One handcuff hung around his wrist; the other dangled, open.

Samir feinted one way trying to make a break for the door. The detective cut him off. Samir doubled back behind the desk. He was trapped. He knew Kek could cover the door and any chance of escape. He relaxed as if defeated. Detective Kek relaxed, too, and smiled. Samir suddenly feinted back, then quickly darted to the far side. Dodging around the detective, Samir made it out onto the terrace, leaping up onto the parapet, balancing precariously on top of the railing six stories above the street.

"Don't." Ari held his breath.

Detective Kek froze for a moment. He spoke calmly, trying to talk Samir down. He approached step by step, as if in a minefield. Inching forward until he was close enough to reach up and steady Samir's precarious balance. Samir grasped both of his hands, poising himself.

"We won't go until you go!" Ari recognized the Arabic. "We won't go until you go!" The sound of the chanting grew. It seemed to arrive on the street below with the cacophony of pelting rocks, boots running, tear gas exploding.

"We won't go until you go!" Samir joined in the chant. An exultant look came into Samir's eyes. "We won't go . . ." He lost his fear. Detective Kek tried to pull away, but Samir simply leaned backward over the street below. ". . . until you . . ." He pulled the small detective up and over the railing. ". . . go!"

"Samir, NO!" screamed Ari as he ran out onto the terrace to catch hold of them, but they were gone.

He heard the sickening crunch. He looked over the edge. The roof of a blue car directly below was crushed. Ari saw a dead hand sticking up, Samir's hand with the open handcuff dangling from it.

The melee in the street below grew silent. At one end was a line of police with truncheons. At the other end were a thousand protesters armed with rocks. Both sides had seen the two men fall.

A few angry protesters ran up to the crushed car to take a look. Samir and Detective Kek lay in each other's arms, peacefully motionless on the crumpled roof of the car. One of the protesters lifted Samir's hand by the handcuff for all to see. Everyone at both ends of the street began to comprehend that the two had fallen to their deaths after some police action.

A protester yelled for vengeance. A roar erupted. All the protesters charged in a wave straight down the street, overrunning the police line, catching the police, beating them. No one stopped. A river of rage flowed past the two dead bodies, unstoppable, unquenchable.

Chapter 52

Mena House was perfectly quiet except for the sprinklers watering the green lawn. The hotel chambermen went around changing the linens. Beth sat out on the terrace going over Omar's budget with a red pen. She enjoyed a glass of mango juice.

The door burst open. Ari came in and started gathering up his belongings. Omar followed him.

"Beth," asked Omar, finding her on the terrace, "did you make the wire transfer to my account?"

Beth picked up a piece of paper and handed it to him.

"Here's the confirmation."

"Six hundred and fifty thousand dollars?" He scanned the page.

"That was the amount you asked for, wasn't it?"

Omar read the number, then folded the paper into his pocket.

"Good, good."

Ari pulled out his suitcase and started stuffing all his clothes into it.

"Did you get the permits?" Beth stood up and looked at Ari quizzically.

"You don't need them now," said Omar. "I've got to close my studio and shut down production."

"What?" She was alarmed. "Why?"

"Later tonight, the police are going to withdraw from the city to create anarchy and make everyone want the army. Cairo will have no protection at all."

Beth surveyed Omar with a piercing look. "Then you need to reverse that wire transfer." She pointed to the paper sticking out of Omar's pocket.

"That is impossible," said Omar. "The banks are closed."

"You're going to steal *six hundred and fifty thousand dollars?*" she erupted.

Omar shook his head earnestly. "No, no, no, Beth. When the revolution is over, come back. Then we'll finish your film."

"But you said . . . you said we would be able to shoot, no problem?"

Omar chuckled, caught for a second. "I lied."

Irate red blotches flushed out onto her face and the tips of her ears. "Ari, Ari! Do something."

"Think of it as an opening bid," said Ari as he walked across the living room with his suitcase.

"Are you crazy?"

Ari stopped packing his things for a moment and looked at her. "There's been an accident, Beth."

"What happened?"

"Samir fell out the window."

"Oh my God." She was calm again. "Is he hurt?"

"He's dead." Ari zipped up his suitcase. "Beth, I've got to head to the airport, try to get to Jordan."

"You won't be with me when everyone comes to Cairo?" She walked over to him. "I . . . need you . . . here. To explain."

Ari looked to Omar.

"Not a good idea," Omar said.

"But . . . ?" Beth reached out to Ari. How many times had he taken that hand? Smiled his smile? Kissed a coward's kiss? To be wanted for whatever reason, no matter what, had taught him how to make himself wanted. She wanted him now more than any one ever had before. He tried to smile from habit, from discomfort, from pity for her adherence to actions that had lost all meaning for him. Ari tried to smile his familiar smile. He tried. The muscles in his cheeks and mouth had forgotten how.

"You're in Omar's capable hands now." Ari couldn't engage. He didn't feel anything anymore. "Isn't that what you wanted?" He started toward the door.

Beth stopped him. "Ari, please don't go."

Ari looked at Omar, who had no trouble smiling, then back at Beth. "I'll leave you two to . . . negotiate."

Ari picked up his suitcase and camera bag and walked out.

Chapter 53

Ari sat in the middle seat as the hotel van sped down the road beside the Sphinx. He saw the scars where Napoleon's cannonballs had shot off its nose for target practice. And still it stood, intransigent, challenging those who pass before it with an age-old question: Do you know yourself, you four-legged, two-legged, three-legged creature? Do you know how brief is man, who lives but a dawn and dusk in my shadow and then is done? Who are you?

Ari had shot the Sphinx, chipped off a piece and taken it with him. He had seen Samir smile in a shaky old helicopter when the world outside turned upside down around them. Some smiles are hard to come by. That was a rare smile, priceless. The van passed the ticket booth for the light show and the café. Ali, the ticket seller, tossed a few coins to the little boys begging, the police nowhere to be found. Then the Necropolis was behind him.

Ari tapped his pocket and felt the crinkle of paper. He drew out Rami's flier and held it in his hand for a minute until he could dare to unfold it. There smiled Farah and her sisters of a new Egypt, of a promise of freedom from the truncheon, and the gun, and the bribe, and torture, and tear gas. He had one last piece of unfinished business, one that might follow him forever. He turned back and looked at the Sphinx. "Who are you?" it seemed to ask.

Do I even know? he wondered. Who?

He handed the flier with Farah's picture on it to the driver. "Take me here, to this concert," said Ari.

"You will miss your flight, Mr. Ari," the driver protested.

"Just for a minute. I need to tell someone . . . who I am."

The driver agreed to take Ari as far as Talaat Harb Square and wait for him on a side street, but they never got that far. They came to a line of police and were diverted up another avenue until the van was engulfed in white smoke. The driver slowed to a crawl.

"What's happening?" asked Ari.

Then, through a break in the smoke, he saw a mass of protesters running toward them. The driver stopped. There was no time to turn around without hitting someone in the crowd running by. Eerie clouds of tear gas floated by completely covering the van in a fog.

The driver locked the doors. A wave of police in riot gear ran past. Rocks started landing on the van's roof. The rear window cracked. A protester slammed up against the window, his face mashed in agony as several riot police whipped up their truncheons and brought them down with quick lashing blows.

Through the glass, Ari saw the panicked pleading eyes of

the protester, his tears streaming from gas down the window, his convulsions with every impact. Unable to look away, Ari could feel an urge ignite in his gut. He was more afraid than he had ever known. His brain commanded him to stay still and frozen, but his hand, as if by itself, reached for his camera bag on the seat. He unzipped the black knapsack and pulled out his fancy digital camera. His thumb switched it on. He raised the eyepiece to his eye and started to shoot.

"Mr. Ari, no!" begged the driver. "The police! They will take your camera! And then they will . . ."

It only took a few moments for one of the police to notice the filming. Then he stopped beating the protester and yelled at the others. They looked at Ari in disbelief, then dropped the beaten man on the ground and hurled themselves at the van's side window, smashing it in. Beads of broken glass spilled with a sudden noise and fury into the van, the muffled protection of it ruptured, violated. They reached inside and tried to grab at Ari. Still filming them, he slid away across the seat away from their clawing hands to the other side. He unlocked the door and jumped out into the gas, which stung his eyes and made his nose run. He dodged as fast as he could away from the van.

Panting shallow breaths, he tried not to draw the bitter steam down deep into his lungs. He found a pocket of clear air and sipped a breath, coughing violently on the awful taste. He ran along between vague human forms also running. He followed them, filming them, all trying to make their way out of the gas.

Ari turned a corner into the clear. He burned. His skin, eyes, nose, throat, lungs—he tried to cough out the acrid film in his throat. Ari noticed a liter bottle of Coca-Cola held out by a hand in front of him. He took it gratefully and swigged, swished, and spat. Ari felt better immediately. There, sitting beside him on the curb, was a young Egyptian with tight wavy hair, shiny sweaty cheeks, and an open generous face. He cupped his hands.

"Pour some," said the protester. "It helps with the gas."

Ari poured Coke into the protester's hands, and the protester slathered it all over his own face, behind his ears, his neck and hands, and all over his exposed skin.

"Now you wash with Coke, to keep the sting away," said the protester, who took the Coke bottle and poured it into Ari's hands. Ari covered his skin with the sticky brown liquid.

"*Shukran*," said Ari, thanking him.

"*Aala wajib.*" The protester took a scarf, poured Coke all over it, tore it down the middle, gave half to Ari and wrapped the other half around his face. Ari copied him.

"For breathing the gas," said the protester as he put the Coke back in his knapsack.

An empty green gas canister rolled by in the gutter. On the bottom it said, MADE IN THE USA. The protester picked it up. On the side it said, MANUFACTURED BY COMBINED SYS-TEMS INC. JAMESTOWN PA. The protester held it beside his masked face and posed, the perfect picture.

"Will you show this film in America?"

"To anyone who will watch." Ari nodded, then nodded again, and once again after that as if convincing himself, girding against his fear.

He picked up his camera, sticky in his Coca-Cola-drenched fingers, and started to film the revolution. The protester gathered up an armful of fallen rocks, broken pieces of cement and brick from around him in the street. He loaded up as many as he could carry. Ari followed him, jogging against a stream of protesters running away from the square, away from the gas and the police, away from the action.

Ari kept chasing into the pandemonium, following the protester from behind as he ran down the boulevard toward the fighting in the square. They dodged exploding gas canisters that landed at their feet. They kept running toward a long barricade made of trash and big sheets of galvanized metal torn from the roof of some building.

Many protesters with armfuls of rocks manned the barricade. They took turns hurling their rocks and fragments of cement and asphalt with all their rage as hard as possible at a line of police in the distance. The rocks landed unpredictably, kicking sideways, or bouncing up off the pavement, driving the police to retreat. Once someone had used up all their rocks, they sprinted back away from the cover of the barricade to gather more rocks and make room for the next protesters.

Ari poked his camera over the top of the barricade, peeking at the police lines. Rubber bullets bounced off the galvanized metal, banging on it like thunder. Ari ducked, trying to become as small as possible. He wished himself away, anywhere else. He prayed to a god he had never believed existed. Deliver me out of here, please, and I will be utterly honest with myself and everyone else for the rest of whatever life you give if you let me live, God.

The hailstorm of bullets fried his nerves. His heart beat in crazy rhythms. He could feel his fingertips swell painfully from wild surges in blood pressure. He screwed his eye into the viewfinder of his camera as if he could disappear behind the lens. Surely the black, sleek, shiny object could protect him and make him invisible.

Crouching, he looked up through the lens. He saw Farah run toward him. She was dressed in black and carried an armload of rocks. She looked into his lens. The rocks fell out of her hands as she saw that it was Ari behind the camera, and she turned on him. A moan, then a torrent of jumbled-up Arabic and English spewed from her lips as she beat with her fists on his back, then his chest, as he stood up and stopped filming. He heard snatches of words above the din: "Pig . . . American . . . Fascist . . . traitor . . . how . . . why . . . ?" Two tracks of tears from gas were already streaming down her face. She was screaming, crying, beating on him until the wave of her fury crashed against him. Her legs buckled and he caught her.

"I know," said Ari holding her up. "I know what I've done." I shot the Sphinx, he thought to himself.

I first went to Egypt in 2005 to shoot a helicopter shot of the Sphinx for the Hollywood action movie *Jumper*. I remember stepping off the plane behind an Egyptian/American family from Great Neck, Long Island: a mom, a dad, and their teenage daughter.

"I can't believe I'm in Egypt!" the teenager kept repeating in an accent as Jewish as any Bat Mitzvah girl from the Five Towns. "I can't believe I'm in Egypt!"

Neither could I.

"Wait, just wait till you drink the water from the Nile," said the mother in the same Jewish accent. "Then you'll believe you're in Egypt."

I remember that romantic feeling: I can't believe I'm in the Egypt of the pharaohs; the pyramids; the desert; the Nile; Ra, the Sun god; Osiris, the first mummy; Isis, the goddess of magic; the treasure of King Tut; Cleopatra, who had bewitched Mark Antony away from his allegiance to Caesar; the

Sphinx's timeless riddle . . . but somehow I knew that my journey into that ancient mystical land would not be an easy one.
It wasn't.

At this point in my filmmaking career, I had filmed in just
one Middle-Eastern country: Israel. The Israelis seemed to
have one guiding principle: Never ask for permission. Do whatever you set out to do until someone stops you. This, as I
soon discovered, was not the Egyptian way.

Jumper, the science fiction movie I was working on, told the
story of a young man, played by Hayden Christensen, who
could teleport, meaning "jump," from place to place instanta-
neously.

Early in the story, he goes surfing on a huge "break" off the
coast of Australia. To establish his "jumping" power for the
audience, the script had him teleport from a surfboard on a
massive wave in the Pacific Ocean to a beach chair perched
on the head of the Sphinx.

The magic of special effects made it possible to shoot
Hayden sitting in a beach chair on a life-sized model of the
top of the head of the Sphinx on a back lot in Tijuana, Mex-
ico, but before we made the model and shot Hayden, I had
to take a technical team to Cairo to shoot a shot of the real
Sphinx—in a helicopter. Then we could combine the two
shots inside a computer and—presto!—it would look like
Hayden was sitting on top of the actual Sphinx.

I needed a local Egyptian producer, and several months before I went to Egypt, I called Cairo-based production companies. I got the first response from a young Egyptian producer
who had done a TV show at the pyramids for Fox, the same
American studio making *Jumper.* By the time the older, more

established producers had called me back, the first producer had already submitted a budget and a sensible bid. In the film business time is money, so I hired the young producer and his company right away.

In Egypt, when you make a movie, you must hire an Egyptian production company whether you want to or not. That company, not your movie, technically "owns" permission to shoot. That company must apply for permits from the Ministry of the Interior, the Crew Guild, and the Actors Guild. Then you have to start paying several thousand dollars in permitting fees. You also have to pay each union a thousand-dollar fee for each crewmember or actor you bring into Egypt. The permitting process takes six weeks. You have to translate your script into Arabic and give copies to the officials and censors who have to approve the content of the script before you shoot a single frame. All these hoops you have to jump through present all kinds of opportunities for corruption to flourish.

And while shooting, you need to hire a social censor to babysit your shoot to make sure you're not filming anything "immoral" or "anti-Islamic." I was, however, told it was a typical practice to pay the censor not to show up. Or more accurately, whether he shows up is his own business, but you have to pay him anyway. I never saw the censor who was supposed to oversee *Jumper*.

The Egyptian Air Force offered us a very old large Soviet helicopter. I wanted to try to rent an American aircraft from any local Egyptian charter company. I found a charter company called Petroleum Air Services. I went in for a meeting. The head of the company was a retired Air Force general who, much to my amusement, looked like a taller, younger, handsomer movie-star version of the president of Egypt, Hosni Mubarak. The general told me that he had retired two years prior as chief of staff of the Egyptian Air Force. President Mubarak had also been chief of staff. I was about to make a presentation to the general when he stopped me and joked, "I'm really just a figurehead here. Let me bring in my number-two man who really runs the company."

I explained to both men what I wanted to do, and they were sympathetic, but they still refused to rent me a helicopter on their assumption that the Egyptian Air Force would want to control any helicopter flight over the nation's most iconic of antiquities. They did tell me about their company and gave me brochures that listed a very large number of aircraft for a charter company. Back in the States, that kind of company would own a couple of helicopters. They had about thirty. This company could transport men and equipment from Cairo International Airport to oil fields all over the Middle East.

"How can you afford to have so many aircraft? Who owns this place?" I asked.

"Oh, we're owned by the American oil companies," they answered. Of course, that made perfect sense. How better to gain access to the top of the Egyptian military elite than to hire a former chief of staff?

The former Air Force commander was right. We would have to shoot from an Egyptian Air Force helicopter in order to fly it around the head of the Sphinx, and we would need the personal sign-off from the defense minister, Field Marshal Tantawi, chairman of the Supreme Military Council. And since we had to work with the Air Force, a military censor would have to look over our shoulders at every shot to make sure that we did not film any of the base we took off from or aircraft stationed there.

After six weeks, we received all the permits that we needed to film except the signature of the defense minister. A week before our requested shoot date, we had given up on being able to shoot the shot. We wouldn't have enough time to prepare. The next day Field Marshal Tantawi approved our application. Almost as portrayed in the novel, I went into overdrive to get ready.

The SpaceCam, a rare and expensive gyrostablized camera that mounts on the front or side of a helicopter, is based in Los Angeles. Overnight, the cameramen had to prep, pack, and ship the seventeen cases to New York. There was no time to ship the cases to Egypt as airfreight, so I had to fly with the seventeen massive pieces of luggage to Cairo International. With a wagon full of heavy black cases in tow, I followed my Egyptian/American friends with the Jewish accents from Great Neck up to the customs desk. The customs inspectors confiscated the SpaceCam.

A young woman from the Press Ministry was there with a letter of authorization to help me clear customs. Vociferously, she argued for customs to return the SpaceCam, but to no avail. The customs inspectors piled up the cases beside a storeroom of confiscated luggage under the watchful eye of a portrait of President Hosni Mubarak.

I spent days trying to reclaim the SpaceCam. I waited on lines. I saw minor officials. I paid small fees to process applications in Arabic that I could not understand. A strange Kafkaesque bureaucracy had cropped up in Egypt. I saw vestiges of British colonialism mated with Soviet bureaucracy.

Both systems had died, relegated to the ash heap of history, but somehow both had resurrected and recombined in Egypt due to the deep institutional and not so contradictory roots of colonialism and socialist Pan-Arabism that run deep into the modern Egyptian governmental psyche.

My technical crew arrived from America. Our shoot date came and went without our camera. We bided our time and did what other work we could, taking still photos at the pyramids and in the vast sand dunes of the Western desert.

During this time, I had one of the strangest meetings of my life. As recounted in the novel, I went to see the head of customs at Cairo International Airport, a general. I drank mint tea and waited in a chair in front of his desk for half an hour while an Egyptian soap opera droned in the background on an old Russian black-and-white TV. The general looked up from his paperwork from time to time and smiled at me. I smiled back; not a word was exchanged. After half an hour, he looked up and said, "Do you like George Bush?"

Was he testing me? I didn't want to give the wrong answer. I studied the man. The customs general sported a Saddam-style moustache. I wondered if he wanted me to insult Bush. But I didn't think that was what he was looking for. After all, there was the ubiquitous portrait of President Hosni Mubarak right behind him on the wall.

I thought hard for a moment and said: "I think Bush made a mistake going into Iraq, a big mistake."

The general smiled a wide and delighted smile. "You are good man. I give you your camera." I knew I had come up with the perfect answer. Then he added: "Saddam is great man."

At that time, by 2005, Bush's quick and easy invasion of

Iraq had just devolved from a "Mission Accomplished" into the quagmire we're still stuck in as I write these words a decade later. As a number of Egyptians told me, "What America does in Afghanistan is your own business, but Iraq is too close to us." The image of Saddam dragged from a hole in the ground, unkempt and unshorn, mumbling to himself, may have planted a seed in the back of every Arab's mind that an all-powerful strong man can be toppled. Saddam was, after all, simply human.

The Iraq War stirred the Arab consciousness, and certainly stirred an Islamic reaction. That Saddam was gone may have excited other possibilities in other countries, but American troops, bombs, drones, raids, and the images from Abu Ghraib and Guantanamo were all an affront to Arab and Islamic dignity. As I was told at Cairo University when I noticed hundreds of girls covering their hair with the hijab, the head scarf, but wearing very tight sexy jeans, "Before you invaded Iraq, five percent of the coeds wore the hijab, now ninety-five percent of them do."

After my meeting with the customs general, I went down to customs and told them that their chief had said that I could have my camera. They didn't know what to do. They kept me there for another three hours identifying every piece of equipment in every case on a manifest. I finished that process and still they wouldn't give me the camera until, finally, a man came into the tiny storage room and handed the customs official a newspaper, presumably with some small tip for the customs inspectors tucked between the pages. Then, at last, they gave me my SpaceCam.

In Egypt I learned that government baksheesh was systemic.

By underpaying government bureaucrats and police, the social norm became that the government paid them to show up, but bribes paid them to do their jobs. If you couldn't afford a bribe, you couldn't get something done. For instance, a large enough bribe could secure a university degree, a practice that makes all degrees suspect and puts incompetent people into positions they are not qualified to fill. The result of this kind of activity is a general lowering of the standards of competence. When police live off bribes they soon become thieves, taking people's money during a routine traffic stop or casual encounter. If someone complained, the police would beat them—in some notable cases, to death.

Access to the regime is another form of corruption. If you had a friend who had a friend who knew the right official, you could get something done. If not, you couldn't. Monopolies were created for friends of the president's children. When entire industries can be controlled or dominated by cronies of the regime, no one will challenge them. As Ayn Rand said to Mike Wallace in 1959: business using government to prevent competition, "is the worst of all economic phenomenon."

Patronage is not new or unique to the Middle East. Before globalization, before the Industrial Revolution, patronage was the norm of economic organization. The tribe, the clan was everything. How far away or close to the leader one was determined wealth and social status. Efficiency and management science abhors bribery and is in conflict with ancient tribal systems of baksheesh. It simply adds an unnecessary cost to doing business in the Middle East.

For most international companies, extensive bribery, often in violation of their own country's laws, means becoming a lawbreaker, risking heavy fines, even jail time. Top oil companies have routinely paid multimillion-dollar fines for making illegal kickbacks in order to purchase oil. U.S. businessmen pay "fixers" who then bribe oil officials in these countries. High-profit businesses such as the oil industry will accept that risk as the price of doing business or hire foreign subcontractors who legally shield them from the risk. The ubiquitous baksheesh, however, gives an unfair advantage to those willing to be corrupt even as it places a burden upon them. This is, perhaps, the foremost reason that region hasn't advanced as fast and as far as the industrialized world despite the vast oil revenues throughout the region.

I had never thought about baksheesh before going to Egypt. I had no experience with bribery in the United States, not that it doesn't occur here. We certainly have soft-core forms of bribery that everyone is familiar with: junkets, "swag," "the red carpet treatment," big donor political fund-raising, the "revolving door" between government regulators and the industries they are supposed to regulate, but retail bribery on a small scale for a government official to do their job was not something I had any experience with. Looking back on it, I was given many opportunities to pay a bribe. I was left alone for long stretches of time with various Egyptian officials in their offices, neither of us saying a word.

We did have to reapply to Defense Minister Tantawi for another flight date around the head of the Sphinx. We were given another date a week later. If that expedited date was on account of any money changing hands, I never knew and never asked.

We did fly our historic mission in three sorties over six hours. In each sortie, we would refuel and load our camera at the air force base adjacent to Cairo International Airport, fly over downtown Cairo to the Necropolis in Giza, and make two dozen passes orbiting the Sphinx. We tried several different flight paths, but the most successful, the one that ultimately ended up in the film, started low down in the valley near the Sphinx. We'd fly low just in front of it, then climb up passing the tops of the pyramids in a line.

After our first sortie, we realized we were flying too high to get the shot in a good way and went to the squadron commander to complain. Our Egyptian producer yelled angrily until the commander consented to let the pilots fly lower. On our next sortie, the pilots flew so low that the helicopter, a massive Soviet Mi-17, about the size of a bus, kicked up a cyclone of dust. The tourists around the Sphinx below us fled in pandemonium as we cast an upside-down mushroom cloud of sand and dust in our downdraft. Inadvertently, we chased hundreds of tourists every which way as we climbed up to the plateau of Giza and the vast desert beyond. Tourists took cover in the bus parking lot, only to find themselves trapped between the buses as our 60 mph rotor wash blew a torrent of desert sandstorm into their faces.

The following day, the Supreme Military Council forbade anyone to fly around the Sphinx in a helicopter ever again, but that shot orbiting the Sphinx became the centerpiece of the marketing of the film—on the poster, in the trailer, and in TV commercials.

I returned to Egypt in 2009 to prep the Middle-Eastern shoot for the movie, *Fair Game*. Our movie told the story of Valerie Plame, the CIA agent who had been "outed" by Dick Cheney to punish her husband for revealing that Saddam Hus-

sein was not building a nuclear bomb. This publicly contra-
dicted the opposite claim by Bush in a State of the Union
address, his justification to the American people for going to
war in Iraq.

In the three years since I'd last been to Egypt, I sensed a
palpable mood change in the country. The Egyptians in the
production company I was working with seemed impatient
with the police and the minor officials we encountered on
our trip to scout Cairo International Airport. Every time an
official said no to a small request, the location manager argued and officials backed down. We were supposed to shoot at
the University of Cairo on a Thursday. Our schedule was set.
The actors Naomi Watts, who played Valerie Plame, and
Sean Penn, who played her husband, Ambassador Joe Wilson, were on the way to Egypt when suddenly we were told
that we couldn't shoot. Fearing that some bribe would be
asked for, I began to press the location manager, who had shot
there many times before to find out what was going on.

We were offered Friday, the day after, to shoot instead. No
bribe was asked for. It seemed that Cairo University would
have a special guest: President Obama was coming to the university to make an historic speech to the youth of the Arab
world. Our movie could wait a day.

Obama's visit made an impression on the Egyptians we
worked with. Obama was the complete antithesis of Bush,
who himself was the son of a president. Bush had walked out
of power voluntarily, a point that was not lost on the Egyptians. Their president, Hosni Mubarak, had been in power for
almost thirty years.

Over breakfast one day, I saw an item in the paper. In an

effort to discourage corruption, the Egyptian government had raised the pay of every civil servant by ten percent. Then I saw another item in the paper about a man pulled over in his car by two policemen. They took his cell phone and a hundred and sixty-five Egyptian pounds, about thirty-five dollars. The next day the man went to the police station to complain. The day after that, the two policemen came to his apartment and threw him out his window to his death. The police were sentenced to two years in prison. I doubt they actually served that much time, if any.

Due to disagreements well described in the novel, we switched production companies, not an easy thing to do in Egypt. The complex permitting procedure made that a nightmare and a "permitting fee" had to be paid to the crew guild to switch the permit over to the new production company.

One of the strangest sensations I've ever had was on the night I had my final conversation with the original Egyptian producer. We had paid him a large amount of money that had not yet been spent on the film. I asked for a meeting to demand the money back. He refused to meet me in his office, which we had always done before. I wondered why. He insisted that we meet out at his country club late at night where we could sit under the watchful eye of an armed guard at the front door and a night porter who could witness us together. He would only sit in sight of this guard.

He was nervous. He refused to return the money to the production, but he was very frightened. I realized that he was physically frightened of me. I believe that he was prepared for me to kidnap him or kill him over the money. Witnessing this fear was so bizarre to me. I'm one of the least threatening people I know. I've never even punched anyone in my life. Why was he afraid? Was it because I was American? Had Iraq and Afghanistan, U.S. raids in the middle of the night, the extra-judicial killings, targeted assassinations, the drones in Yemen and Pakistan, and the mistakes, the dead civilians, women and children and parents in wedding parties and funerals, made me a source of terror? Had the War on Terror made me an object of fear? I believe so.

This novel is based on personal experiences, but it is a fictional account. I had no affairs with coworkers or Egyptian revolutionaries. No one was murdered because of the movies I made. The revolution did not interrupt our filming. The hope of the Arab Spring in Egypt was a great source of inspiration and the spark that rekindled my memories of doing business in Cairo that led me to write this story in the first place.

You can taste fear when you see it, smell it even. For me it was an intoxicating moment, but one to back away from, for sure. Yet, I can now see how seductive it becomes, when one is presented with the easy temptation to solve a problem by paying money to a pesky policeman or a customs official or even a general, whether it's simply to get an official to just do his job on time, or to make some troublesome person disappear.